LOST
ANGELS

BOOKS BY STACY GREEN

The Girls in the Snow
One Perfect Grave

LOST
ANGELS

STACY GREEN

Bookouture

Published by Bookouture in 2021

An imprint of Storyfire Ltd.
Carmelite House
50 Victoria Embankment
London EC4Y 0DZ

www.bookouture.com

ISBN: 978-1-80019-676-6
eBook ISBN: 978-1-80019-675-9

Secrets are like a stain. They seep into your life, often undetected, until their true colors bleed through.
—Unknown

PROLOGUE

He watched the movers load the trucks for a while. The house owners emerged from the red-brick colonial home a few times, checking the progress or carrying a smaller box to one of their personal vehicles. She came out more than he did, her dark hair held back in a ponytail. Even at this distance, he could tell she was the one in charge. She knew who she was, and he envied that about her. As he stood there, he fantasized that she would somehow sense his presence and ask him to step out of the shadows. He knew that if she just gave him a chance, he would fill the hole in her life. She might be happy with her husband, but he could show her an entirely new world if he just had the chance.

It was a warm day, and at times she stopped to catch her breath, shaking her head. Was she questioning her decision to move? His insides twisted every time one of the movers brought something else out of the house and put it on the truck. He knew he was running out of time, and he had to know where she was going. The idea of losing her now was unthinkable.

He waited down the street in his car until the movers stopped for a cigarette break. He slipped on his expensive suit jacket and set off toward the small, colonial home. He was just a businessman out for a walk, busy on his phone.

When the opportunity came, he was ready. He looked up, as though trying to figure out his surroundings, and caught the eye of one of the movers. "Hey, man, can you tell me where 322 Cyprus is?"

"Two blocks south," the bigger of the two men answered. "Past the intersection. You won't miss it."

"Thanks." He pretended to check out the house. "You guys got a long haul ahead of you?"

"Freaking Minnesota," the man answered, lighting another smoke. "Who moves from a place like this to the frozen tundra?"

"I hear it's only frozen part of the time." He smiled and continued walking. "Safe travels."

She was going home.

CHAPTER ONE

Nikki stared out of the window, her stomach rolling as the expanse of water below her grew larger. She didn't mind flying, but small planes always made her feel like she was about to crawl out of her skin. The flight from the ranger station in Ely to their destination was only about twenty minutes long, but she would be happy when it was over.

The Superior National Forest was four million acres of wilderness that stretched along the United States and Canadian border. It was a coveted area for outdoorsmen—the reserve known as the Boundary Waters Canoe Area was one of Minnesota's crown jewels. The interconnected waters stretched for a hundred and fifty miles, and it was a popular destination year-round. Canoes and kayaks dominated the water during the warm months, along with fishing boats. Cold weather brought out dog-sled teams, hikers, and ice fishermen. Snowmobile tracks still crisscrossed some of the waterways, but it was hard to imagine that just a few weeks ago, the ice was thick enough for the machines to safely travel across the water.

Despite the year-round activity, the Boundary Waters area was secluded, especially in winter. The victim had been spotted this morning during a routine flyover by the forest service. Rangers quickly confirmed the victim was dead and called the FBI. Nikki had been half-asleep when she took the call. She'd worked late the previous night, tidying up notes from recent cases.

"Looks like the ice is really starting to break up," Liam said from behind her. "How are we going to land?"

"The area we're landing in is still thick enough for a ski plane," Mayberry replied. "Ice-out's not for at least another few weeks."

Mayberry had been Nikki's first point of contact when they arrived at the Kawishwi Ranger Station less than an hour earlier. He was around thirty, with a round face and an eager-to-please attitude. Nikki could tell how keen he was to help, but she knew he'd never been part of a death investigation.

"Have you been to the scene yourself?" Nikki asked.

"Not yet," he said. "When the report came in, my boss went to secure it. Although you won't find any campers or hikers in the area, there's plenty of wildlife to keep away. The black bears will be coming out of hibernation soon, and there's a female we hope to see emerge with a cub or two. There are also about fifteen hundred wolves in the Superior National Forest area, and a large pack was spotted near the area last week."

"But the body wasn't found then?" Nikki clarified.

"Correct," Mayberry said. "It was only spotted this morning when our supply plane flew over Deadman Lake." Mayberry laughed nervously. "You think Frost chose the location because of the name?"

"It's possible that's why the killer chose that specific site, yes," Nikki said. "But it may have been a special spot between him and the victim. We won't know until we find out more."

Mayberry twisted his hands in his lap. "I have to tell you, I never expected to be hanging out with a famous FBI agent when I woke up this morning."

Nikki smiled. "I wouldn't say I'm famous."

Nikki had first found herself in the news twenty years ago when she'd found her parents murdered and helped put the alleged killer in prison. She'd become a household name again in the past several months after DNA results proved the wrong man had been convicted.

"You catch serial killers and murderers," Mayberry said. "That's pretty badass."

"Not really," Nikki said. "It's much more glamorous on television, right, Liam?"

"That's an understatement," Liam said. He was Nikki's partner and the first agent she'd trained when she'd established the behavioral unit she had been running for the last few years in the Minnesota office. "How close are we? My legs are cramping," he complained.

"Poor baby," Courtney Hart replied and Nikki watched Liam roll his eyes. Courtney was the team's forensic specialist, and even though she'd only brought the necessities, Courtney was jammed into the small space like a sardine. The big leather bag containing the crime scene markers and yellow tape had been wedged between Courtney and the window, blocking her view, while the protective equipment and various evidence collection tools had been packed tightly behind her seat. "I can't even see out the window."

"Just a few minutes." Mayberry paused. "You haven't found a Frost victim this year, have you?"

Nikki sighed. One of her ongoing cases was well known. The Frost killer still hadn't been found—he was believed to be responsible for killing five women, leaving their bodies frozen solid in several different locations. Nikki had been chasing him for years. There was a lot they didn't know about Frost, but Nikki was sure that there was something significant in how he positioned them. Each woman was preserved, with her clasped hands resting on her torso as though she'd been placed in a coffin. She supposed she shouldn't have been surprised that Mayberry knew there hadn't been a Frost victim yet this year. Nikki's name had been in the media on a regular basis since DNA evidence exonerated the man who'd spent twenty years in prison for murdering her parents. She'd also been involved in a couple of high-profile cases and had been asked about Frost numerous times.

"This may not be one of his victims. For one, it's a little late in the year," Nikki told him. She knew Frost timed the discoveries of his victims so they were hard to examine, and he'd have known that the ice was beginning to break.

"Meaning the body will thaw too quickly, right?"

Nikki shifted uncomfortably. She was used to people asking her about Frost, but it didn't make answering their questions any easier. "You've followed the cases, I take it?"

"Not in detail, but we're always prepped at the beginning of winter on how to handle any criminal activity, and Frost's name always comes up." Mayberry tapped the small window. "I'm surprised he hasn't left a victim here before. It's the perfect place to disappear."

Nikki glanced at Liam and knew he was thinking the same thing. Frost didn't want his victims to disappear. He always dumped them where they'd be found.

"How are you planning to get the body out of here?" Nikki asked. "Will the medical examiner be meeting us?"

"He's coming on another plane," Mayberry replied. "Should land around the same time we do. He'll take the body back to be autopsied."

"We're going to land in a couple of minutes." The pilot's voice crackled over the radio. "The ice was solid enough to land on this morning, but it could get a little dicey. The plane can float, so if we break through the ice, don't panic."

Courtney whimpered from the back seat. She wasn't the only one uncomfortable in the tiny plane.

Liam paled. "That's reassuring," he said sarcastically.

Nikki tightened her seatbelt, grateful she didn't eat much this morning. She peered out the small window, watching the lake grow larger. She could see large chunks of ice floating in the water. "Ranger Mayberry, it's really safe to land on the ice?"

He patted her hand. "Absolutely. The guy flying us has been doing this for thirty years. We're in good hands."

Nikki tried not to clench the armrest too hard as the ski-plane descended. The shore and the ice loomed larger and larger, until the runners scraped the ground. Ski-planes didn't fly at the height or speed of a regular plane, but the landing was still bouncy. As Nikki felt it jerk up and down, she was certain the plane was beginning to skid out of control, and every horror story she'd heard about drowning in freezing water ran through her head, even though her practical side knew that wouldn't happen. Nikki couldn't relax her hands until the plane had completely stopped.

"We exit onto the dock," Mayberry said. "It can be slippery, so be careful."

Icy cold air shocked Nikki when she stepped out of the plane. It never ceased to amaze her how much colder it was just a few hours north of the Twin Cities.

A gray-haired ranger strode toward her.

"Agent Hunt, I'm Terry Smith, head ranger. Thanks for coming so quickly."

"We appreciate how quickly you called us. As I'm sure you know, time is of the essence in cases like this."

Smith nodded and then addressed Mayberry. "The medical examiner is landing in a couple of minutes. Let's go help him with his stuff."

Liam and Courtney exited the plane carrying Courtney's equipment. Nikki introduced her team.

Smith pointed down the snow- and ice-covered shore. "The body is about three hundred yards east. Go ahead, we'll join you when the medical examiner arrives," he said.

Liam shouldered Courtney's heavy bag, and the three of them started walking. The pit of dread in Nikki's stomach suddenly felt like a big rock. She never looked forward to seeing a body, but this was different. Electricity seemed to crackle through her, as though her body was preparing her.

Nikki had requested the scene not be processed or touched until the team arrived. Yellow crime scene tape created a larger perimeter around the area where the body had been found. No matter how many cases she worked, seeing the absolute stillness of the body and realizing it was no more than a shell of a human always gave Nikki pause. Her mentor in the behavioral analysis unit at Quantico had told her that the moment death stopped affecting her, she'd know it was time for a career change, and she'd lived by that rule ever since.

She ducked under the crime scene tape, taking stock of the woman's lack of obvious physical injuries and clothing. She still wore a heavy winter coat—something they'd yet to see on a Frost victim. But his victims never showed immediate signs of injury, always appearing to be asleep, and this woman looked similar. "Is that a Burberry jacket she's wearing?"

"Yes, it's a $2,000 coat," Courtney said.

"Looks like she's almost in the right position." Liam sounded resigned. They'd kept the staging of Frost's victim's out of the media, stating only that they were "laid out in the snow."

The woman lay with her arms folded over her stomach, her small hands clasped together. Her head was turned toward the lakeshore, the cold wind blowing her dark hair over her face. Nikki slipped on a pair of latex gloves and then crouched next to the victim. She appeared to be around Nikki's height, with a stockier build.

Nikki's nose burned from the chemical scent surrounding the body. "I can smell the bleach."

"He didn't use bleach on that coat," Courtney said. "I'm pretty sure even color-safe bleach would have messed up the exterior. I'll get it bagged first."

"Is she wearing a ring?" Liam asked.

"Looks like it," Nikki answered.

Liam crouched on the other side of the body and gave Nikki a pointed look. "Frost has never left jewelry on his victims."

Nikki couldn't see her face yet, but the woman's exposed skin also didn't have the same ghostly pallor as the other five victims. A sense of dread settled into the pit of Nikki's stomach as she examined the thick ribbon tied around the victim's head. All of Frost's previous victims had a red velvet ribbon tied in their hair like a headband. "No, he hasn't, but this ribbon is definitely velvet." The ribbon's material had also been kept out of the media, and even without Courtney's expertise, Nikki could tell the ribbon was the same as the ones found on the other victims. "The bleach odor is stronger than any other victim."

Nikki's adrenaline had started to spike. They'd been called to numerous crime scenes over the past five years by local law enforcement who were certain they had a Frost victim on their hands. Nikki and her team could usually rule them out fairly quickly because of specific details that had been intentionally kept from reporters. But this woman had what Liam had once referred to as the Frost trifecta: the positioning, the velvet ribbon, and the bleach.

Nikki was beginning to think this could be Frost's work, and she could see Liam and Courtney's faces harden as they realized it too. The bleach was so strong that the body couldn't have been here very long, which meant the killer could still be nearby.

Liam's face was flushed from more than the cold wind, she knew. He paced back and forth, shading his eyes and scanning the shoreline before unzipping his coat, his hand lingering over his holstered weapon. "I'd assume she's been here a while. But he could still be in the area."

"If he were still here, surely one of the pilots would have spotted him from the air," Nikki said quietly. She understood why Liam had jumped to that conclusion, but the staff were used to spotting and tracking wild animals, and they would have seen him. Liam looked only slightly reassured. "But we might be able to find evidence or figure out how he brought her here. We need as many people as possible to search the area and the connecting lakes."

"How could he have just come and gone in the area unless he flew in?" Unease colored Courtney's usual confident tone. "The ice isn't broken up nearly enough for any sort of boat."

"I'm not sure yet. Let's ask Mayberry."

Nikki edged closer to the body, trying to get a better look at the ring the victim was wearing on her right hand, but her other hand partially covered the jewelry. Hopefully it was a wedding band, or perhaps something engraved that would help them identify the woman. Nikki needed to get a better look at the ring's gemstone. The glare from the sun made it impossible to tell if the stone was red or onyx. Still on her knees, she shifted until her face was nearly parallel to the ring. She gently touched the woman's hand.

"She's in rigor." Nikki looked up at her team.

Courtney's eyes widened. "Then she really hasn't been here long."

"Christ." Liam stalked around the body. "I'm trying to get a decent signal so we can call in searchers, but evidently T-Mobile doesn't work in the frozen tundra."

Nikki wasn't listening. A low buzzing had formed in her head. Her heart galloped in her chest. She grasped the ring and tried to work it off the stiff finger.

"Boss," Liam said. "The medical examiner's going to be pissed if he catches you messing with her before he gets here. He just reached the shore. Mayberry's helping with his equipment. Can you check your phone and see if you have a better signal?"

But Nikki ignored him and tugged harder. She had to get the ring off before she looked at the face. She had to know.

The ring wouldn't budge.

The buzzing had turned into a relentless hammering.

"Nikki." Courtney's voice echoed from somewhere behind Nikki. "What's wrong?"

Her throat was too tight to answer. On her hands and knees, Nikki moved to the other side of the body. She couldn't stop her fingers from trembling as she brushed the dark hair off the victim's face. Watery blue, sightless eyes stared back at her.

Barely managing to stifle the wail in her throat, Nikki touched each of the victim's stiff cheeks.

A hand tightened on Nikki's elbow. She hadn't noticed Courtney coming to kneel next to her. "Nikki?"

Nikki still clutched the dead woman's face. "I know her…"

CHAPTER TWO

Her eyes blurry, Nikki tried to pull herself together. She knew she shouldn't cry at a crime scene, but it was almost impossible to hold back the tears threatening to come out. "Her name's Annmarie Mason. She was my best friend growing up. We haven't spoken since…" Nikki's voice caught, and she realized that she wasn't going to be able to say the words without losing the remaining pieces of her composure.

Courtney fished a wad of tissues out of her pocket and pressed them into Nikki's hand.

"Mayberry's helping the medical examiner get his equipment out of the craft, but they'll be heading this way any minute," Liam said, taking two steps to his right, effectively blocking Nikki's view of the others. He knelt down on the other side of Annmarie's body and cleared his throat, his cheeks pinker than usual. "You haven't spoken since around the end of high school?"

"She sat next to me every single day during my parents' trial."

Nikki studied her old friend. Annmarie's face was rounder than Nikki remembered, with deep wrinkles around her eyes. The eyebrow piercing she'd been so proud of was gone, but Nikki could still see the faded scar in Annmarie's graying eyebrow.

Nikki had to stop herself from holding Annmarie's rigid hand. "I gave her this ring for her sweet sixteen. It's inscribed 'best friends forever, love, Nikki.'" Annmarie had stood by Nikki during the worst days of her life. When the dust settled, Nikki had decided that the only way she could survive life without her parents was to push everyone away and focus solely on school. Raise her grades, graduate, get into college, get the hell out of Stillwater and away from the living nightmare. She'd abandoned Annmarie.

"She's in good condition," Courtney said. "Even if the wolves Mayberry talked about weren't in the area, there are a lot of scavenger birds around here. But they don't seem to have touched her."

Liam pointed to the red ribbon tied in Annmarie's hair. "It's definitely velvet," he said, but quickly straightened up, looking at Nikki. "Mayberry's coming," he told her.

Nikki nodded and wiped her tears with her sleeve as best she could. She tried to remember that she was the senior FBI agent in a murder investigation. She knew that if anyone found out that the case was a person Nikki had a connection to, she'd be thrown straight off it. Better to keep her emotions to herself.

"Doug Larsen's with him."

Minnesota had several assistant medical examiners scattered throughout the state, and since Nikki's unit covered all of it, she'd worked with just about all of them, including Doug Larsen. He was short, barely an inch taller than Nikki, but his personality made up for what he lacked in stature. He was kind and funny, and he always brought a sense of calm to the scene. He was also the only one-night stand she'd had after her divorce. They'd both attended a forensics conference a few years ago, and Nikki had wound up doing the walk of shame from Larsen's hotel room at the Four Seasons to her own, two floors above. He'd always told her he was fine being single, that what had happened had been with no strings attached, but he invited Nikki for drinks every time she saw him.

Nikki stood and jammed her trembling hands into her coat pockets. She nodded at Larsen. "Doug, thanks for getting here so quickly."

Doug smiled grimly. "No problem."

"I've identified our victim as Annmarie Mason." Nikki forced herself to sound as nonchalant as possible. "We attended the same high school, but we haven't spoken in years."

Larsen laid his equipment next to the body, crouching down to begin his examination.

"Mayberry, how do you think our killer got here?" Liam asked. "What about a ski-plane like we did?"

"Not without us knowing about it." Mayberry rested his hands on his utility belt. "Air traffic control keeps better track of them than you think, and I already checked with them. No one but us has been in during the last twenty-four hours. He's probably got a Wilcraft."

"A what?" Liam asked.

Nikki turned her back on Larsen's examination of Annmarie's body. If her superiors got wind of how close Nikki had once been with Annmarie, she'd have to fight to stay on the case, and she wasn't about to let Annmarie down again. "A Wilcraft," Nikki repeated. She'd heard of it. "Basically, it's an ATV that's also equipped for ice and water."

"Sounds expensive," Liam said, glancing at Nikki. They'd long believed that Frost's ability to keep his victims frozen for long periods and his skill at going undetected pointed to access to plenty of money.

"New, yeah," Mayberry said. "We can't get the federal government to spring for one. But every once in a while you find a used one for a reasonable price."

"They're supposed to be registered, just like a boat. We'll try to get a list of owners in the state. Given the price, I'd think the number would be relatively low," Nikki said. "Doug, can you confirm she hasn't been out here very long?"

Larsen gently touched Annmarie's arm. "She's still in rigor mortis. Cooler temps can slow that, but even so, I don't think she's been dead for more than twelve hours, if that."

"Can you slip the ribbon off and check her neck for any marks?" Nikki asked. Frost always killed his victims with a fatal dose of a strong sedative, and the injection point was always at the back of the neck. All of his victims also had bruising on their wrists that indicated they'd been kept under sedation before he killed them. Nikki kept her question deliberately vague, knowing that Liam would step in and examine Annmarie's neck without cluing Larsen or Mayberry into specific details.

Larsen slipped the ribbon off Annmarie's hair and slotted it into an evidence bag at the side of the body. He gently grasped her shoulder. "Agent Wilson, can you give me a hand?"

Nikki walked a few feet toward the lake, trying to focus on the sound of Courtney's camera instead of watching Liam and Larsen move Annmarie's stiff body in order to see the back of her neck.

Liam's voice was grim. "There's an injection mark on the base of her neck."

Nikki shared a look with Liam and Courtney and knew they were thinking the same thing. It was another Frost marker that was kept out of the media. They both walked over to her, out of earshot of the other two men.

"Why is she looking in the wrong direction?" Liam asked quietly. Frost's victims always faced the sky, likely held in place by some device until the bodies were frozen well enough to maintain the position. "The positioning of the body is right otherwise. This is the first crime scene we've been called to that's ticked this many Frost boxes. It's just the time of year and the positioning that's awry. It could be him…" He looked worriedly at Nikki.

As hard as she tried to keep her personal life out of work, she and her team worked so closely together, and Liam and Courtney both knew how hard the last several months had been for Nikki. Liam looked braced for a reaction from her. If this was Frost, he had killed Nikki's friend.

"I agree," Nikki said, but she kept her emotions to herself. "It could be him. But we don't know for sure. Let's consider both lines of inquiry."

Liam nodded.

Nikki couldn't help but think about the positioning. Was Annmarie's face fixed so that she could see the water? She remembered how much Annmarie had loved the water—she'd wanted to move to the North Woods one day. Nikki's stomach soured. She wondered if perhaps Annmarie's killer knew her. Perhaps he cared about her in some capacity—he could have injected her right here so she could see the lake as she died.

"Courtney, I want this area triple-checked for evidence." She went on, "In particular, anything that might have been used to administer the lethal dose."

Courtney had already finished with her camera and started labeling evidence bags. She gave Nikki a skeptical look but grunted her acknowledgment. They all knew the chances of Frost panicking and disposing of evidence carelessly were slim to none, but Nikki couldn't leave anything to chance. And they couldn't be certain it was him yet, despite Nikki's gut instincts. She had to eliminate all other possible suspects.

Nikki glanced around Liam to make sure the medical examiner was still focused on the body.

On Annmarie's body.

It's Annmarie.

Nikki ignored the voice in her head and hoped she sounded in control. "Maybe Frost saw the interview with Caitlin a couple of weeks ago," she told them.

Since Frost had gone past his usual timeframe of leaving a victim, Nikki had decided to do a news interview to remind people to make sure they reported any females missing, and if they had any information, to call the FBI. She'd given Caitlin Newport, a respected journalist, five minutes of her time to discuss Frost's methods. They had gone over each of Frost's victims and questioned his lack of action this year. "While we are very thankful he hasn't left a victim, we're concerned she just simply hasn't been found yet," she'd said.

Caitlin had asked about the possibility of Frost being dead. "It's definitely possible. But even so, we need the public's help to identify him. These families need closure." She'd ended the interview by urging the public to call the established tip-line with any information related to any of the victims, even if they believed it wasn't important.

Courtney touched Nikki's arm as the weight of what Nikki said set in. "You think you provoked him?"

Nikki nodded—she didn't want to tell her team that she was already starting to feel guilty, but she did. She had to keep her emotions in check, or she'd end up being kicked off the case. She looked up at Liam, knowing she needed to remind him why she was the only person who should work this case and keep him on her side. "Let's think about it, if this is Frost and he targeted Annmarie, then his motives are changing. We can't ask another team to get up to speed in time to find him." Nikki said bitterly, "Annmarie's death isn't going unsolved. I will find out who murdered her."

Nikki could see that Courtney still looked worried, but both of them seemed convinced by what she had to say.

"Agent Hunt." Mayberry cleared his throat and came over, nervously adjusting his skullcap. "I don't want to sound like I know more than Mr. Larsen, but because of the eagles, I don't think she's been here more than a few hours."

Nikki stared at him. "The eagles?"

He gestured to the group's left, farther down shore. "You probably saw the eagles' nest about three hundred yards down shore. That pair of eagles is tagged, and they have a routine. They hunt in the morning, and when there's ice breaking up, they keep an eye on the water. I saw one this morning not two hundred feet from here, around 8:30 a.m., which is their normal time. The call came in about the body some ninety minutes later. I don't think the eagles would have left her alone. At the very least, I would have expected to see some tracks or scraps near her, and I can't see anything."

Nikki had forgotten to put her watch on this morning. "What time is it now?"

"11:30 a.m.," Liam said. "He could have killed her and then waited here for a while. We know Frost wants his bodies found, is particular about how he leaves them. He may have even wanted to protect the body until he was certain a plane was going to discover her."

Nikki nodded at Liam in agreement. She addressed Mayberry. "The pilot who spotted her this morning, around 10 a.m.—was that a routine flight?"

"Not exactly, but it's common knowledge that we're going to be in the air this time of year, looking for the black bears we've tagged to come out of hibernation, plus keeping track of the wolf pack." Mayberry scowled. "We've had an increase of poachers in the past year, so we've been flying more."

"That's common knowledge around here too?"

Mayberry nodded. "It's on the BWCA website. Not specific times, but we always have estimates."

"Annmarie's body was spotted ninety minutes ago. If you're right about this, the killer could still be close by," Liam said.

"Ranger Mayberry, how fast do the Wilcrafts go?" Nikki asked.

"Up to twenty miles an hour for the top-of-the-line ones. I think the average is fifteen."

Adrenaline was starting to mask Nikki's grief. "Let's say he departs at 9:30. Two hours later, he can't be more than thirty miles away in any given direction…" Nikki surmised. She turned to Mayberry. "I need you to call every ranger in a thirty-mile radius with a BOLO for the Wilcraft," she told him. "Can we get a pilot in the air too?"

Mayberry was looking at his phone. "Just got a text from my boss." He shook his head. "There's a snowstorm coming this way. They're expecting six to ten inches of snow with heavy winds."

"A blizzard in the Boundary Waters in April." Liam rolled his eyes. "Mother Nature can't even give us a break."

The incoming storm helped Nikki to stow her grief and focus on the present. "How long before it hits?"

Mayberry shrugged. "National Weather Service radar shows it hitting here in about two hours. But if the wind speed changes, it'll be sooner."

"Then we need to get moving." They walked back over to Larsen. "Doug, how long will it take you to get the body loaded onto the plane?"

"Not long once I've finished the preliminaries here."

Nikki kept her eyes on her team, knowing that looking at Annmarie would mess with her ability to compartmentalize. "Liam, you stay here and help Courtney process the scene. Doug will probably need help getting the body onto the plane too. Mayberry, can you put the BOLO out on the Wilcraft?"

"On it," he said, pulling out his phone.

"Doug, please see to it that she's taken to Dr. Blanchard's office in St. Paul. Blanchard handles all bodies that could be the work of Frost."

Courtney glanced at Liam and then started unpacking her equipment. Nikki knew they supported her working the case or they wouldn't have helped hide her personal connection with Annmarie. But she also knew they were becoming increasingly uncomfortable with the circus around Frost killings, and how much Frost might be enjoying the attention Nikki's name brought to his crimes. A few years ago, Minneapolis hosted the Super Bowl, and Nikki had assisted with security on game day. Frost's victim had been found at the end of the third quarter, just a few hundred yards away from the building. Leaving the body in such a high-traffic area ensured that she was found quickly. Nikki arrived on scene within minutes of the 9-1-1 call, and she'd enlisted a team of officers to help her discreetly scour the stadium for any sign of Frost. The massive crowd made finding him impossible, and he'd vanished as usual, but Nikki felt like she was being watched the entire time. Liam had remarked then that he thought Frost reveled in the attention Nikki's name brought to his crimes.

"I know you're still worried that I'm too closely connected," she said quietly. "But no one knows Frost better than me. From the way he chooses his victims, to the way he carries out their murders, to the specific way he leaves their bodies. Even if he targeted Annmarie on purpose, I'm still the right person for this case."

Courtney nodded, but Liam still seemed wary.

"So you agree that Frost could be goading you?" he asked.

"Yes, but I understand the game he's trying to play. I can separate myself from it."

Liam sighed, his arms crossed over his chest. She knew he was struggling with the right thing to say. Nikki was his superior, but his concerns were valid. "You can compartmentalize better than anyone I know, but this is a lot to process."

"I promise to be transparent about everything," she told him. "I'll step back if it gets to that point. Right now, we've got to search the area."

"I'm going to start processing the scene. We don't have much time." Courtney looked pointedly at Nikki. "But I'm here if you need me."

Nikki shot her a grateful look and tried to focus on the wrinkled map that Mayberry had retrieved from his backpack.

"This is our main map of the area." He held the map so they could all see it. "We're here, at the southeast edge of Trout Lake. There's one main entry point not far from here. We checked it this morning as soon as the body was spotted and didn't find anything unusual. It's still fairly frozen, and we're not allowing ice fishing right now. But there's also a portage entry from Lake Vermillion, which is just south of us. Again, we're in mid-thaw, so no one is supposed to be on the lake at all."

"You said the campsites in the area have already been searched?"

Mayberry appeared to be fighting his excitement. "There's only two campsites, and there's no sign anyone has been there recently."

She doubted Frost left a scrap of evidence behind, but she wanted to see if they could find where he came onto the shore. They could likely confirm he'd been in a Wilcraft from the tracks left and maybe give the other rangers an idea of where to focus the BOLO. "We have ninety minutes to search the area. We meet back here in eighty to get back on the plane," she said, looking around at her team. "Let's go."

CHAPTER THREE

Nikki and Mayberry headed east, walking along the edge of the deep woods. Nikki had only been in the Superior National Forest once, the summer before her parents died. And like many of her childhood trips, it had been with Annmarie…

She and Annmarie, along with a few other friends, had come up to the area to camp. Annmarie had relented and had a few drinks. She'd gone a short way into the woods to pee when a screech owl scared her. Nikki could still see her running towards them, pants around her knees. The boys had howled with laughter, and the owl continued to voice its displeasure through the night.

Before they left on the search, Mayberry assured her he knew the woods like the back of his hand and would be able to spot anything unusual. She kept her eyes on the ground, looking for anything that Frost might have left behind, and let him lead the way. According to Mayberry, the area only had three locations the Wilcraft could have come ashore. "Even with things melting during the day and freezing again at night, we should see tracks."

The first two had been a bust, and Nikki prayed the third time would give them something useful. "Those Wilcrafts are heated inside, right?" she asked, stepping over a fallen tree.

"Yeah, they're pretty awesome. Basically, a heated icehouse on ATV wheels. I've been saving up for a used one."

"Do you know how many dealers there are in the state?"

"Only a few." Mayberry seemed impervious to the increasing wind, his jacket partially unzipped and his skullcap riding up over his ears, revealing dark hair.

Despite the warm winter hat, Nikki was still freezing. She yanked her hood over her head and tried to match Mayberry's pace.

"I'm sorry that the victim is someone you know." Mayberry paused. "It must be horrible being able to identify a body. I don't know how well you knew her, of course."

"Thank you," Nikki said. She was grateful for his condolences, but she didn't want to linger there for too long or fill in any of the gaps he clearly wanted her to fill. "Would you walk me through your morning again, if you don't mind?"

She wanted to distract him, but she also wondered if Mayberry might object to her questions. He was a federal officer and, like the other rangers on duty, he had already been alibied for this morning. He didn't seem to realize this, though, and launched into his day, which started at 7:30 a.m. sharp.

"Winter's slower, especially during the ice breakup. I clock in at the ranger station and then do a quick walk around to make sure no pipes have broken or frozen. If there's a dog sled tour scheduled or a hiker requesting any sort of permission or assistance, I'll deal with that." He glanced at her, a sheepish look on his face. "I never take personal calls unless they're an emergency, but an old friend had left me a message, and I was distracted. I'm afraid I screwed up and missed something that could have helped us."

"That's not a screwup." Nikki spoke over the wind. "If Frost killed her, I guarantee he'd already scouted this place and knew your routine. He wants his victims found quickly, and I'm betting that he knew the flight schedule too."

"But why come all the way up here to leave her body? If he wanted her found, surely there would be easier places to access."

"That's a good question." Nikki had been wondering the same thing. When the call had first come in, she'd assumed that if this was a Frost victim, he'd chosen the Boundary Waters because it was still cold, and the body wouldn't thaw very quickly. Her gut told her he'd scouted the location and intended to use it for a victim, but she couldn't figure out why he hadn't taken Annmarie weeks ago and gone through his usual methods.

She and Liam had been keeping an eye on missing persons reports for weeks, and Annmarie's name had never come up. If this was Frost, why had he taken her and killed her so quickly? If he'd been sick or injured, he might have been forced to adjust his routine. But why Annmarie?

After DNA proved who killed her parents and helped free Mark Todd from prison, Nikki's past had been rehashed by every news outlet. Frost might have chosen Annmarie because he knew it would get to Nikki, but she still couldn't figure out the change in his timing.

"Look at the sky." Mayberry's worried tone drew her out of her thoughts. "The storm is moving closer."

Nikki looked up, shocked at how quickly the northeastern sky had darkened to a blue purple, the storm clouds stretching across the entire horizon. "How close are we to the third outlet?"

"It's just right up here." Mayberry headed closer to the shoreline, and Nikki followed.

Walking was difficult, as much of the slushy ice covering the weedy beach remained dangerously slippery. Sharp, cold wind gusted from the northeast, and Nikki pulled her coat collar up to her nose.

They walked in silence for several minutes, and Nikki warred with her emotions every step. She prided herself on her ability to compartmentalize her life. Most cases, she could walk the line between remembering the victim was an actual person with a grieving family whose life had been tragically cut short and staying neutral enough to remain laser focused. She had to figure out a way to do the same thing with this case.

Nikki was so lost in her thoughts that she nearly missed the frozen tire tracks.

"Mayberry," she shouted over the increasing wind. "Here."

He jogged down to the shore as though it weren't frozen solid. "Those are definitely Wilcraft tracks." He shaded his eyes against the wind and scanned the lake. "See the ice? You can tell where the machine started to break through."

"That's southwest, right?" Nikki said.

"Towards the portage route into Lake Vermillion, is my guess. There are a bunch of little islands in that area he could hide out in. No shelters, but as long as the Wilcraft has fuel, he could hide it."

"Let the rangers know." Nikki followed the tracks from the shoreline to the trees. There was a break in the trees large enough to drive into the woods. "He could have easily camouflaged the craft, even in winter."

She and Mayberry walked slowly in opposite directions around the area, looking for any usable evidence.

"Agent Hunt. Come look at this."

Nikki tried to hurry and skidded, nearly losing her balance. He steadied her and then pointed to one of the evergreen bushes. High winds had stripped most of the pine needles in places, but she could see a piece of dark fabric attached to one of the branches. She carefully removed it. "It's silky. Like an inner lining of something."

Mayberry looked above him, as clouds gathered in the sky. "I think we've run out of time…"

Nikki slipped the material into the evidence bag she'd been carrying and started taking pictures. The weather seemed to worsen by the moment.

"Agent, we need to go," Mayberry called over the wind. "I don't see anything else here, and if we delay much longer, the plane won't be able to take off."

She snapped a couple more photos before she and Mayberry hurried back to join the others. They made it back just as snow flurries started to fall.

Courtney shaded her eyes against the increasing snow. "I was getting worried."

Nikki handed her the evidence bag. "We found a piece of fabric attached to a bush along the water towards Lake Vermillion."

Courtney's eyebrows furrowed as she examined the fabric. "Looks like silk."

"Perfect timing," Liam yelled over the wind. "We're ready to go. No one else has reported any evidence from their searches, and I managed to get Annmarie's address just now. She lived at The Pointe in Woodbury. That's as much as I got from the office before my signal went to shit."

A wave of relief crashed over Nikki. "That's Washington County. As soon as we land, I'll call Kent and have him pull up as much information on her as possible." Kent Miller was the interim sheriff for Washington County, and Nikki had worked with him on several intensely complicated cases in the last few months. He was a skilled cop, and Nikki trusted him as much as she did her team. "Did Larsen take off with Annmarie?"

Liam nodded, and the three of them hurried over to where Mayberry stood with the waiting plane as the snow began to fall in bigger flurries around them. Nikki climbed on board, followed by the others. She secured her seatbelt, trying not to think about the increasing wind.

"Good thing is, we're flying away from it," the pilot said. "And we're taking off, so everybody strap in. It's going to be bumpy."

CHAPTER FOUR

After a very long journey, most of which was spent in white-knuckled silence, Nikki and her team taxied into the municipal airport in Ely, where the nearest ranger station was located. Nikki asked Liam to drive back to the metro area with Courtney so she could have some time alone in her car. She needed to decompress, and she didn't want to get emotional in front of them.

Nikki could tell Courtney was worried about her as they said goodbye. "Drive safe and stay close to us," she told her.

"I will." Nikki ducked her head against the wind and headed to her jeep. She closed the door and started the engine, listening to the hum and fighting tears. After more than a decade in law enforcement, Nikki had seen horrific things, including murdered children. Knowing that she was providing justice for the victim and closure for the family always got her through the emotional moments, but Annmarie's murder had shaken Nikki to her core.

While she waited for the engine to warm up, she texted Rory to let him know she was on her way back to Stillwater. She'd been at his house when the call came in, and she knew he'd want to know that she was on her way back in the storm. Rory had been the bright spot in Nikki's return to Stillwater. He'd never blamed Nikki for his brother's wrongful incarceration, and his compassion had helped her push her pride aside and catch her parents' real killer.

The snow started picking up, and Courtney flashed her SUV's headlights as they were each ready to drive off. Nikki motioned for them to go first and then called Chief Miller. His phone went to voicemail, so Nikki left him a message letting him know they had a case in his county and needed his assistance. Miller had gone to high school with Nikki and had known Annmarie, so she didn't use her name in the voicemail. She'd tell Miller when he returned her call.

By the time she got on the interstate, snow was pouring from the sky, and the heavy wind made for lousy visibility. The front was moving northwest, so they just needed to stay on the road until they drove out of the storm.

For the first hour, Nikki managed to concentrate on driving and keeping Courtney's taillights in sight. But once they'd driven through the worst of the bad weather and could relax a little, Nikki could no longer keep her emotions in. She was devastated. Acid burned Nikki's throat. She could picture Annmarie perfectly, sitting on Nikki's bed when they were kids, listening to Nikki tell ghost stories about the farmhouse she lived in. The two of them had scared themselves silly and even tried to have a séance until Nikki's mother intervened and made Nikki get rid of the Ouija board.

"Ghosts aren't real," Nikki's mother had said, "but we don't need that kind of bad juju in the house."

Nikki scrubbed the tears out of her eyes, thinking about the years after her parents had been murdered like they were yesterday—she'd methodically pushed everyone away, obsessively focusing on graduating and going to college. Getting away from Stillwater and anything that reminded her of the past had been her sole endeavor for several years. Annmarie had stuck around longer than anyone. She'd even managed to get Nikki to have a joint graduation party with her, and Nikki had gone through the motions. But by the middle of her freshman year in college, she'd successfully shut Annmarie out just like everyone else.

Her eyes stung with tears. How could she have been so cruel, even in her grief? Why hadn't she swallowed her pride and apologized when she got her head straight? She'd told herself that Annmarie was better off without her.

Tomorrow, Nikki knew she would have to go to Annmarie's apartment, to find out where she worked and what she'd been doing for the past twenty years. She also knew she'd need to go to the nursing home first thing in the morning, although she had no idea if Howard, Annmarie's father, would be able to comprehend what she had to tell him.

Her phone rang loudly through the Bluetooth, startling her.

"Courtney." She'd waved to them as she took the exit for Stillwater, while they drove on to the Cities. "You guys okay?"

"Fine, fine. But Liam was looking at that piece of fabric you found, and it hit me where it's from. The coloring and the texture looked familiar to me. It looks like a piece of Annmarie's coat pocket. I'll double-check when I get the clothes, but it's the same blue as the inside of her coat, and if you hold it up to the light, you can see the Burberry logo superimposed on it."

"Maybe it snagged on a branch. But she could have torn it out and left it." Nikki's chest felt tight. "I mean, the bush came up to about my chest, and the fabric was left a few inches from the top. I guess she could have caught it. But it was an evergreen bush. There weren't any needles." Had Annmarie known what was about to happen and torn the fabric from her coat in the hopes someone would piece things together?

"I'll have a better idea once I get it under the microscope. I just wanted you to know it belonged to her."

Nikki's hands tightened on the steering wheel. "We're going to get him this time, Court."

"From your lips to God's ears, my friend," Courtney replied and hung up.

It was nearly midnight by the time Nikki made it to Rory's house. Aside from a couple of texts, she hadn't spoken with him since this morning, when she told him about flying into the Boundary Waters.

She hung her coat on the hook by the garage door and slipped out of her boots. Upstairs, the television droned on. Exhaustion seemed to set in deeper with every step. By the time she reached the top floor of Rory's split level, Nikki's grief was barely contained.

She found Rory asleep on the couch, the remote in his hand. Wordlessly, Nikki laid her head on top of him, resting it on his chest.

"Hey." He kissed the top of her head. "You're finally home. Were the roads bad up there?"

Nikki lifted her head to look at him, the tears already building in her eyes.

"Oh my God, what's wrong?"

CHAPTER FIVE

Tuesday

Nikki peeled her eyes open, wincing from the morning sunlight streaming through the blinds. They were crusty and swollen from crying. Rory had soothed her as much as he could, but she had obsessed over the case half the night, going through old Frost notes trying to look for anything they'd missed. She didn't remember falling asleep, but Rory must have woken up and brought her into the bedroom.

She gently prodded his arm until he grunted. "It's past seven. Aren't you usually at work by now?" Rory owned a successful construction company, and he was hands-on, always running from one site to another, juggling various jobs and working out the details of new contracts.

He opened his eyes. "I'm going in later. I wanted to be here when you woke up." Rory moved his arm so she could slip underneath it and snuggle against his chest.

She traced the big tattoo on his sternum. "You didn't have to do that."

"I wanted to." Rory's voice was thick with emotion. He had been a few years behind her in school, but he'd known Annmarie. Back then, before the murders, Nikki had been fairly close with Rory's older brother, Mark. She and Annmarie, along with a couple of other friends, had spent a lot of nights in the Todds' kitchen. "How are you holding up?"

"Okay," she said. "Being able to compartmentalize comes in handy at times like this."

His fingers trailed down her back. "You don't sound compartmentalized. You sound numb."

"That too," Nikki said. "Will you tell Mark for me? We're trying to keep it out of the news for as long as possible, but I'd hate for him to hear it that way."

Rory squeezed her. "Sure. He's working with me today."

She reached for her phone and saw that Miller had returned her call. "I need to tell Chief Miller. He knew her when we were kids too. We've got to process Annmarie's apartment, and I have to tell her father." The thought made her half-nauseous.

"I'll make a pot of coffee." Rory slipped out of the sheets. She could see his back muscles flexing as he slipped on sweats, reminding her of the relaxed nights they had spent together before she got the call yesterday.

She waited until Rory left the bedroom to call Miller back.

"Hey, Nikki. Sorry I missed your call yesterday. I had the day off and my daughter had a recital. What's up?"

Nikki exhaled shakily. "A body has been found in the Boundary Waters. I was called because there are elements of the scene that look like Frost..." Nikki swallowed hard, hoping the knot in her throat would go away. "It's Annmarie Mason."

"My God," he replied, shock in his voice. "But I haven't had any missing person reports."

"Because something's different about this one," Nikki said. "I just don't know what exactly that is yet. Her dad's in a nursing home, so I'm going to stop there and see when she last visited, but we don't think she'd been there long."

He was silent for a moment. "Nicole, I'm so sorry."

"Don't be. I'm not the one who deserves your pity. Howard is," she said. "I never even had the guts to call her, even after I found out about Howard being in the nursing home."

"That doesn't mean you aren't allowed to grieve, Nikki," he said, pausing for a moment. "Do *you* think it was Frost?" Miller had investigated a case of his own that he'd thought was Frost's work at first.

Nikki quickly explained the anomalies in the case, before acknowledging that this one had more hallmarks than they'd ever seen before. It was a possibility. "Blanchard is doing the autopsy today, but it will take a little while for toxicology to confirm that Annmarie had the same drugs in her system as Frost's other victims."

"But when you first came back to Stillwater, you told me that Frost doesn't deviate from his routine," Miller said. "So why deviate now?"

"We're not sure yet," Nikki admitted. "While the consistencies stand out, we can't ignore the anomalies, either. My gut tells me this is Frost's doing, but we're still casting a wide net to begin with."

"Do you know anything about Annmarie's life since high school?" Miller asked. "I don't; we barely crossed paths."

"Nothing," Nikki replied. "We found out that her last name is still Mason and she lives at The Pointe in Woodbury. Her last name *was* Mason," she corrected herself. "Can you get ahold of property management and get a warrant to search her place? See what else you can find out about the last few years of her life too." Nikki was relieved to have Miller's help. She knew he could be trusted with details about Frost they normally didn't share with local police.

"No problem," Miller replied.

"Let's meet at The Pointe later this morning. I'll have a better idea on the time after I get to the nursing home."

"Sounds good," Miller said. "Can I say something? I'll only say it once, I promise."

"Go ahead."

"I know there's zero chance of you taking a back seat in this case, but you do realize that your personal connection to Annmarie might mean you're the wrong person to investigate it. If you feel yourself getting overwhelmed, take some time off…"

Miller had witnessed the emotional toll returning to Stillwater had taken on Nikki over the past few months, so she wasn't surprised at the question. He was too good at his job not to ask. "I will."

She ended the call just as Rory returned with steaming coffee, loaded with French Vanilla and sugar, just the way she liked it. She took a few sips, relishing the burn in her throat.

Nikki loathed to leave the warm bed, but she wanted to visit the nursing home before meeting Liam and Miller at Annmarie's apartment as they'd arranged via text in the wee hours of the morning. The nursing home, Heritage House, where Annmarie's father lived was on the west side of Stillwater, not far from Rory's. She'd been so close to Annmarie over the past few months and hadn't seen her. And now it was too late.

The only thing Nikki could do for her old friend was to catch her killer, and that's exactly what she intended to do.

Heritage House was a large, single-story brick building with two expansive wings. One side housed long-term patients, while the other served rehab patients who just needed to get their strength back.

Nikki found a parking spot and took a few minutes to clear her head. She was here as an FBI agent, but she also knew Howard. He'd always treated her kindly, and after Nikki started coming to Stillwater to see Rory, she'd asked around about Annmarie's father in the hope that she would get the courage to go see him. Rory found out through his parents that Howard had Alzheimer's and had even tracked him down to Heritage House for her, but she'd never mustered the courage to visit for fear of running into Annmarie.

Nikki hated the idea of him suffering from Alzheimer's, but part of her hoped he wouldn't be able to understand that his only child was dead. Telling a parent that their child was gone was the hardest thing any cop ever had to do.

Nikki walked through two sets of double doors into a large, cheerful lobby. There were floor-to-ceiling windows on the northeast side, which brought in plenty of light, the walls were painted a soft yellow, and artwork, which seemed to be by local artists, lined the big room. To her left was a reading nook with a television and comfortable chairs.

"Hi." A young woman in maroon scrubs smiled at Nikki from the front desk. "How can I help you?"

Nikki forced a smile and held up her badge. "I'm Special Agent Nikki Hunt with the FBI. Unfortunately, I'm here on business. Is the charge nurse available?"

The girl looked surprised and then glanced at the clock. "Umm… she's finishing rounds. She should be available in a few minutes." She pointed to the small laptop sitting open on the counter. "If you'll just sign in and have a seat, I'll let her know you're here. The gray recliner is the comfortable one."

"Thank you." Nikki did as she was asked. "Every visitor has to sign in and out, correct?"

"Absolutely," the girl said. "We know who's in the building at all times."

"Good to know."

Nikki went to the gray recliner and sat on the edge, unable to relax. She had to stay alert and on point, or her emotions would get the best of her.

Her phone vibrated, and Liam's number flashed on her screen. She answered quietly. "I'm at the nursing home, waiting to speak to the head nurse. Are you on your way to Stillwater?"

"Yeah," Liam said. "I have a list of registered Wilcraft owners. I haven't had a chance to do more than skim it, but one name caught my eye. You'll never believe who reported a registered Wilcraft stolen, roughly four years ago, out of a storage unit."

"Who?" Nikki asked.

"Ernie Hoff."

"You're kidding." Kimberly Hoff had been Frost's first victim. Her body had been left in Kalamazoo, Michigan, five years ago. Kimberly's face still haunted Nikki's dreams, along with Frost's other victims. "Are you sure it's Kim's father's?"

"Positive. He still lives in the area, but the cell number we have on file for him is disconnected. I left a message on his home phone. And don't worry, I made it clear we were still looking for Frost." Nikki and Liam made sure to touch base with the victims' families a few times a year to let them know they weren't giving up, but she hadn't talked to the Hoffs in several months.

Dread washed through Nikki as a heavyset woman in navy blue scrubs approached her. "I've got to go. I'll see you at the apartment in an hour," she said to Liam before hanging up the call.

"Agent Hunt? I'm Lynn Norway, the day charge nurse." The two women shook hands. "I have to admit," Lynn continued, "we don't see a lot of FBI agents here."

Nikki stood and showed her credentials again. "Well, that's a good thing. Thank you for speaking with me. Is there a place we can talk in private?"

"Of course," Lynn said. "My office is just down the hall. Fair warning: it's small and messy. We're short-staffed, and I'm swamped with paperwork."

"That I understand," Nikki said as she followed Lynn down the corridor. "There's no shortage of paperwork in law enforcement."

Lynn unlocked the first door to her right and flipped on the light. She hadn't been lying about the mess, but Nikki could tell it was an organized one. Lynn removed a box marked "medical equipment" from the chair next to her desk. "Please, sit."

Nikki sat down and waited until Lynn had done the same. "I'm afraid I have some terrible news," Nikki began. "Annmarie Mason was murdered."

Lynn flinched as though she'd been slapped. "Pardon me? You're talking about Annie? Howard's daughter?"

Her dad had been the only person Annmarie allowed to call her that. She always said the nickname sounded too babyish. "I'm afraid so. Her body was discovered yesterday."

Lynn opened a desk drawer and dug around, finally pulling out a smashed box of tissues. She took a handful and dabbed her watering eyes. "Murdered? You're certain?"

"Yes," Nikki said. "I'm not sure if you're aware, but I grew up with Annmarie."

"Yes, I did know that actually." Lynn smiled. "She talked about you." Lynn paused. "Especially with everything in the news in the past few months."

Nikki smiled tightly. "You spent a lot of time with her, then?"

"More than I do with some family members, yes. Annmarie was very attentive to her father. She came to visit him every single day." Lynn's mouth trembled. "I wondered why she hadn't been here since last Tuesday. I thought of calling, but…"

"She visited her father last Tuesday? What time?"

"1:30 or so. She usually came from 10:30 to 1:30. All of the CNAs liked her. She was desperate to ensure that her father was treated with care, but she wasn't overbearing like some family members can become."

"Did she spend the entire time with Howard?" Nikki knew that certified nursing assistants were underpaid and that many facilities had a hard time keeping staff, which often led to various forms of neglect in assisted living facilities. Family members had to be diligent about making sure their loved ones were treated well.

"Most of it," Lynn said. "He's not very coherent most days and rarely recognizes her, but she doesn't let it stop her from coming every day."

"That had to have been tough for her," Nikki said. Annmarie had always been close with her parents, and she would have kept an eagle eye out for any issues.

"She took it in her stride, I think. Fortunately, Howard is still pretty good-natured."

"He didn't mind someone he thought of as a stranger spending so much time in his room every day?"

"Howard sleeps a lot," Lynn said. "Annie brought her laptop and worked. I think she just wanted to be with him."

"You saw her every day, then," Nikki said, almost to herself. "Did anything seem different the last few times you saw her? Did she seem worried or scared?"

"No," Lynn said. "She was always quiet and focused on her computer. We usually discussed her dad's state, and once Howard agreed to let her visit with him, I'd leave them alone."

"Did Howard have any other visitors?"

"As far as I know, she was the only one." Lynn shook her computer mouse and then started typing on the keyboard. "As I'm sure you know, everyone has to sign in at the front desk on the computer. Let me check the visitor logs."

Nikki wondered if the night shift ran as tight of a ship as Lynn did. In her experiences, nursing homes were usually short-staffed, especially in the evenings.

"Here we go. Howard Mason." Lynn peered at the screen. "Annmarie is the only one—wait. There was someone else. He visited a few weeks ago, in the evening. He signed in as Howie Doe." Lynn's cheeks turned pink. "That's a fake name, isn't it? We should have caught it, but we're busy and unless we know there's a possible security threat—"

Nikki's heart galloped in her chest. "That's all right. I noticed you have security cameras in the lobby and at the front door. Can you look through the footage from that day?"

"I'm afraid not. We only keep that footage for a week. The director says we don't have the budget to store it permanently."

"Can you tell me who worked that night?"

"I'm already pulling up the schedule. Myself and the evening charge nurse are responsible for it. Let's see, Paula Silver is the evening charge nurse, she would have been on the floor, along with a few CNAs."

"For the whole memory unit?" Nikki asked.

"I'm afraid so. It's hard to find people who want to do this sort of work. CNAs cap out at less than twenty dollars an hour, and it's brutal work."

Nikki shook her head. It was hard to believe the people responsible for providing humane care for the elderly were paid so little, while professional athletes and entertainers made ridiculous salaries.

"Here we are," Lynn said. "Kyle Wood and Theresa Park were on the memory unit that night."

"What about the regular unit?"

Lynn shook her head. "The memory unit has a separate entrance. Unless you're accompanied by one of us, you must enter through that door."

"I'd like to speak with everyone working that evening, just to cover all bases. I actually need a list of all your employees. Could you give me a list of names and their contact information?"

Lynn nodded. "Absolutely. I'll make sure my people know to expect your call. And, of course, you're free to speak to anyone on the floor today, although we have two new intakes in the memory unit, so it's very busy."

Nikki slid her business card across the messy desk. "You can email me at the address on the card." She couldn't put off talking to Howard anymore. "How do you suggest we tell Howard? Will he even know who we're talking about?"

"Probably not, unless we catch him at a lucid moment. But I can take you to see him. We owe it to Annmarie to try at least."

Nikki's feet felt like bricks as she walked down the wide, carpeted hallway with Lynn. The good-natured woman clearly cared about her patients and their families, and she beamed with pride when Nikki asked her about the framed artwork lining the walls. Some were nothing more than scribbles, but others were quite good.

"Our wall of fame," Lynn said. "Several of the residents like to draw and color, even the memory patients. We frame and hang them for a while so they can see their drawings on the way to eat or physical therapy. Even the memory patients who likely don't recognize their own work seem to enjoy them."

"That's wonderful," Nikki said. "It must be exhausting but rewarding to work with the elderly."

"It is." Lynn smiled. "But you have to have a thick skin. Death is a part of life. I guess you understand that given your job."

"I do. And I've learned the best way to deal with it is to try and live in the present. Appreciate all the little things in life."

"Good advice." Lynn stopped in front of a closed door with a whiteboard hanging in the center. Someone had written Howard's name on it, along with what looked like a note about his condition after breakfast.

"How is he on a day-to-day basis?' Nikki asked. "Does he recognize any of the regular staff?"

"Sometimes," Lynn said. "But if he does, it's brief. Fortunately, he's not prone to violent outbursts like some people, as long as no one else in the room is agitated. But if he senses you're frustrated with him, he'll react. He's good-natured about things, and we try to use humor when he does have memory issues. Just remember to keep the conversation casual and relaxed. Like a friendly chat. He seems to handle those situations best." She knocked on the door before peeking her head inside. "Howard, you have a visitor."

"I hope they brought some chocolate." Nikki heard his gravelly voice through the door. "I'm dying for an Andes."

Lynn laughed. "I don't think she has candy, but I'll see what I can do." She stepped aside so that Nikki could enter.

Nikki tried not to flinch at the sight of the man. She remembered him as stout and tan from working outside on the farm, but he had been reduced to a pale, thin frame with a shock of white hair, and seeing him like that was a surprise to Nikki. She hadn't expected him to have changed so much physically.

Howard was propped up in his bed, and a smile spread across his face as he noticed Nikki in the doorway. "You're back early. I thought you were spending the summer doing that college thing," he said.

Nikki looked at Lynn for reassurance, and when the woman nodded, she introduced herself.

"My name is Nikki," she said as she stood in the doorway. "I'm friends with Annie, your daughter."

Howard's smile started to fade. "I swear you look like a friend of mine," he said. "Who's Annie?"

"Your daughter," Nikki repeated, slipping inside the room. She knew the conversation was going to be difficult, but she had no idea she'd struggle even to explain who she was.

"Not ringing any bells, Val," Howard replied.

Nikki smiled, the name slowly sinking in. She didn't know what to say.

"Valerie Nolan. I took her to junior prom. She was a nice girl," he continued.

Nikki found herself gripping the tall bed rail. Valerie was Nikki's mother. Her parents and Annmarie's had gone to Stillwater High School together. They'd continued to run in the same social circles until the murders.

Howard looked at her with sad eyes. "You look just like her."

Nikki did bear a strong resemblance to her late mother, but nobody had told her that in years, and the memory of her mother hit her in the chest. She tried to remind herself of what she was doing, that she was there in Howard's room to tell him that his daughter had died. But before she could say anything, Howard's expression changed. He looked angry, upset, confused.

"Valerie and her husband were murdered. Their daughter Nicole found them. I wonder if she ever found out what happened." The words were a sucker punch in the gut, and Nikki couldn't help but feel the pain of her parents' deaths as if they had happened yesterday. Howard shook his head, his expression almost childlike. "I'll take that secret to my grave, Val. Promise."

And then Howard's eyes started to close. Nikki wanted to ask him what she meant, but he looked so sad and tired. She wanted to pull the blankets to his chin and make sure he was comfortable to sleep, but she didn't want to agitate him by invading his space.

"I'm afraid you won't get much more from him," Lynn said from behind her. "This doesn't seem like a good day. He gets really tired after conversations. He'll be asleep before we make it to the door."

Wordlessly, Nikki went round to the side of the bed and patted Howard's gnarled hand. Her parents had suffered unimaginably, but at least they hadn't lived to become trapped in their own heads like Howard. And it was clear that it was pointless trying to tell Howard the news about Annmarie. In some ways, it was a blessing to never learn of her murder, but in another, it was sad that Nikki had no one else to inform.

Lynn walked with her to the main entrance. "I'll email you the employee list right away, and I'll make sure the night staff know you'll be stopping by."

"Thank you," Nikki said. She could see her jeep from the front doors and hit the remote start. "By the way, did you ever see the car Annmarie drove?"

"I think it was a red truck," Lynn said. "I know I saw her driving it at least once."

Nikki left the nursing home in a daze. She shouldn't have been surprised that Howard had mistaken her for her mother; they'd always looked similar, and Nikki looked more like her as she'd gotten older. But what secret was he talking about? She reminded herself that Howard was an old man with Alzheimer's. He could have been mixing any number of memories together.

Lynn had already emailed over a list of all the nursing home employees. There were only twelve medical staff: four nurses and eight CNAs, plus two janitorial employees. Nikki knew she'd need to ask for every staff member's alibi, but in her heart, she doubted any of them were involved.

CHAPTER SIX

Annmarie lived in Woodbury, a small city in the metro area not far from Stillwater. The Pointe at Woodbury was a newer, higher-end apartment building that advertised luxurious exclusivity. Nikki was surprised that Annmarie had been living in a place like this. When they were in high school, they used to make fun of all the town girls with their designer clothes and bad attitudes. Annmarie had never been materialistic, and she'd even talked about spending a couple of years in the Peace Corps before going to college. Nikki spotted Miller's cruiser as she arrived out front and parked next to him. Before she joined him, Nikki drained her coffee, already wishing she had another. It was going to be a long day, and she was already exhausted.

Miller exited his vehicle, his dark skin slightly ashen. He'd told Nikki that he hadn't stayed in touch with Annmarie since high school, but Stillwater was small enough that he likely had memories of her. With a sigh, Nikki slung her bag over her shoulder and got out to meet him.

She shook Miller's outstretched hand. "Thanks for meeting us. Liam should be here in a few minutes."

"No problem," he said. "How are you holding up?"

"I'm okay honestly," she reassured him. "What did you find out?" Nikki had asked Miller to dig up all the information he could on Annmarie. The media would be foaming at the mouth once they learned that Nikki was yet again connected to a case, so she was glad to be in Miller's jurisdiction, knowing he would keep things close to the vest.

A silver Prius drove past and then parked in the space across from them, distracting Miller from Nikki's question. Liam looked as jammed in and uncomfortable as usual, and Nikki was always amazed at how easily he managed to get out of the car.

He joined them, shaking hands with Miller.

"Kent was just getting ready to tell me what he found about Annmarie's past."

Miller checked the small notepad he always carried. "Annmarie graduated from Mankato State in '99. She went to grad school for computer engineering at Purdue and then worked at an Indianapolis technical firm for five years."

"I'm not surprised she went into tech," Nikki said. "She was always in the computer lab, even in middle school. Where did she go after Indianapolis?"

"According to her tax records, over the next few years, she lived in Colorado, Washington State, Nevada, and California to work for a company called VPCloud," Miller said. "They're a private cloud service with a lot of bells and whistles. She stayed in California until a couple of years ago, when she returned to Minnesota. Best I can tell, she still works for them, just remotely most of the time. No registered vehicle in her name, but I ran her dad's. Howard Mason owns a red GMC Canyon pickup. She might have been driving it since he stopped being able to."

"She was." Nikki couldn't picture her friend driving such a big truck. Annmarie had loved the little hatchback she drove in high school. Her parents wanted Annmarie to drive something bigger and safer, but she'd insisted on something that didn't "suck up gas and pollute the air." "The nurse at Howard's place saw her driving a red pickup. Did you find any reason why Annmarie moved so much?"

Miller shrugged. "Her tax status was self-employed after she moved to Colorado, until VPCloud. Looks like she did a lot of consulting work and freelance. Maybe she liked the change of scenery?"

"Maybe," Nikki said. "But Annmarie was never an adventurer. She was a planner, always carefully debating things before deciding to do something. I can't see her as some kind of nomad. Then again… I didn't know her anymore. People change." She cleared her throat.

"Married? Kids?" Liam asked.

"No," Miller said. "Which probably made it easier to move around."

"But why move so much?" Nikki asked. "Was she hiding from someone? Running from a horrible job? A toxic relationship?"

Miller's dark eyebrows knitted together. "What did you make of the signs that this was Frost? You said that was why they called you to the scene?"

So far, Nikki had only entrusted her team with Frost's signatures, but this was the first case in a long time that looked likely to be him. If she was going to find out, she needed Miller's help, and Miller had earnt her trust over the past few months. "Yes. Frost has particular signatures, ones, unlike the bodies being frozen, that we keep out of the media." She told him about the ribbon used to hide an injection, his use of bleach and the body positioning. "It's hard for me to believe there are any other explanations other than Frost killing her, given those details, but until we know more about her life, we have to keep all our options open."

Miller still looked overwhelmed, but he held himself together. He glanced at Nikki. "I haven't gone inside yet. Is Courtney on her way? I didn't call my forensic guys because I assumed you'd want her to handle things."

"Thank you," Nikki replied. The lump in her throat ached. "I spoke to her on the drive over from the nursing home. She'll be here soon, so we might as well go on inside."

"How'd it go with her father?" Liam asked, falling into step beside Nikki.

She bypassed the question, ashamed she hadn't had the nerve to tell Howard about Annmarie. Instead she informed them about the male visitor a few weeks ago. "Unfortunately, the security footage is already wiped, but I'm hoping to speak with the night staff this evening." She didn't mention Howard's strange ramblings about her parents. "Did the Hoffs call you back?"

"Not yet. I'm waiting to hear from them before I send anyone to track down the other registered owners."

"Call again if you don't hear from them soon." Nikki didn't want to give anyone false hope, but it was good intel. The vehicle could provide another strong connection between Frost and the case. "We need booties. I think I have some in the jeep," Nikki said absentmindedly. "I'll run back and get them."

"Already on it." Liam dug into his backpack. He held up three pairs of paper booties and latex gloves.

Miller gestured to the impressive, contemporary apartment building. "I went to the judge this morning and requested a warrant to search Annmarie's apartment and phone records, along with security footage from The Pointe. The security team is currently going through the last few days of closed-circuit footage to see when Annmarie last left the building, but they haven't had any complaints of stalkers or strange people. They do several drive-throughs at night, and this place is pretty quiet."

They walked in unison toward the entrance, and Nikki's anxiety ticked up with each step. She wasn't sure she was ready to walk into her friend's intimate space after so much had happened, but she had a job to do.

"Who owns this building?" Liam asked.

"Martin Property Management," Miller replied, reading once again from his notebook. "They own several higher-end apartment buildings throughout the city. Stellar record, pride themselves on security, et cetera."

Miller held the door open, and they walked into the lobby. Trendy black tile floors shined beneath warm lighting, a small bubbling fountain the centerpiece.

A man in gray slacks walked eagerly toward them. The only thing shinier than the gel he used to comb his hair back was the likely fake Rolex on his wrist. "Sheriff Miller?" he asked.

Miller shook his extended hand and then introduced Nikki and Liam. "This is Declan Simpson. He's the building association president. Martin Property Management said he would be the best person to answer our questions."

"I'm stunned to hear about Annmarie," Declan said. "She was a model tenant."

"And a good person." Nikki couldn't keep the edge out of her voice. She knew Declan was probably uncomfortable, but Annmarie had been a hell of a lot more than a good tenant and for some reason, Nikki was feeling defensive. "Did you know her?" she asked him.

"Not well," Declan said. "She attended a few resident meetings, but I don't think anyone knew her very well. I'm her neighbor, and I only spoke to her during those meetings."

"You're her only neighbor?" Liam asked.

"It's on the top floor, so the spaces are larger. I have the two-bedroom, she has the single. The studio unit is currently empty."

"Do you remember what the meetings she attended were about?" Miller asked.

"Security. There are only twelve units in this building. Everyone tries to look out for one another. Last year, our main building system was targeted by someone trying to get past the lobby. We never found out who did it, but Annmarie was very angry. She worked in computer engineering and said that whoever tried to get into the system and figure out key codes was smart, and that our firewalls were 'pathetic.'" Declan looked sheepish. "For a quiet person, she was a firecracker. Within twenty-four hours, we had rock-solid cyber protection."

Nikki had heard of hackers figuring out how to access smart locks, but she'd assumed that luxury apartments like The Pointe would have top-of-the-line security.

"Here, let me show you," Declan said.

They followed Declan across the lobby to the elevator, where a large video screen had been mounted into the wall. "Prior to the hacking attempt, residents of each floor had a code allowing them inside." Declan touched the screen and swiped to his left, revealing a map of fire exits for each floor, along with basic floor plans for each apartment. "Once they're on their floor, a second, individualized code gets them into their unit."

"Who monitors the system?" Miller asked.

"Our security team," Declan said. "We have a night guard in the lobby, and our video control room is staffed twenty-four hours a day. They're able to remotely unlock every door in the building and manage visitors. But they don't have full access to all the information the system holds. That is reserved for the property managers."

"What can they access?" Nikki asked.

"Everything," Declan said. "It's basically a web portal that streamlines things. They can extend lease dates, issue day passes, that sort of thing."

"You're the building president," Liam said. "Do you have access?"

Declan shook his head. "Only what security is cleared to show me. My job is more about keeping the residents happy and making sure things run smoothly."

Liam folded his arms across his chest.

"What changed after the hacking attempt?" Nikki asked, still studying the map on the screen.

"Mostly increased firewall. Stuff that's on a par with government buildings. We also changed the codes so that everyone's floor code is different, along with their apartment code."

"But security can remotely unlock a door," Nikki said.

"Yes, but the resident has to give them their code and answer security questions. The officers don't actually have access to the codes."

"I assume the codes are changed frequently?"

"Every two weeks," Declan said. "And if someone needs remote unlocking, the code is changed immediately after." He typed a code onto the screen and the elevator opened. "Annmarie wanted to add facial recognition, but I couldn't get it approved by management."

Nikki nodded.

"Has the head of security gone through the CCTV footage?" Miller asked.

Declan slipped the tablet out from his arm. "It seems we've had a bit of a technical difficulty with our closed-circuit cameras in the parking garage."

"What sort of difficulty?"

"We store footage for up to a month." Declan opened the tablet. "Annmarie seemed to have a routine. She normally left around 10 a.m. and then returned around 1 p.m. This is the last footage we have of her, from last Wednesday, at 10:07 a.m." He tapped the screen, and the black and white video began to play.

Nikki sucked in a raw breath as she saw Annmarie in an elevator, a messenger bag hanging on her shoulder and a pair of keys in her hand. She didn't appear to be under any duress. Nikki wanted to pause the footage and soak in the image of her friend alive. Had she known she was in trouble? The doors opened, and Annmarie exited into a large, concrete corridor.

"That's our underground garage," Declan. "Unfortunately, this is where our footage stops. It would appear our cameras in the parking garage were offline for about thirty minutes. Our people fixed it quickly, but they're still not sure what happened."

"Convenient hiccup in your system," Nikki said dryly. Annmarie had been taken some time on Wednesday and then found by rangers on their Monday morning flyovers. She didn't believe the timing had been a coincidence. Frost knew she'd be found quickly, just like all of the others.

"It's never happened before."

"If the system was hacked, doesn't that mean anyone could access the elevator?" Liam asked.

"That's the unusual thing," Declan said. "Only the garage cameras were down. Every other system stayed intact."

"I'd think a network engineer could probably create some sort of bug to pull that off," Liam said. "But why would she do that?"

Nikki didn't think she had. "Take us to the parking garage."

As they stepped inside, she asked, "There's only one elevator in the building?"

Declan nodded and pushed the "B" button. "As I showed you, it takes a code to even open it."

The parking garage was small and confined, Nikki thought as the group exited the elevator. Her chest tightened when she saw the red pickup. Either Annmarie hadn't made it out of the garage, or her killer had driven the truck back to the garage after leaving her at the Boundary Waters. If it turned out to be the latter, Courtney might be able to get viable evidence from the pickup. Nikki counted roughly twenty spaces to the red GMC pickup parked in the center, beneath a security lamp, just like every woman had been taught to do since she started driving.

"Declan, would you mind staying here while we check out the truck?" Nikki asked.

He looked disappointed, but Declan nodded, jamming his hands in his pockets. "Just let me know if you need anything."

"I don't see any apparent signs of a struggle," Liam said when they were out of earshot. "If the killer approached her here, could she have gone willingly?" he asked her.

"Maybe," Nikki replied.

Miller checked the pickup doors. "It's locked."

"What about the bag she had in the elevator? Can you see it anywhere?"

Miller shaded his eyes and peered in the windows. "Nope. The inside looks spotless."

Nikki remembered that Annmarie was a perfectionist: she hated a messy car, so the lack of personal items didn't strike her as odd. "I want this thing towed to the lab so Courtney can get it open and do a full search."

Miller knelt down to examine the tires. "The dirt on the side panels shows that she's been driving through the city like the rest of us. It hasn't been driven on any sort of gravel or anything ice-covered in a while. There aren't any signs of driving over ice melt or sand. I'd expect to see something like that if it had been driven in the Boundary Waters area."

"You're probably right," Nikki said.

"There's something here." Still crouched next to the truck, Miller snapped on a latex glove and reached behind the front driver's-side tire. He held up a business card. "Annmarie Mason, Network Engineer at VPCloud. Her cell and a PO Box are listed." He turned the card over, and Nikki could tell by his shocked eyes that something important was on the back.

"What is it?" she asked.

"'If found, call FBI Special Agent Nikki Hunt.' Your office number is on here."

Wordlessly, Nikki put on a glove, and Miller placed the card in her hand. She immediately recognized the neat cursive she'd always envied. "Oh Annmarie," Nikki whispered. She couldn't believe what she was seeing. "What did you get yourself into?"

CHAPTER SEVEN

Nikki stood, still reeling from seeing Annmarie's message. It was confirmation that Annmarie had known that she was in trouble. But had she known more than that? If she'd known she was in danger from Frost specifically, she could have left the message to ensure Nikki was informed. Nikki was certain Annmarie had been afraid of someone.

"Courtney's about ten minutes away." Liam slipped his phone back in his pocket. "I told her to text when she arrived and to plan on towing the pickup back to the lab."

Miller had come prepared and had slipped the card into a small plastic bag, which he was now holding. Nikki couldn't help but steal glances at it. "Declan, could you have the building's security stay with the truck until our CSI arrives?"

Declan nodded and made the call to the front desk of the building.

A few minutes later, a stocky, middle-aged man in a gray uniform joined them. "This is Tom Caves. He's head of security."

"We looked through all the parking garage footage taken after she was last seen in the elevator Wednesday," Caves said. "This truck hasn't left the garage in a week."

Nikki had expected as much, but the location of the card made it appear that Annmarie had dropped it when she was accosted. Either her killer had been close enough to the truck to possibly leave trace, or he'd been inside the vehicle with Annmarie and driven it back. Either way, they had a decent chance of getting prints. "Liam, make sure Courtney knows where the card was found. I want the entire exterior of the truck scoured for prints and physical evidence.

Mr. Caves, have you had any reports of strange people around? Is Wednesday morning the only time you've had issues with your security cameras recently?"

"Yes, ma'am." Caves sighed, staring at the truck. "We still don't know what happened to put us offline that day, and it just makes me sick. We could have helped her."

"We're dealing with an incredibly bright and manipulative individual," Liam said. "Don't beat yourself up about it. He likely would have found another way to Annmarie. That said, I'm sure you know it's protocol for us to speak with all of your staff so that we can eliminate them from our suspect list. The sooner the better."

"No problem," Caves said. "Just let me know when to expect you, and I'll make sure everyone is available."

Caves stayed behind to wait for Courtney's team while the others headed upstairs to Annmarie's apartment. The four of them rode the elevator to the top floor in silence, but Nikki was certain the others had to hear her stomach churning. When they were young, she and Annmarie had their lives planned out. They would graduate, go to the same school and always live close to each other. Nikki knew it wasn't her fault that things hadn't worked out that way, and she'd been working on forgiving herself for cutting Annmarie out of her life, because at the time, it had been the only way for her to emotionally survive.

She followed the men out of the elevator, fighting for control. Liam and Miller wouldn't judge her for showing emotion, but Nikki knew that if she allowed one tear to fall, she'd be useless to the investigation. Declan seemed like a nice enough man, but she didn't need someone running to the press about how she was too emotionally involved to handle the case.

Still, Declan essentially had all-access to Annmarie and would have been able to learn her routines easily without being noticed. Until he was alibied, Declan was also a suspect.

Gleaming, dark gray tile covered the long hallway. The walls were also painted a soothing gray, with metal wall decorations in the shape of various trees lining the walls.

"This is hers." Declan stopped in front of a gray door labeled 4B. "After Chief Miller spoke with property management, I was given a temporary key code for her lock." Declan pulled a piece of paper out of his pocket and then typed in a series of numbers. There was a click and then the door opened an inch. Declan stepped aside. "I'll stay in the hallway, of course. Please don't hesitate to ask questions. I'll try to answer as best I can."

Nikki donned her booties and gloves; Miller and Liam did the same.

Nikki hesitated in front of the door, her hand hovering above the silver knob. *You buried your parents. You can do this.*

Even though Annmarie's body wasn't inside, Nikki had no idea what they would find. They might be investigating Annmarie's murder, but the idea of entering her apartment and learning about her life made Nikki feel like she was about to open Pandora's box. Her guilt over her friend's murder was growing rapidly. She had to get it together. She double-checked to make sure her booties and gloves were on properly and then slowly pushed the door all the way open. High-quality wood floors lined the long hall in front of them.

"Straight down the hall is the bedroom and master bath," Declan said from the doorway. "The guest bath is the second door on your right. First door is a small closet. Kitchen and living room on the left. It's an open floor plan."

"Thank you." A pair of Nikes and heavy-looking snow boots sat on the mat beside the door, and Nikki could tell by their size they belonged to Annmarie.

"She put on a deadbolt." Liam pointed to the large lock on the inside of the door.

"What?" Declan asked. Nikki could see that he looked surprised. "Residents aren't allowed to do that. That's why they pay extra for high-end security."

It seemed like Annmarie had been scared and hiding from someone. Nikki was fairly certain the door would have to be busted by a sledgehammer or axe, because the deadlock was solid and virtually impenetrable.

"How long did she live here?" Nikki asked.

"Almost four years," Declan said. "She was one of our first tenants, along with myself."

"Yet you rarely interacted?"

He shook his head. "I barely knew her." Nikki turned back towards the door to look at him; he seemed genuine. "She worked from home, I believe. She had her groceries delivered."

"Right to her door?" Nikki asked. "How does the delivery make it through security?"

"Security confirms who the tenant is expecting and then sends them up. A resident is never surprised by a visitor."

Nikki had more questions for Declan, but she wanted to get the initial search of Annmarie's apartment over. "Chief Miller, would you mind canvassing the other tenants? I'm sure they'd rather speak with the county sheriff than the FBI." Nikki looked at Declan. "Please keep this out of the media. We'd like to keep them out of our hair as long as possible."

"Absolutely," Declan said.

Miller clapped him on the back. "Why don't you get me a list of all the tenants so I know who I'm speaking with? You'll see the warrant covers it."

Declan nodded. "No problem. I can do that as soon as we're finished here."

Nikki sighed. "This is a murder investigation. We can't let you tag along."

"Of course not." He reddened. "But I'm supposed to make sure nothing in her apartment is damaged."

"You have my word on that. We'll be along shortly."

Nikki closed the door, expecting to hear the code being put in again, but Declan must have gotten the picture, because he didn't try to get back into the apartment. She, Miller, and Liam made their way through the small, open floor plan. The kitchen was lovely, with a floating counter separating it from the living room. It was clean, the counters devoid of clutter save for a Keurig and a Ninja-Foodi blender.

"Annmarie was always thinking about the future, even when we were kids," she said. "She never liked material things because they weren't going to put food on the table or help her retirement. We teased the hell out of her for being so practical." Nikki could tell by the modern and minimalist decor that Annmarie hadn't changed on that front. Her small kitchen table only had two chairs, and both were neatly tucked in. The living area was pretty but cold. A gray, plush carpet was the centerpiece, placed between an average-looking entertainment system and a couch. Nikki noticed there wasn't a lot of seating for guests.

Liam opened a set of pocket doors near the back corner of the living room. He let out a low whistle. "Damn, Nikki. You were right."

Nikki's chest tightened as she hurried to see what Liam was talking about. Right that this was Frost? Right that she should feel guilty?

"Oh my God," Nikki gasped. She was looking into a small room, which Annmarie must have once used as an office. But it looked like a task force room for a major murder investigation. Two large monitors were attached to what appeared to be a custom-built computer, a bulletin board hung above, but it was the opposite wall that caught Nikki's attention. She moved closer to it. There were large maps of Minnesota, Wisconsin and Michigan on the walls. The states where Frost had left his victims. She couldn't believe what she was seeing.

Annmarie had written a red question mark on the map next to Kalamazoo, Michigan, where Frost's first victim, Kimberly Hoff, had been found in February 2015. She had a couple of old newspaper articles printed out and pinned to the wall. There was another red circle and question mark over the University of Madison-Wisconsin's campus, the location of Susanna Robins, victim number two, but no articles.

"Why are there no question marks next to the last three?" Liam asked.

Tessa Randall, Frost's third victim, had been discovered in the North Woods a year later, near several popular fishing resorts. Marina Bishop had been left in the winter village near the stadium the following year, during the Super Bowl, and last year, Karissa Larson had been left less than a block from First Avenue, the downtown Minneapolis club that Prince helped make famous.

"Maybe she didn't start following the case until the third victim was left in the North Woods," Miller said. "That's the first in Minnesota, and I remember you being on the news. The question marks on the first two could mean she was still researching."

"Maybe." Nikki bent down to look at the shelving below the maps. The space was lined with books, many on coding and computer software, but Annmarie also had the latest version of the DSM and a couple of books about profiling and psychology. The books on the second shelf had collapsed, as though whatever was holding them upright had been moved. "I think we can focus our investigation on Frost now," Nikki said, and Liam nodded, still looking stunned. "And I think Annmarie knew that Frost was targeting her."

CHAPTER EIGHT

"It makes sense," Nikki insisted after she'd explained her theory. They'd spent the last twenty minutes searching Annmarie's office for anything that might give them a lead but had come up empty. "If Annmarie was researching Frost, this explains why he deviated from his routine. Frost could have found out what she was doing and saw her as a threat who had to be eliminated."

"Then why leave her like he did the others?" Liam asked.

"He wanted to make sure that I knew he killed her?" Nikki guessed.

Liam looked out of the small window in Annmarie's office, chewing over what Nikki had said. "How could he know she was a threat?" he asked her.

"I'm not sure yet," Nikki replied. They also didn't know *why* Annmarie had been doing this research. Was she simply fascinated by the case she knew Nikki was working on? There were a lot of people out there who saw themselves as vigilantes or amateur sleuths—was Annmarie one of them? And had she got close? "I'm going to talk to Declan and see if I can get any more out of him. You keep going through her office."

"We haven't found any financial files or bills." Liam pointed to the monitors. "I'm betting everything is on her computer, but all we have is monitors."

"Remember she was carrying a large bag in the elevator footage; I'm betting that she had her laptop in it," Nikki said. "According to the staff at the nursing home, she took it there every day, and it appears that she left around her usual time on Wednesday. If you were a cybersecurity expert, wouldn't you keep your most important information with you at all times?"

"I would," Liam replied. "But Annmarie also worked for a place that offered private cloud hosting, so we might be able to access some things through them. We should get a warrant and see if she had anything stored at work. Did you call VPCloud?" Liam asked.

"I left a message for the CEO this morning," Miller said, "but they're two hours behind us, so we may not hear from him until later. I gave him your number as a call back," Miller said to Nikki. "I assumed you'd want to speak with him."

They heard the code being punched into the door, and Nikki gave Liam a pointed look. "Would you mind continuing the apartment search while I ask Declan a few more questions?"

Nikki hated for someone else to be going through Annmarie's personal things, but she wanted to interview Declan instead of relying on someone else's interpretations of his facial expressions and reactions.

"No problem."

Nikki found Declan standing in the doorway, chewing his lower lip. He held up a print-out. "I have that list of tenants and security staff. I'm sure everyone will be happy to assist in any way they can. Which brings me to a bit of a sensitive question. Have funeral arrangements been made? The residents and I would like to send something."

"She didn't have a lot of family," Nikki said. "So, things are kind of in limbo. I can let you know when something is scheduled. In the meantime, I have a few more questions for you."

"I'm not sure I can be of any more help," he said.

Nikki tried to smile. "You'd be surprised how many people say that and don't even realize they know something crucial, especially since you live next door. Do you work from home like Annmarie? I assume being building president doesn't pay the bills."

He smiled and leaned against the doorframe, his arms over his chest. "No, it doesn't. I work in marketing and public relations at Hewlett Packard."

"Not in the tech field?"

"God, no," he laughed. "I'm more of a people person. That sort of thing is way over my head."

Declan's charm and good looks likely helped him at work, but Nikki wasn't going to humor him. She wanted him off guard and as nervous as possible. "I hear you. So you worked regular hours? How often did you see Annmarie?"

Declan nodded, his expression unchanged, but Nikki could tell by his shifting posture that he was getting impatient. "Like I said earlier, I rarely interacted with Annmarie. Her help with security is the most I've spoken with her."

"And she's lived alone the entire time she's been here?"

"As far as I know. I never noticed visitors."

"No noise complaints or anything?"

He shook his head, slouching back against the doorframe once again. "Not a peep."

"What about other residents? Is there anyone Annmarie interacted with?"

"I don't think so," Declan said. "We want to foster a sense of community, which is part of the reason for the small number of apartments. We have once-a-month meetings, and there's always a potluck after. But, with the exception of the security meeting, I've never seen Annmarie at any of them."

Declan appeared to be telling the truth despite his nerves. Nikki thanked him for his time and promised to let him know of any memorial or funeral arrangements.

Annmarie's isolation wasn't entirely unsurprising to Nikki. She'd always preferred the company of one or two close friends. Nikki had dragged her along to parties in high school, and Annmarie had been miserable every time.

"When Courtney's finished with the car, she'll come up here and process the apartment, so we will be here a while. You understand that we can't allow you access to the apartment?"

"Oh, I see." Declan rocked back and forth on his heels, his hands in his pockets. "That's no problem." Nikki wondered if he was trying to keep an eye on things for the management firm, or was he actually afraid of what they might find in Annmarie's apartment? "The security staff is available right now if anyone wants to speak to them."

"Perfect timing. Give me a couple of minutes." Nikki closed the door and returned to the office. "Kent, can you go with Declan and talk to security? There are a couple of staff you can begin interviewing. And could you call the office and get them to do background checks on everyone who's listed?" She handed him the list Declan had given her. "Let me know if there's anything suspicious about any of them."

"Will do," Miller said. "I'll see if I can get any more out of them about the prior security issues."

Liam was still methodically looking through the paperwork and books that Annmarie did keep in the office. He glanced up at Nikki. "Do you want me to go through her bedroom?"

"No, thanks," she replied. Nikki knew that she needed to do this herself.

He nodded. "Holler if you need anything. I'll keep an eye out for Court."

The bedroom was across from the office. The door was open, and Nikki could already see that Annmarie's bed was neatly made, just as Nikki would expect her to have left it.

She stood in the doorway for several long seconds, trying to make her legs move. Finally, she slowly inhaled and reminded herself that she'd endured even more painful things in her life and stepped inside.

Like the rest of the apartment, the room was minimally decorated, with cream-colored walls, plush beige carpet and blackout
drapes. Nikki went into the bathroom first. Annmarie had been
a creature of habit, and Nikki had to smile when she realized
that hadn't changed after all this time. Her toiletries were in the
medicine cabinet, alongside over-the-counter allergy medication
and an antidepressant. Skincare products were stored in the top
drawer of the vanity, makeup in the second, and various shower
products in the bottom drawer. Annmarie had definitely intended
to come home that day.

Nikki went to the nightstand first. She found a couple of tubes
of lip balm, a box of Kleenex, and a manicure kit. Nothing useful.

Nikki walked over to the closet door and slowly opened it. Her
knees immediately weakened. The closet was large, with built-in
shelves, but it was the antique mahogany armoire in the back of the
closet that took Nikki's breath away. It had belonged to her mother.

It was a family heirloom. Nikki had considered hiding inside it
when she'd found her parents murdered, but her mother always kept
it full of odds and ends, so she'd known it would have been full.

How in the world had Annmarie come to own the armoire?

Nikki had only been sixteen when the murders happened, and
she'd gone to live with her aunt Mary, who was her mom's older
half-sister. Aunt Mary had hired a lawyer to take care of her parents'
so-called estate, which was really just the house and ten acres. It
had been sold and put into a college fund for Nikki. She'd never
gone inside the house again, and she'd been too traumatized to
think about what she wanted to keep, so her aunt had put most
of it in storage.

Nikki hadn't felt ready to go through any of it until the summer
after she graduated high school. She was counting the days until
she left for college and could leave Stillwater in the past. Those
days were still fuzzy in her memory, but Nikki remembered that

she hadn't wanted the armoire or anything else from her parents' bedroom. Aunt Mary had said something about continuing to pay for the storage because one day Nikki might change her mind.

She hadn't, and she'd never set foot in Stillwater after she arrived at the University of Minnesota. Aunt Mary came to the city to visit and they stayed in touch for a while, but Nikki eventually phased her out as she'd done everyone else, and Mary died when Nikki was in grad school.

Standing in Annmarie's bedroom, she couldn't recall if she had ever thanked Mary for taking her in and caring for her. Her aunt's lawyer had been the one to tell Nikki about her death, bringing her the personal items and mementoes her aunt had wanted Nikki to have. She vaguely remembered him saying something about an auction.

Annmarie must have wanted the armoire and could have purchased it then. She'd cared about Nikki's parents too.

Her mother had kept family heirlooms, including two quilts and a shawl knitted by Nikki's great-great-aunt. Mary had insisted she take them out of the armoire and keep them, and Nikki had promised that she would, but she never had. She knew her mother and aunt would be furious with her for letting the quilts go, and the decision had haunted her for years.

Heart pounding, Nikki went to the back of the closet and slowly opened the armoire.

She let out a little cry before sinking to her knees. The quilts were inside, along with the shawl. Her father's newsboy cap was there too. It had been hanging in the entryway of her house, and Nikki had refused to take it with her. Her mother's collection of tawdry romance novels took up part of the top shelf, carefully covered in plastic. She and Annmarie had learned about sex from the novels, sneaking them out of her mother's room and into Nikki's. Her father's three ties were inside, along with two of the cross-stitch pieces her mother had done.

At the time, Nikki couldn't bear to see any of those things.

But it was like Annmarie had known. She'd known that Nikki would want them one day, and she'd saved them.

The sobs she'd been fighting for the past hour finally won. Nikki covered her face with her hands and quietly cried, hoping the others didn't hear.

She didn't know how much time had passed when she felt a soft hand on her shoulder.

Courtney pressed a wad of tissue into Nikki's hands and then wrapped her arms around Nikki.

Nikki blew her nose and cleaned the tears off her face. She knew that crying didn't make her weak, or bad at her job, but she couldn't sit in here all afternoon. It wouldn't help Annmarie, so she shook the sadness off and tried to refocus. "Did you get anything more from the material?" she asked Courtney.

Courtney nodded. "Annmarie's fingerprints, which means she spent a lot of time pressing her hands into that material, either out of fear or because she was trying to leave the print so we knew it was hers. Unfortunately, there were no other prints."

A soft knock startled them both.

Liam poked his head into the closet. His eyes widened. "This a bad time?"

"No," Nikki said. "What do you have?"

"Kimberly Hoff's mother just returned my call about the Wilcraft," he said flatly. "Kim's sister has been missing for three weeks. Look at her picture." Liam held his phone out.

"As in, Frost's first victim, Kimberly Hoff?" Courtney asked, incredulous.

"The very same."

"She looks just like Kim." Nikki got to her feet, blood boiling. "Who's handling her disappearance, and why the hell weren't we brought in?"

"The Eagan police," Liam said. "And that's a damned good question."

CHAPTER NINE

Nikki left Courtney in charge of the apartment search while Miller finished with security and any residents he could track down, and she and Liam drove to the Eagan police department. Nikki was thankful they were in separate vehicles. She needed to be alone with her anger for a few moments.

Why hadn't they been informed that Darcy Hoff was missing? Why hadn't the Hoffs called the FBI? It was unusual for a serial killer to take a family member, especially six years later, but Frost wasn't the usual serial killer. His victims had very little in common in life: three had been white, one black and one Latina; the youngest victim had been twenty-one, and the oldest thirty-two. Each victim came from different socioeconomic backgrounds, but none were from higher-risk situations like involved in prostitution or afflicted with drug addictions. Nikki and Liam both agreed there were only three things each woman had in common: shoulder-length dark hair, a stable family background, and mercifully, none had children.

Liam had long argued that Frost chose women without kids because they were easier to take, but Nikki disagreed. There was no more powerful weapon against a mother than the threat to her child. Frost could have used that as a way to control the women. Nikki firmly believed the decision not to take women with children wasn't a tactic—it was about Frost himself. Something in his background drove this choice, and she had always felt that if they could figure out what it was, they might be able to figure out how to catch him. Over the years, they'd investigated countless suspects who fit the profile, but they'd always come up empty.

Darcy Hoff lived with her parents in Eagan, one of the larger upscale suburbs in the Twin Cities area. Eagan's municipal center had always reminded Nikki of the YMCA, and she half-expected to smell chlorine as she and Liam strode inside. Nikki hadn't bothered to call ahead. If the police didn't think her team should have been notified when Darcy disappeared, Nikki saw no reason to extend them the courtesy of a warning call.

They both showed their badges to the front desk sergeant. "We need to see whoever's in charge of the Darcy Hoff investigation. And if they're not available, we'll speak to their commanding officer."

The surprised desk sergeant turned to his computer for a moment before reaching for his phone. "Detective Engle, the FBI is here to see you about Darcy Hoff." He paused and looked up at Nikki. "Yeah, I don't think she's going to take no for an answer." He ended the call, and the door to their left buzzed open. "Walk straight ahead and you'll see the bullpen. She's in one of the first cubes."

"Thank you." Nikki and Liam walked inside, the door buzzing shut behind him.

A fit-looking black woman in jeans and a dark blazer greeted them, her expression wary. "Detective Marjorie Engle. How can I help you?"

"FBI Special Agent Nikki Hunt," Nikki said. "This is my partner, Agent Wilson. We need to speak with you about Darcy Hoff."

"Believe it or not, I was going to call you in next week. We have a new police chief, and he is…" Engle exhaled and shook her head, "running a tight ship, and he does not believe Darcy was kidnapped. She does have a history of disappearing, and a couple of people who worked at the same delivery service she did told us she was talking about leaving town and starting over. There was no sign of foul play, no prior issues—"

"Except the murder of her sister," Liam said.

"Right," Engle said. "And the op-ed."

"What op-ed?" Nikki asked.

Engle motioned for them to follow her. Her cubicle was larger than many others, which likely meant she had some seniority. Nikki knew that seniority in law enforcement was a double-edged sword. It often earned the respect of the department, but it also put them closer to retirement. In times of upper-level change, a senior officer butting heads with a new boss was a good way to get on the fast track to early retirement. She would try to give Engle a pass for not involving the FBI as long as she was willing to work with them now.

"In February, Darcy published an online op-ed in the *Star-Tribune*." Engle handed Nikki a printed copy of the op-ed.

"*To the coward known as Frost*. Oh, God." Nikki couldn't believe the paper allowed the letter to be published.

"*You're nothing but a skulking shadow who only has the courage to act once a year, and only when your victim is most vulnerable,*" Liam read over Nikki's shoulder. "*I know women who fear you. I am not one of them. Had I been with my sister Kimberly Hoff the weekend you stole her from us, you would have failed.*" Liam sighed and looked at Nikki. "She should have just come out and said come get me, bro."

"What was she thinking?" Nikki asked.

Engle shook her head. "I don't know. Her parents told us that she believed Frost wouldn't have the guts to take a victim's relative. And if he did, you would capitalize on the mistake."

"Me?" Nikki said.

"That's what she told her parents." Engle's tone mirrored the challenging look in her eyes.

"Why haven't they called us?" Liam demanded.

"Chief convinced them not to, especially as we found out she'd bought a suitcase and other necessities at Walmart two days before she disappeared."

"By credit card receipt?"

"Of course not." Engle's voice was sharp. "I'm a little better at my job than that, Agent. She's seen very clearly on their security videos. We went over them from every angle, and there's no sign she was under duress or that she wasn't alone."

"I'm sorry." Nikki barely kept her anger reined in. She'd been in Engle's position before and could tell the detective was just as frustrated. "I get that you're in a bad position, and I'm sure you know how to do your job. What can you tell us about her actual disappearance?"

Engle nodded and opened the file on her desk. "Darcy was living at home, taking college courses again and doing deliveries. You're aware she went off the rails for a couple of years, I assume?"

"Yes. She blamed herself for what happened," Nikki said softly. Darcy had been only seventeen when Kim was killed. The sisters were six years apart, but they'd been close. Kim had worked at an accounting firm in Minneapolis, and the weekend she was abducted, Darcy had cancelled a visit with her sister. The two of them had planned to visit various colleges, as Darcy was a senior and still figuring out life. "Instead of going to see Kim, she cancelled at the last minute to go to a big party. If I remember correctly, a boy she really liked was going to be there. I told her that Frost would have just found another time. I don't think she ever believed me." Nikki hadn't spoken to Darcy in several months, but her parents seemed to believe her life was turning around. "I thought she was getting her life back on track."

"It appeared she was," Engle said. "She was back taking college courses, kept a steady job. She was still living at her parents' guest house, but her parents told me that they thought her psychiatrist believed she'd made a breakthrough in therapy, and they'd found an antidepressant that worked."

"What happened?" Liam asked. "Why did she write that op-ed?"

"She told her parents it was to honor Kim on the anniversary of her death, to make sure the public hadn't forgotten her name."

Nikki kicked herself for not seeing the article. She remembered that Darcy had been the outgoing risk-taker, while Kim had been quiet and focused on her job. She was one of the youngest junior accountants at a major firm and well-liked by all.

"Self-destructive behavior," Liam said. "I wasn't working the case back then, but I know every victim's file by heart. Darcy did a lot of risky, dangerous things after her sister died. Way beyond the usual."

"She wanted to be punished," Nikki said. "What was she doing when she disappeared?"

"Delivering groceries," Engle said. "In Woodbury. She works for Lunds and Byerlys. We found her car about a block from The Pointe at Woodbury, where she was supposed to deliver groceries."

Nikki and Liam exchanged a look. "To apartment 4B?"

Engle slipped on a pair of reading glasses and opened the file she'd picked up off her desk. "4C. He called after she missed her estimated time. When other deliveries were missed, her parents were called. They called us."

"Declan's apartment," Nikki said. "He mentioned a grocery delivery to Annmarie." But not to himself, Nikki thought. He might not know that Darcy was actually missing, but it still bugged Nikki that he had a connection to two victims.

"How many grocery orders were still in her car?" Nikki asked.

"Two. 4C's were missing, and he said he never got them. The Pointe has good security, and we're certain she never made it to the building."

"I don't understand why your chief thinks she would run off and leave her car with a bunch of groceries in it," Liam said irritably. "If she wanted to run away, seems like she'd take her car and the free supplies."

"That was my issue," Engle said. But we didn't find any car keys or phone, no sign of her purse."

"What about a cell phone?"

Engle shook her head. "It must be turned off because we can't get any GPS tracking."

"You said she bought some things at Walmart a couple of days before," Nikki said. "Is it possible she was working as a personal shopper there as well?"

"We checked all of that out," Engle said. "Right now, Walmart doesn't do their own delivery, so we checked out Instacart and Shipt, plus a couple of smaller, local places. Darcy isn't employed by any of them."

"What did her friends say?" Liam asked. "Do they believe she might have taken off?"

"As far as we can tell, she didn't have any close friends. Her cell carrier gave us three months' worth of records, including texts for the last month. She texted her parents and her boss, along with a cousin in Nebraska. None of the conversations were helpful. And she doesn't have a social media presence."

"And I assume no sign of the suitcase or other things she bought at Walmart at Darcy's place?" Liam asked.

Engle shook her head. "They weren't in the car, either."

"Which bolstered the local police's theory that despite her car still being in the parking lot, she left on her own," Nikki said.

Nikki could see how some might think Darcy had snapped, but the FBI still should have been called in. She could tell Engle had been stuck in a lousy position, and Nikki would eventually speak with the new chief who had decided to keep the FBI out of the loop, but right now she needed everyone's cooperation.

"We're working a murder case, and Darcy delivered to the victim's neighbor. We just came from there. 4C is occupied by a Declan Simpson."

Engle nodded. "We ran his information. He has a couple of traffic tickets, but that's it. He said Darcy never came inside, but he allowed us to search his apartment. We didn't find anything of concern."

"What did you find out about him specifically?"

"I don't follow."

"His apartment. What did it tell you about him?"

Engle shrugged. "His place is nice. Better than a bachelor pad. Is that what you mean?"

"No, but that's fine." Nikki would get her own tour of his apartment, hopefully catching Declan off guard when she asked to come inside. They might not have found any red flags yet, but he was tied to both women. She knew she felt wary of him for a reason. "Can you get me a copy of the case file?" Nikki asked.

"My boss—"

"Here's the thing." Nikki tried to keep her tone respectful. "We believe the cases are connected, and ours has connections to Frost too. If he's taken Darcy, there's a chance she could still be alive. I have no doubt you're a competent detective, and I understand you're stuck between a rock and a hard place. But I'm sure once I speak with the Hoffs, they'll want us to handle this, and your boss will have to agree. He can call me if he takes issue."

"Fair enough," Engle said. "I'll do everything I can to keep things between us, but I'm going to hold you to that phone call if he blows a gasket."

Nikki smiled tightly. "Please do."

Engle agreed to get Nikki a copy of everything, including the security videos her department had already gone through.

Nikki and Liam decided to stop at the grocery store Darcy worked at before going to visit the Hoffs.

Nikki left the station with her emotions in a knot. This was the closest they'd come to finding Frost in years. She finally managed to slip her arm inside the sleeve. Nikki yanked up the coat's zipper and marched toward the car. Her team should have been called about Darcy's disappearance immediately. They may not have been able to save Annmarie, but the delay could have already sealed Darcy Hoff's fate.

*

Lunds and Byerlys was an upscale supermarket chain in the metro area. Large and spacious, with perfect-looking produce and pretty much any item a person needed, the store had been a treat for Nikki as a kid. Her mother usually did the grocery shopping at the local Cub Foods, but every once in a while, she would splurge at Byerlys. Nikki's favorite thing had been the sampler trays. The store always had two or three set up on the weekends, and she'd do her best to sneak as many pieces as possible while her mother shopped.

They went to the customer service desk and showed the teenaged clerk their identification. "Is the store manager available? We have some questions about an employee."

The young man's eyes popped wide. "The FBI is going to arrest one of our employees? For what?"

"We have questions," Liam said evenly. "For the store manager. And we don't have a lot of time."

"Right." The clerk picked up a phone and dialed, talking excitedly. "Yeah, I'll send them in." He pointed to his right. "Go that way and turn right. You'll see the nutritionist office and then the manager's office."

"Thank you."

When they reached the office, a dark-skinned man with silver hair and a bright tie shook both their hands. "Bob Davis, day manager." He motioned for them to sit in the padded chairs next to his desk. "What can I do for you?"

They sat, and Nikki jumped into their reason for the visit. "We're looking into the disappearance of Darcy Hoff. She delivered for you until recently?"

"Disappearance? The detective said they thought she took off. She was having problems or something. Came as a complete shock to me. She was a good worker."

"Did you notice anything different about her behavior in the days leading up to her disappearance?"

"Not at all, but she was a quiet person. She came in and did her job. I'm not sure if anyone would have noticed if there were signs. And her customers liked her."

"Her customers?" Liam asked. "Aren't the grocery deliveries randomly assigned?"

Bob shook his head. "It's one of the perks of shopping with us. We allow customers to request a specific shopper, providing they are on the schedule."

"Did Darcy start in delivery?"

"No, she started in the stockroom because that's what was available. She moved up to personal shopper a couple of months later. Darcy worked for us for nearly two years," Bob said. "She was a reliable employee, so we were surprised to hear she missed a delivery. After the complaint about the second one came in, and Darcy didn't answer her phone, we alerted her emergency contact. I believe they called the police."

"Her parents were the emergency contact, I assume?"

The manager nodded. "Her mother is. That poor family. I had no idea their other daughter died several years ago."

"Would it be possible to see a list of Darcy's customers over the past couple of months?" Nikki asked.

"Well, to be honest, I don't know. We've never had a request like this, and there are privacy issues, including HIPPA, since shoppers also pick up medication. I'd like to help, but—"

"We just want names," Liam said. "We'll track them down ourselves."

"I guess that would be all right. I can put the list together and email it to you."

Nikki handed him her business card. "That's fine, but we need it today so that we can start eliminating suspects."

"No problem," he said. "I was surprised the police didn't ask for something similar, but they were satisfied with the security footage the last week she worked."

Detective Engle had already sent Nikki a copy of the video, and she'd perused it while Liam drove over here. Darcy had been easy to spot, methodically filling her cart, a clipboard balanced on the child seat. She'd handled three smaller orders that day, and nothing out of the ordinary had appeared on the video. The store had been busy, and Darcy passed several other shoppers who only seemed interested in their own grocery lists.

"Thank you for your help," Nikki said. "What about co-workers? Was Darcy friendly with anyone?"

"I wouldn't say friendly. She was very closed off. Not rude, just kind of on her own. She came in on time, got her customer lists and did her job. We never had a single complaint about her."

Nikki stood up. "I'll keep an eye out for that customer list. If you think of anything else, please reach out to me."

She followed Liam out of the store, checking her phone to make sure she hadn't missed any calls. A shiver went down her spine and Nikki jerked her head up, certain she was being watched. She scanned the parking lot and stopped in her tracks. Rory's mother stood in front of an SUV parked in a handicapped space, her bag tucked beneath her arm, glaring at her. Rory desperately wanted his parents to warm to Nikki and forgive what happened with Mark, but they refused, and Nikki didn't think it was right to push them. Nikki felt like a little kid getting caught sneaking something out of the kitchen. She had to try to say something, but before she could get the courage, Ruth turned on her heel and got back into her vehicle. Nikki decided to wait for her to leave, and when she had, she couldn't get out of the parking lot fast enough.

CHAPTER TEN

The Hoffs lived in a gated community in Eagan, and the two-story, Tudor-style house was the gem of the cul-de-sac. Ernie Hoff made a good living as a tax lawyer, and his wife, Irene, ran her own small but successful interior design company. They'd both been so devastated about Kimberly and worried constantly about Darcy's well-being. Nikki still couldn't believe they hadn't called her when she'd gone missing.

Irene opened the front door before Nikki could knock. "Thank God you're here." She swept Nikki into a tight hug. "My baby has to be alive."

Nikki hugged her back. "We're going to do everything possible to find her."

Irene pulled away and then ushered Nikki and Liam into the large foyer. She looked thinner than the last time Nikki saw her, and her dark hair had gone almost entirely white. For some reason, the Hoffs had always liked Nikki, even though she had yet to find their daughter's killer. She suspected it was because Nikki somehow reminded them of Kimberly, as they'd told her more than once.

"This is my partner, Agent Liam Wilson. He's worked the last few Frost cases with me."

"Please, come into the kitchen and have a cup of coffee. It's decaf, but it's fresh."

Nikki and Liam followed her into the large kitchen, where Ernie sat alone in the breakfast nook, nursing a glass of whiskey. He looked like he hadn't slept in days. Nikki couldn't imagine the pain of losing both your children.

Darcy might not be dead, she reminded herself. Unless her body was found, Nikki intended to act as though she were still alive.

"Hey, Ernie," Nikki said softly as she sat down across from him. "How are you holding up?"

He looked up at her with bloodshot eyes. "Where have you been? I called you the day Darcy didn't come home. I left a message."

Nikki felt like she'd been struck in the chest. "I never got any messages. Did you call my cell phone?"

"I lost that number. I called your office. March ninth."

Six years ago, when the FBI offered Nikki the job to head a new criminal profiling unit in the Minneapolis–St. Paul office, she'd been given a shoestring budget and housed in a small room at the administration building in downtown St. Paul. They'd finally been able to move to new offices this year, and while the bigger space and access to the lab and other services had been a godsend, the move itself had been a headache-inducing event. "Ernie, I'm so sorry. We moved into a new building that week; perhaps there were some issues with the phones. If you'd called my cell—"

"I don't care," he said flatly. "Instead, we've been dealing with the incompetent assholes at the Eagan police department."

"It's not Detective Engle's fault." Irene placed a steaming cup of coffee in front of Nikki, and gave one to Liam, along with cream and sugar. "I remembered how you like it, dear."

"Thank you." Nikki dumped a couple of creamers and sugars into the cup and slowly stirred. "Ernie, I'm not happy with the Eagan police, either. We should have been called, but it sounds like the new police chief—"

"Is a bureaucratic bastard," Ernie cut her off.

"It does sound like it," Nikki said. "To her credit, Detective Engle was in a really bad position, and I can see that certain things would make them think Darcy just left. That said, I've already issued new BOLOs for the entire tri-state area."

Liam took the seat next to Nikki, holding his cup of black coffee, and Irene sat down next to her husband. Nikki could tell that they were reassured that she was here and that she'd already acted so quickly. It was true that it wasn't Engle's fault that she wasn't called, but she could understand the anger towards her.

"You don't think she just left, do you?" Liam asked.

Ernie banged his fist on the table, seeming to ignore Liam's question. "How does this happen to the same family twice?" he said angrily. "Did Frost take her too?"

"It's possible," Nikki replied. She wanted to be honest. "We're investigating the murder of another woman…" Nikki almost choked on her words. She still couldn't believe she was talking about Annmarie. She cleared her throat. "Her name is Annmarie Mason. We think she might have had a connection to Frost, and she lives at The Pointe at Woodbury. Darcy delivered groceries to at least one tenant in Annmarie's building."

"I know who she is," Irene said. "She was a witness at your parents' murder trial. Did Darcy deliver groceries to her?"

"We're waiting for a list of delivery clients from Lunds and Byerlys," Nikki said. "Does the name Declan Simpson ring a bell to either of you?"

The Hoffs glanced at each other and then shook their heads.

"Darcy didn't date," Irene said. "She was singularly focused on finishing her general ed courses so that she could get her degree."

"It sounds like she's been doing well," Liam said. "Did you know she was going to run that op-ed?"

Irene sighed. "We knew she had submitted a piece about Kim to the paper. When I read it, I couldn't believe she'd been so brazen."

"Stupid, you mean," Ernie snapped. "She had this theory that a smart guy like Frost would never come after a victim's sister. We told her that was ridiculous. She looks like Kim. Isn't that supposed to be part of these psychos' hang-ups?"

"Some of them, yes," Nikki said. She agreed with Ernie, but she didn't want to make them feel any worse. If Frost was going to come after Darcy, there was nothing she could do to stop him—yes, she had goaded him, but he was still evil.

"She knew she was baiting him," Ernie said. "A couple of years ago, I would have said she did it because she didn't care if she lived anymore. But not now. She was on the right track."

"Anniversaries of traumatic events can be almost as crippling as the event itself," Liam said. "She never mentioned anyone strange in her life? Did she ever feel unsafe on her deliveries?"

"If she did, she didn't tell us," Irene said. "Not that she shared much with us, anyway. But she enjoyed the job. She loved being able to make people's lives easier, and she was able to work around her classes. Her tips were very good."

"You didn't even call us about Darcy at first," Ernie said suddenly. "You called about the missing Wilcraft. What's that got to do with anything?"

Nikki tried to think of a way to answer without giving away too many case details. "A Wilcraft was used to transport Annmarie through the lakes up north where her body was left. We ran a check for registered owners, and yours came back reported stolen."

Ernie looked thoughtful for a moment. "About a year after Kim died," he said. "It was insured, and I would have sold it anyway. She loved going ice fishing with me." He smiled sadly. "Not sure I could have even sat inside it without losing my mind."

"Did she ever take it out by herself?" Nikki asked.

"No way," he said. "That's something Darcy would do. Kim was a rule-follower. Darcy's the one who breaks them."

"Had Kim gone out on the craft with you around the time she disappeared?"

His graying eyebrows came together to form one single line. "Couple of times, yeah. Why?"

"We've always considered the idea that Frost followed his victims before taking them," Liam said.

"Detective Engle said Darcy wasn't social." Nikki knew her sister's death had sent Darcy into near seclusion, something she'd always understood. But she'd hoped that getting her life on track meant some new friends too.

"She has trouble connecting to people ever since Kim," Irene said. "She said it feels like she lives in a world separate from everyone else."

Nikki nodded; they knew she understood. "Did she seek out any grief support groups? There are a couple in the city that are exclusively for the families of murder victims."

"Her therapist and I tried and tried, but she refused."

"Could we see Darcy's room?" Nikki asked.

"She's staying in our guest house," Irene said. "The Eagan police already checked it out and said they didn't find anything. We'll grab our coats and take you out there."

Nikki and Liam followed the Hoffs through the sliding glass doors at the rear of the big kitchen onto a large deck that wrapped around the in-ground swimming pool. Several inches of snow and ice layered the pool cover, and Nikki wondered if the couple had even bothered to clean and fill it in the summer since they didn't have young kids anymore. Her five-year-old daughter Lacey had been campaigning for a pool for at least two years, ever since she took her first swimming lessons. Tyler didn't have the backyard for it, but Nikki technically did. She just didn't want the burden of taking care of a pool.

"The apartment's on the second floor of the pool house." Ernie led them up a short set of stairs on the side of the small building and unlocked the door. "It's just a studio size, but she likes it." His voice cracked, and he handed the keys to his wife. "I can't, Irene. I can't go in there when she's out there. Agent Hunt, please find our little girl alive soon." He clambered back down the stairs before Nikki could respond, but the tension between her shoulder blades tightened into a painful knot. If Darcy was still alive, Nikki had to find her, because the thought of telling the Hoffs both their children were dead was more than she could handle.

Shivering, she followed Liam into the small apartment. It couldn't have been more than six hundred square feet, with a tiny kitchenette, a daybed, and a large desk with a couple of textbooks.

"Psychology," Nikki murmured. "Is that what she wants to do?"

"She's talked about it, yes. I think she just wants to understand why people hurt other people, how someone could do such a horrible thing to her sister." Irene pulled a tissue from her coat pocket and wiped the tears out of her eyes.

"Sometimes there is no understanding," Nikki said. "Nurture does play a large part in things, but some people are just born bad."

During the last year of graduate school, Nikki had worked on a major study about sociopathy in children. At the time, experts disagreed on whether or not sociopathy could be spotted in young children. During the study, Nikki had observed that sociopathic traits such as lack of empathy or sense of guilt at their wrongdoings and lying could be spotted in children as young as three. Since then, more long-term studies showed similar results, and child psychologists had begun working on being able to spot the traits for an early intervention. Antisocial personality disorder couldn't be cured, but current thinking focused on teaching empathy and other skills to children with multiple sociopathic traits, with the goal of the children learning that even if they didn't feel empathy, they had to consider others' feelings and well-being. Since the vast majority of people with antisocial personality disorder didn't become murderers, Nikki believed the effort to teach empathy wasn't in vain. But there were still the select few—and Nikki believed Frost belonged in this group—who would have killed no matter their upbringing.

"Detective Engle looked through here when she first disappeared." Irene stowed the tissue away, new resolve in her voice. "She didn't find the suitcase that Darcy bought, and we didn't know if there were clothes missing, so they didn't see a reason to be concerned."

"Any idea why she was buying a suitcase?" Liam asked.

Irene laughed shakily. "Darcy wanted to pay her own way—she paid us rent—and she loved a bargain. She found that roller carry-on for half-price when she went shopping and couldn't resist."

"But the police didn't believe that?" Nikki asked.

"They acted like we didn't know our own daughter," Irene said. "But we do. Darcy told us about that suitcase. If she'd been planning on taking off, she wouldn't have."

Nikki slipped on her latex gloves. "Has anyone else been here since the police?"

"No," Irene said. "Darcy still kept a lot of things in her old room. Most of her jewelry, some books. She didn't have much out here, but the police seem to think she could have taken some with her just because it's kind of sparse. It doesn't look like she took a bunch of things from her old room, either."

"She didn't store the suitcase in her old bedroom?" Liam asked.

Irene shook her head. "No, we've looked through the entire house. And they didn't find it in the car."

"Was her car paid off?"

"It was a gift for her high school graduation," Irene said. "It's my old Camry, although it's only seven years old. We wanted her to have something reliable that wasn't too expensive to insure."

Nikki couldn't imagine anyone running away and leaving their car behind unless they didn't want to be found, especially if they owned it outright. Engle had confirmed that Darcy hadn't made a big bank withdrawal in the days leading up to her disappearance, and there hadn't been any activity on her credit cards up to this point. "Did she carry a lot of cash?"

"I don't think so. She made tips from her deliveries, but she tried to use that for daily spending and save as much of her paychecks for bills as possible."

Nikki thumbed through the textbooks. *Sociology of Crime and Deviance*, *Intro to Psychology.* "Was she thinking about studying criminology?"

Irene smiled sadly. "Big surprise, isn't it? She wants to get her AA of Arts with an emphasis on criminology and go from there. She plans to get her four-year degree as well, but…" Irene's face paled. "Should I stop talking about her in the present?"

"No," Nikki said. "Right now, you do whatever you need to get through this. Thinking positive isn't going to hurt."

Liam looked at Nikki, and she shook her head. She knew what Liam was thinking: Frost never held a woman for more than a few months, and he always left their bodies in the snow. The snow was melting fast…

She couldn't say any of this to Irene, but she guessed by the expression on the woman's face that Irene got the point.

"Right now, we're treating this as a missing person's case," Nikki said. "I can't imagine what you and Ernie are going through, but hang on to all the hope that you can."

Nikki skimmed through the textbooks. Darcy had highlighted several passages and made notes in the margin, but they all appeared to be related to her coursework.

"Engle noted in her file that Darcy's Chromebook hasn't been found. Would she have it with her on deliveries?"

"She carried it everywhere so she could do her assignments if she had unexpected downtime. It's small and fits into her big purse. That's gone too. And her cell. Detective Engle said they can't trace it because the GPS is off, which means the phone must be off. She said that could be another indicator that she didn't want to be found."

Nikki and Liam shared a knowing look. Engle wasn't wrong, but it was just as likely that the phone was off because whoever took Darcy got rid of it.

*

Before they left the Hoffs, Nikki and Liam planned their next moves. "I have the list of Darcy's deliveries over the past couple of months," Nikki said. "I'll forward it to you. It's a fairly big list, so see if Miller can help with the interviews." Detective Engle had spoken to a few of the clients, but Nikki wanted someone from her team to follow up. "We need to run as many background checks as we can."

"On it." Liam donned his silly-looking winter hat with the big ear flaps. "I'll check in with Courtney and our computer techs too. Eagan police are supposed to get Darcy's car to us by tonight."

"Thanks," Nikki said. "I'm going back to the nursing home to talk to the staff on the night shift, and then I'll head back to St. Paul. Call me if you hit on anything."

"Where's Blanchard on the autopsy?"

"She was in court part of the day," Nikki said. "She's doing it this afternoon."

Liam's cheeks flushed, the tension rolling off him. "I know I don't have to say this out loud, but I'm going to do it any way since it's eating at me. Annmarie chasing Frost down is one thing, but if he went after her because of her connection to you, that changes things."

"I know," Nikki said. "But we don't know if that's what happened yet. She still could have somehow drawn him out."

"Yes, she could have," Liam answered. "And we're closer to Frost than ever. We can't make any mistakes."

Nikki knew what he was getting at—a good defense attorney could use the connection to throw a serious wrench in the case, and Frost could walk. "Don't worry, Liam. As long as you and I keep an open dialogue, we'll be okay. If there comes a moment when I should step aside, then I will."

Liam nodded, seemingly reassured. Nikki was already thinking about their next step. Another woman had been taken, and Nikki wasn't going to let Frost ruin more lives. They would catch him this year if it killed her.

CHAPTER ELEVEN

Lynn had left a message for Nikki to stop by that night after dinner service, but the staff was still busy getting residents back to their rooms. Nikki decided to check in with Howard before talking to the staff. Seeing him again was probably a mistake; she wanted to tell him about Annmarie even though she knew he most likely wouldn't recognize the name and if he did, he wouldn't retain the information very long. But the idea of coming to the nursing home without stopping to check in on him felt wrong. Annmarie would have wanted her to keep an eye on him.

The corridors were eerily empty as she walked through them, and when she reached Howard's door it was closed, so Nikki knocked softly.

"Come in," she heard him call out.

She took a deep breath and braced herself before opening the door. "Hi, Howard," she said as she walked through. He was sitting up on the bed again, in almost exactly the same position. "Do you remember me?"

He stared at her for a moment, and then he smiled. "Is that you, Nicole Walsh?"

Nikki was surprised and she could feel the tears suddenly building in her eyes. "It sure is," she replied, standing by the door. "Mind if I sit and talk with you for a bit?"

"Why, I'd like nothing better. I'm so glad Annie finally called you. I told her it was the right thing to do." Despite the gravelly voice, he sounded more like his old self at the moment, and Nikki struggled with the dilemma of telling him about his daughter. He was lucid right now. She should tell him, but she just couldn't get the words out of her mouth. How could she tell him that his daughter was dead? Could she put him through that pain?

She sat down in the chair next to the bed. "Me too. How are you feeling?"

He waved a pale, thin hand. "I'm fine. But look at you, all grown up. How's college, kid? Doing okay?" Howard grinned. He'd always called her "kid."

He was off a couple of decades, but at least he knew who she was. Nikki decided to keep her responses as general as possible to play along and keep him talking. "I'm doing well. Busy with work and school."

"Your parents would be proud, God rest their souls." He looked around the room, his expression shifting. "Where's Annie? She's supposed to bring me some real ice cream. Having your tonsils taken out as an adult is no joke. It feels like I'll never get out of here. Where's my bell?"

Nikki couldn't help but laugh despite the sad truth about his failing memory. She remembered Howard's tonsillectomy clearly. His timing was off again because that had happened their sophomore year. Nikki remembered getting ready for the homecoming game at the Masons' while he recovered at home. Someone had given him a little bell as a joke, and he drove Annmarie and her mother nuts ringing for every little thing.

"Your mom woulda been proud of you," Howard said. "She took some college courses one summer during high school, but she never got the chance to go. It was real important to her that you got your degree."

That was the second time he'd mentioned her mother taking college courses. "What year was she in high school then?"

Howard stroked his chin, and Nikki remembered with a chill that he had a beard when she and Annmarie were kids. "Between freshman and sophomore years. I was so impressed. And jealous."

Nikki was too. She had never heard of her mother being academically inclined. The opposite, actually. She'd always been on Nikki about taking school seriously and not making the same mistakes that she had. "She took them at the University of Minnesota, right?" She hoped her questions might help Howard remember. But he shook his head.

"No, out of state. She stayed with family over the summer..." Howard scowled. "I can't remember where."

This was the first Nikki had heard of any family out of state. Her father had been an only child, and her grandparents had died before the murders, thank God. Aunt Mary had been her mother's half-sister and only sibling, and their mom had mostly raised them as a single mother. Grandma Jen had died when Nikki was twelve, but her own mother rarely talked about her father, other than to say he wasn't worth talking about. Could Valerie's father have lived out of state? Maybe her mother had gone to visit and try to have a relationship that summer and taken the college courses too. But she'd never mentioned the college courses. It was always "I wish I'd gone to college."

"Have you decided which school you're going to? Annie told me you had scholarships to more than one," Howard continued.

Nikki smiled. "I think I'm going to the University of Minnesota. It's either there or Michigan." She'd received academic scholarship offers from both the University of Minnesota and the University of Michigan. Nikki had wanted to leave Minnesota altogether, but the university had offered her a full ride, while Michigan had only offered half as much. She'd initially worried about being constantly recognized on campus, but once she'd arrived she'd fallen in love.

"Michigan, Michigan." Howard's voice sounded strained. "Why does Michigan feel so important to me?"

Nikki perched on the edge of the chair, trying to anticipate his next words. Was he getting confused? Should she touch him? Would that have an adverse effect?

Nikki patted his arm gently and saw the quick shift in his expression and the sudden darkness in his pale eyes.

"Valerie, I didn't tell anyone. I promise," he said.

Nikki tried her best not to react. "I trust you, Howard."

He grabbed her hand, his grip stronger than she'd expected. "Tell the truth, Valerie. He deserves that."

"You really think that I should?" Nikki had no idea what to do other than play along, and the idea of learning something new about her mother after all these years was too tantalizing to resist.

"Michigan, Michigan. Tell him about Michigan. It's important."

Howard's eyes fluttered closed for a few moments, and Nikki tried to catch her breath. Was this real memory breaking through, or was it driven by the Alzheimer's? Could it be a mixture of both?

Howard's eyes opened again. He dropped Nikki's hand. "Who are you?"

"It's me, Valerie."

"I don't know no Valerie. And I don't know you." He fumbled with the call button and Nikki could see that he was panicking even before he spoke. "Nurse! There's a strange woman in my room."

Nikki stood up and started backing out of the room; she knew she needed to give him some space and let him relax and she was taken aback by how quickly his mood had changed. "I'm sorry," she told him calmly. "I didn't mean to scare you. I must have the wrong person."

"Damn right." He hit the call button again, and a skinny guy in scrubs with peach fuzz hurried into the room.

"Mr. Mason, it's all right," he said, putting himself between Howard and Nikki.

"You let a stranger in my room," he bellowed.

The sudden change in Howard was unnerving; he'd been chatting so happily with her one second and the next saw her as a complete stranger. How had Annmarie dealt with his illness every day, not knowing which Howard she would be seeing?

The CNA glanced at her. "She's leaving."

Nikki scanned the CNA's nametag. "Kyle, I'm so sorry." Nikki turned to leave, but Howard's words stopped her in her tracks.

"There's still time, Val. You can tell the truth."

"What truth, Howard?" Nikki asked gently.

"You know what I'm talking about," he bellowed.

The CNA ushered Nikki into the hallway. "Look, Paula's catching up on paperwork at the charge station. I don't know what you did to get him all riled up, but he's not usually like this." He went back inside, shutting the door behind him.

Nikki could still hear Howard yelling as she walked slowly down the hall, her mind spinning. What was he talking about? And what the hell had happened in Michigan? What if Howard knew something about Nikki's family that she needed to know?

Nikki pushed the idea out of her mind. She'd just witnessed how quickly Howard's mental state changed. Between Annmarie's death and seeing how she'd saved the armoire despite Nikki's shutting her out, her own emotions were all over the place. She had to put all of that aside and focus on her investigation.

A gray-haired woman sat at the front desk, her glasses perched on the end of her nose.

"Excuse me, are you Paula Silver?" Nikki held up her identification.

"Oh yes, Agent Hunt. Lynn said to expect you." Paula's warm smile faltered. "I can't believe Annmarie was murdered. I only met her a couple of times when I filled in for someone during the day, but she was devoted to her dad." She drew a ragged breath, fighting tears. "We get used to losing our patients, but this is simply awful. I guess in some ways it's a blessing her father's not able to understand what's going on."

"I know," Nikki said. "I actually grew up with Annmarie, so I knew her parents pretty well. Not telling him that she's gone feels wrong, but I don't want to hurt him if it's something he's going to forget."

Paula patted her hand. "I think you're doing the right thing. He won't be able to process it. How can we help you tonight?"

Nikki told her about the visit by Howie Doe a few weeks ago. "It was during the evening shift. I'm hoping someone remembers him. The smallest details can make a huge difference in these cases."

Paula slipped on a pair of reading glasses. "Lynn left me the notes." She fished through a pile of papers on the desk next to her. "I would have been on rounds, distributing meds."

"I realize it's a long shot, but do you remember seeing anyone in Howard's room that night?"

"I don't," Paula said. "But I've usually given him his nighttime meds by then. Have you spoken to Theresa or Kyle yet? They were on the floor that night."

Nikki felt her cheeks redden. "I just met Kyle in Howard's room. Howard knew who I was, but his time frame was all messed up. I was trying to go with the flow and see if he was able to remember anything, and he got upset. I'm so sorry. I'm not sure how long it takes Howard to calm down after getting upset, but Kyle might be in there a while."

"It's all right," Paula said. "It happens frequently with memory patients."

The reedy CNA appeared then at Nikki's elbow. He tossed a clipboard onto the counter, clearly irritated. "I managed to get Howard settled down."

Nikki knew that CNA work was incredibly taxing, but she also understood that it took a special, compassionate person to do it well. She wasn't sure Kyle had many of those qualities. He definitely wasn't worried about pissing off an FBI agent, but Nikki couldn't tell if he was being defensive because he was nervous, or simply frustrated with the situation.

She held up her badge. "Special Agent Nikki Hunt with the FBI. I'm sorry about earlier. Annmarie was my best friend growing up.

I've known Howard since I was a kid. You're aware his daughter has been murdered?"

Kyle's expression turned somber. "Yes, we were all briefed about it." He looked at Paula. "Are we going to tell him?"

"Lynn and I agree that telling him would be a mistake, given his condition." Paula pointed a ringed finger at him. "Do not go against that decision."

"I won't." Kyle looked at Nikki. "I've seen you on the news."

Nikki smiled tightly. "Do you have a few minutes to answer some questions?"

"Sure." Kyle looked at his watch. "But I have to help with med rounds soon."

"This will only take a few minutes." Nikki told him about Howie Doe signing the log. "We're not sure if he's connected, but since he's the only other person who's visited Howard, we'd like to track him down."

"That's, like, more than a month ago," Kyle said. "It's hard enough keeping up here on a daily basis."

"Do you remember a man visiting Howard that evening?" Paula asked testily.

"No, I really don't."

"Did he mention a visitor?" Nikki wondered why someone as apathetic as Kyle had chosen to work at a place like Heritage House.

Kyle worried his lower lip. "No, but I usually don't pay much attention to visitors. The patients are my job."

A red light on the panel next to the desk started flashing. "Agent Hunt, do you have other questions for Kyle?" Paula asked.

Nikki handed him a business card. "No. Thanks for your time. Please call if you do think of anything."

Kyle nodded, and then hurried down the hall, in the opposite direction to Howard's room.

Paula sighed. "He's not exactly the nurturing type. I'm surprised he's lasted as long as he has."

"Which is?" Nikki asked.

"Nearly a year, I think. It's not that he mistreats anyone. He's always willing to do the back-breaking work. But he's inexperienced and likes to be right all the time. If he weren't kind to the residents, I probably would have let him go based on his know-it-all attitude. Let me call Theresa up here so you can finish. You look exhausted."

"Perks of the job," Nikki said.

Paula laughed. "Don't I know it." She called Theresa on the intercom, and a few minutes later, a woman around Nikki's age joined them. Her burgundy scrub top had a stain near the bottom.

"Mr. Hardin sweats more than anyone I know." Theresa grabbed tissues out of the box on the counter and tried to sop up some of the moisture. "What's up?"

Nikki stiffened, tension embedding between her shoulders. "Did you say Hardin, as in the former sheriff?"

"Yes. He's in our rehab section," Theresa said, looking at her quizzically. "He fell and broke his hip."

Nikki had known Hardin all of her life. He'd been the first responder to her parents' murders, but the two hadn't been getting along. When Nikki had returned to Stillwater a few months ago, they'd fallen out; the man Hardin had convicted for Nikki's parents' murders all those years ago had turned out to be innocent, and Nikki blamed him for the mistake. He'd retired before he was officially fired and Nikki had heard that he was struggling since losing his pension. Breaking a hip was bad at any age, but Hardin was nearing seventy and morbidly obese. She couldn't help but feel sorry for him despite everything that had happened.

"How is he doing?" she asked.

"Healing. Albeit slowly," Theresa said. "But he's lost a little weight, so that helps."

Paula introduced Nikki to Theresa. "Agent Hunt has a question about a male visitor that Howard had a few weeks ago. He's the only other visitor—"

"Mr. GQ?" Theresa's eyes lit up. "He signed in as Howie Doe, but I don't think that's his real name."

Nikki's pulse accelerated, and she was suddenly hot inside her coat. "You saw him? The guy I'm referring to?"

"God, yes," Theresa replied. "I remember the day perfectly. I've been thinking about him ever since… He looked like George Clooney during the *ER* years," Theresa said.

Nikki couldn't help but smile. Theresa seemed more in tune with everyday activities than Kyle, and her enthusiasm appeared to be genuine. "I take it he was well dressed?"

Theresa nodded. "He had a dark wool peacoat, and a scarf that probably cost about a month's salary for me. Leather shoes and gloves. It was like he had stepped out of a magazine."

"Can you give me any details about his face?" Nikki asked. "Eye color, facial hair, any moles or tattoos?"

"Not on his face," Theresa said. "He was clean-shaven, and his jaw was sharp enough to cut glass. I didn't get close enough to see his eye color."

"So he went in to see Howard?" Nikki quickly took notes on her phone. "How long did he speak with him? Did you hear any of the conversation?"

"No," she said. "I was down the hall, but I don't think he was in the building more than fifteen minutes or so."

Nikki opened her phone and found the picture of Declan Simpson on The Pointe's website. She showed it to Theresa. "Was this him?"

"No. This guy had kind of darker skin. Olive-toned, like he was Italian."

"Theresa, if we had you sit down with a sketch artist, do you think you would be able to describe him well enough for a composite?"

"I can try," she said. "Is he in trouble?"

"We just need to talk to him," she said. "What's your schedule tomorrow?"

"I've got my kids all day tomorrow, but my daughter is autistic and doesn't like strangers, so I don't think someone coming over is a good idea. I'm here at five in the evening."

"That's no problem," Nikki said. "I will get a sketch artist here tomorrow night, if that's okay with Paula."

"Sure," Paula said. "As long as they know we're understaffed and Theresa might have to take breaks."

Nikki made a mental note to call the sketch artist later. "Before I forget, has anyone named Darcy Hoff visited Howard or anyone else in the last several months?"

Paula slid her glasses up and typed something onto the keyboard. "No one's signed in with that name as far as I can see." She tapped away, then began scrolling through her records.

Nikki appreciated all the help Paula had given her, and she was happy to see that the staff cared about Howard and his daughter. At least Annmarie had some kind people in her life and was able to feel safe, even if she'd been scared enough at home to put an unauthorized deadbolt on her door. Paula looked up and shook her head.

Nikki showed them both the recent photo of Darcy that Darcy's mother had emailed earlier. "Recognize her?"

Both women shook their heads.

Paula stood and peered down the hall. "Kyle, can you come here if you aren't busy?"

He came out of a nearby room, walking at a snail's pace.

Nikki held out her phone. "Does this woman look familiar to you? Has she ever visited the home?"

"I wish," he replied. "I wouldn't forget a face like that."

Nikki managed not to roll her eyes. Kyle and the other employees appeared to be telling the truth, but she'd have the office run background checks on all of them.

Nikki thanked them for their time and promised to confirm the sketch artist's visit to Heritage House tomorrow night during Theresa's shift. She hurried outside and called Liam.

"Someone named Howie Doe visited Howard, and one of the nurses remembers him well enough to sit for a sketch artist," she told him.

"Howie Doe?" Liam snickered. "How big is this guy's ego?"

"If it's actually Frost, you know the answer to that question. But that could be his real name too. We can't get too excited yet."

Nikki couldn't rule out other options, but the employees and the computer system had confirmed that Howie Doe had only visited Heritage House once.

"One of my contacts at KARE channel eleven said they'd picked up the story about Annmarie's death. They're going to run the story tonight, with the angle that Frost might be targeting people in your life."

Nikki scowled. "I suppose they're putting some so-called expert with zero inside information on the case on camera. We have to get a statement out first."

"I'm already on it," Liam said. "I told my contact that our official statement is that we are working Annmarie's death as a homicide pending autopsy results, and that we're currently looking at several suspects. We haven't determined if her death is tied to Frost."

"That's perfect," Nikki said. "Once we have the composite, we'll release it. If it's Frost, we're one step closer to finding him and saving a life than we've ever been before."

CHAPTER TWELVE

Nikki could barely contain her excitement on the drive back to St. Paul. In each of the other cases, they'd only ever had a body. No suspects, no witnesses, and nothing to go on but what Frost had left for them to see. Could this sketch really be a description of the murderer she had been hunting for years? Nikki knew she needed to quell her excitement and not get ahead of herself. There was still a chance this man had nothing to do with Annmarie's death. Still, they finally had a witness able to give them some kind of composite, and that was a good starting point. She'd called the sketch artist as soon as she got into the car and arranged for him to come to the nursing home during Theresa's shift tomorrow.

Even though she knew everything about her visit needed to be taken with a grain of salt, she still felt unsettled after speaking with Howard. It had to have been heartbreaking for Annmarie to experience his memory loss and confusion every day. Had there been anyone in her life to confide in when things with Howard became too overwhelming? Liam and the FBI computer experts would dig as deeply as possible, but given that every employer had praised Annmarie as being one of the top security experts in her field, Nikki had to assume it would take too long to break through her safeguards, and Darcy Hoff didn't have that kind of time. They were still waiting on Annmarie's cell records, but Nikki had a feeling they would be just as unhelpful. Annmarie appeared to keep things as close to the vest as possible, and Nikki's gut told her she wouldn't share too much information via text.

By the time Nikki arrived at her house in Highland Park, a St. Paul suburb with great schools and family neighborhoods, news of Annmarie's murder and possible Frost connection had taken center stage on all of the local media outlets. She'd avoided several calls from reporters that had been redirected to her mobile from the administrative office, but there was one reporter she did want to talk to.

Caitlin Newport was a shark in the water, always circling, and ready for a good story, and she and Nikki frequently butted heads. But last month, her son had been kidnapped and would have died if Nikki hadn't found him in time. Caitlin was also dating Liam, and while she trusted him not to reveal information, she knew that Caitlin had a lot of connections and might be able to get information without the delay of a warrant.

Caitlin answered on the first ring. "I just heard about Annmarie on the news. I'm so sorry, Nikki. How are you doing?"

"I'm fine." Caitlin had spent countless hours trying to prove Mark Todd's innocence, so she'd known that Nikki and Annmarie had once been close. Nikki knew her concern was sincere, but Caitlin was still a reporter. She couldn't let on how broken up she was over Annmarie's death, or she'd end up riding the bench on her case. "I assume you also heard our official statement on the news?"

"I did," Caitlin said, a hint of excitement in her tone. "I'm trying really hard to be a friend first and not start bombarding you with questions."

"Well, it's better that discussion about active cases comes from me instead of your boyfriend," Nikki said as she pulled into the garage. "Work and relationships don't mix."

"You also don't want me to feel like it's okay to pump him for information." Caitlin's dry tone came through the jeep's Bluetooth.

Nikki laughed. "That too."

"Do you think Frost killed her?" Caitlin asked, her tone somber. Nikki doubted Liam had shared important information with her, but Caitlin had a lot of sources in state and local departments. "That's what the news is going with, despite the statement about looking at all angles."

"It is the most sensational." Nikki chose her words carefully. "And a real possibility. But if that's an official question, then my answer is no comment."

"Is that why you're calling your favorite reporter? Are you giving me an inside scoop?" Caitlin's arrogance bothered Nikki at times, but she was very good at her job and once she dug her teeth into a story, nothing would stop her. Normally Nikki would be irritated by her persistence, but she knew it could be useful this time.

"Well, my answer is no comment," Nikki replied, knowing this would do nothing to stop Caitlin from being so suspicious.

"I see," Caitlin said. "And off the record?"

"Off the record, I need a favor." With Annmarie's death public knowledge, Nikki knew she had to get ahead of the media on Darcy Hoff's case. Any capable reporter could discover the link between the two women with a little research. Annmarie's connection to Nikki would be center stage, and she needed to focus the case on Darcy Hoff. "Darcy Hoff wrote an op-ed about Frost, essentially challenging him. Now she's missing, and I'm certain that Frost took her," Nikki said.

"Isn't that Frost's first victim's sister?" Caitlin interrupted.

"She hasn't been missing for very long," Nikki said. "We'll be having a press conference in the next few days."

"And you have specific questions you need asked," Caitlin guessed. "Does that mean I get a front row seat at the press conference?"

"We're still working on the specifics." Because of her past, Nikki had always shied away from working with the media unless it was an absolute necessity. Darcy's disappearance certainly qualified as exactly that, and Nikki was banking on Caitlin's relationship with Liam to keep her from overstepping in her questions.

"I'll be there," Caitlin said. "Zach's staying with me for a few days, and I don't want him to feel neglected. I can leave him for a couple of hours, but that's all the time I can give you."

Nikki hadn't seen the teenager since she'd rescued him from a serial predator several weeks ago, but Liam had told her that Zach was in therapy and seemed to be making progress. She was happy to hear that he and Caitlin seemed to be mending their relationship. "I'm so glad he's spending time with you," Nikki said. "How's he doing?"

"Better," Caitlin said. "He's talking to me more and more, and to someone professional…" Caitlin broke off, and Nikki could tell that she was likely stifling a sob. "I'm so proud of how brilliantly he's doing."

"Well, he's got a great role model." Nikki heard Caitlin take a steady, purposeful breath. Caitlin had been through a lot and though she wouldn't go as far as to call Caitlin her friend, she certainly knew her well enough now to respect her.

Caitlin sniffled. "He'll be home from school in a few, so I'd better go."

Nikki knew that if she didn't go inside and eat something, she would end up passing out in her jeep without getting to spend any time with Lacey, so she thanked Caitlin and ended the call.

But before she made it inside the house, her phone rang, a California area code on the touch screen. She stood outside, hesitated for a moment before answering.

"Agent Nikki Hunt."

"Agent Hunt, this is Ross Kuhn from VPCloud, returning your call. I'm sorry it took so long to get back to you. I've been in meetings all day." The man's voice was brash, professional. Nikki wondered if he knew Annmarie himself, if he had seen the news, or if his professionalism might falter once he found out the news.

"No problem." Nikki cradled her phone on her shoulder and wrested the garage door open.

"You wanted to talk to me about a current employee," he replied, "but you didn't leave a name."

Nikki was about to reply when a mass of dark curls and giggling attacked her legs—she had only just opened the garage door, but Lacey had obviously heard her pull up. "Come play UNO with me and Daddy," she said, her arms wrapped around Nikki's leg. "He's not very good, but I think he's letting me win."

Nikki squeezed her daughter and then motioned to the phone. "Give Mommy a couple of minutes," she mouthed.

Lacey gave her a thumbs up and skipped back through the garage door that led to the living room. Nikki left the door open but went to the other side, sitting down on an old plastic chair she'd been meaning to get rid of, along with a couple of gallons of paint that had gone bad over the freezing winter.

Nikki continued, hoping Ross hadn't heard Lacey. "Yes, the employee I wanted to speak with you about is an Annmarie Mason."

"Annmarie's fantastic," Ross said admirably. "She's one of my best network engineers, but she's on vacation this week, I think." Nikki could hear typing, and she assumed Ross was checking his records. "Is she in trouble?" he asked, almost absentmindedly.

There was no easy way to tell someone about a death, especially over the phone, but it was always better to rip the band-aid off, so she soldiered on. "I'm afraid so. She's been murdered, Mr. Kuhn."

Nikki heard Ross suck in a sharp breath. "She what?" he replied. "There must be some mistake."

Nikki sighed. "I wish it was, Mr. Kuhn, but I made the positive ID myself."

"My God, poor Annmarie. She was such a good person. Who would do this?" he asked.

"That's what I'm trying to find out," Nikki said. "It looks like she moved pretty regularly until she started working for you. Did she ever talk about why?"

"When I interviewed her, she told me she wanted to have a good résumé before applying to a major company like VPCloud, so maybe it was simply a case of going where the work was."

"Right," Nikki replied. She hadn't thought of that. "Did she ever mention any issues with past coworkers or employers?"

"No, and her references were impeccable. Her old employers were sad to see her go. We were just lucky she was willing to stay on remotely when she had to move back to Minnesota."

"How often did you check in with her?"

"Nearly every day by email. She's one of our most reliable engineers. She never gave me the impression anything was wrong, and even though she worked from home, that didn't mean that she wasn't fully integrated with the rest of the office."

"Are you the only one she would have had contact with?"

"No, there are a couple of people in human resources she dealt with on a regular basis. Some project managers as well, but our corporate headquarters is fairly small."

"I'm going to need the names of those employees, Mr. Kuhn."

Ross agreed to send her a list and Nikki pressed on. There was a lot she didn't know or understand about Annmarie's job.

"Annmarie's desktop computer is password-protected, and her laptop is missing. Is that company-issued, by chance?"

"No," he said. "We have the option, but she declined. She wanted to use her own computer because of security issues."

Why would she do that, Nikki wondered to herself, especially since she'd helped to design the company's network security? "Does she store everything at home, or does she have access to a Dropbox account, or perhaps your private cloud server?"

"Possibly," he said. "I would have to check with accounts and get back to you. But if you want to see any communication or the contents of her cloud space, we'll need a warrant."

"Understood," Nikki said. "We should be able to have one drawn up in the morning and sent over."

"Please do," Ross said. "I'll give you access to everything I possibly can."

"Thank you," Nikki replied. "I'm hoping we can find something in her company email once we're allowed to access it."

"She was a private person, you know," he mused. "I probably had the most interaction with her out of anyone, and even I don't know that much about her. Everyone liked her, though, if that helps?"

"It does," Nikki replied. "I really appreciate your help, Mr. Kuhn."

"Please, if there's anything else I can do, let me know."

"Any chance we could get a copy of her references and personnel file? It would save a lot of legwork tracking them down."

"I can do that," he agreed.

After she finished speaking with Mr. Kuhn, Nikki shut the garage door quietly and headed into the living room to find Lacey and her ex-husband, Tyler. Tyler also worked for the FBI, in white-collar crimes, and his schedule was much more consistent than Nikki's. She'd already arranged for Lacey to stay with him tonight, but Lacey had begged to have pizza with Nikki. She nudged Lacey's shoulder as she was sitting on the couch. "Smells like the pizza's about done. Why don't you clean off the table and get out some paper plates and disposable forks? They're on the bottom pantry shelf."

"Bringing out the fine china." Tyler nodded approvingly as he took his homemade pizza out of the oven.

"Pizza tastes better when you don't have a big mess to clean up." She was grateful for the relationship she had with Tyler. They divorced a few years ago after realizing they were better as friends, and their good co-parenting relationship made Nikki's hectic life easier.

Lacey set the paper plates and plasticware on the table. She held up a fork and studied it as though she were looking into a microscope. "I thought fine china was a lot prettier."

Nikki smiled. "It is. That's just Daddy's way of teasing me about not using real plates."

Tyler cut the pizza and put a slice on each plate while Nikki handed her daughter a pile of napkins.

"Let's try to get most of the sauce in your mouth instead of on your face." She took a bite and moaned in appreciation. "Still the best pizza I've had."

Tyler grinned. "I'm glad I still have that title, at least."

Nikki resisted the urge to roll her eyes. Ever since Tyler had found out that she and Rory were dating, he'd been making comments like this. Fortunately, Tyler made sure not to let any jealousy he might feel affect their daughter, and Nikki was grateful for that. If it only came out in a comment here or there, she didn't mind.

"I want another piece." Lacey wiped her chin and then rubbed her tummy. "So good."

"A small piece." Nikki cut a slice in half. "You're going to have a tummy ache."

"No, I won't. We're still going to the Mall of America this weekend, right? I know all the rides I'm going to ride on, and we have to go to the aquarium." Lacey rattled on about the aquarium, talking so fast Nikki had to concentrate to understand her. "I want to see the sea turtles. Do you know they leave their baby eggs on the beach and then when the little baby turtles hatch, they have to make a run for the water? Bunches get eaten."

Nikki had been putting off taking Lacey to the mall's indoor theme park for weeks, and she'd sworn to her that she would take her this weekend since she'd caught up on some things at work. Now she had to break her promise again.

"Bug, I'm so sorry, but Mommy is probably going to be stuck at work. There's another bad man I have to catch."

Lacey sat her half-eaten piece of pizza on her plate, her big blue eyes solemn. "You promised."

"Mommy doesn't like it either," Tyler said gently.

Nikki gave him a grateful look and then took her daughter's hand. "I know, and I'm sorry. I would much rather be at the mall than working."

"Rory said we could do the mirror maze."

Tyler's jaw tightened. He rubbed Lacey's back. "I know it stinks, but Mommy can't help needing to go to work."

"Yes, she can." Lacey pushed her chair away from the table and stood, her eyes glistening with unshed tears. "She's the boss. She can do whatever she wants."

"That's not true, Bug." Nikki wanted to sink into the floor. Lacey was always good-natured about Nikki's schedule, and she hated disappointing her like this.

Lacey turned on her heel. "I'm going to my room until it's time to go."

Lacey's small feet pounded the hardwood floors to her room, followed by the slam of her door.

Nikki pushed her own plate away, no longer hungry.

"She'll get over it," Tyler said. "She always does."

"That's the problem," Nikki said. "She's getting used to this. She thinks my job is more important than her." She tried so hard to shield Lacey from her work and spend as much time with her as possible, but moments like these made her feel like a complete failure as a parent.

"Remind her that it isn't," Tyler said. "And when you are able to take her, maybe don't take your boyfriend and just focus on your daughter."

Glaring at him, Nikki gathered the empty plates. "Don't start."

"Not starting. Just making an observation."

"Good for you." She sighed. "I'm going to talk to her so you can get her home and to bed. It's getting late."

"Seriously, Nikki? You're just going to blow me off?"

"Seriously. Frost has another girl. And he killed Annmarie." She hadn't even thought to tell Tyler until now. Before Rory, he would have been the first person she told.

His expression softened. "Your friend from high school?"

"Yep. Left her in the Boundary Waters." Nikki dumped the paper plates in the garbage and grabbed the cleaning wipes from the counter. She started scrubbing the table harder than necessary.

Tyler gently took her elbow. "Hey, don't shut me out. And don't shut yourself off. You have to grieve."

Nikki kept scrubbing. She couldn't talk about how she felt right now, and she was angry at Tyler. He couldn't question her decisions one minute and try to reassure her the next. "I will," she said. "After I find Frost."

Tyler sighed and held up his hands. "Okay. I guess it's not my place to push you anymore. But you need to be easier on yourself. I get frustrated with things being changed around so often, but I understand it. You're a good mom, Nikki."

"Thank you," she said thickly.

Nikki walked down the hall and knocked on Lacey's half-open door.

"Can we talk?"

Lacey looked up from her art table, where she was coloring a red and pink blob. "Sure."

Nikki sat down on the bed across from her daughter. "I know my job is hard on you. And you're still too young to understand."

"You catch the really bad people." Lacey chose a black crayon. "I know it's really important."

Nikki scooted forward and grabbed her hands. "Not more important than you. I love you more than anything in the world. But my job doesn't have a real schedule, and I'm always juggling things."

"I know." Lacey reached for a stuffed bunny she'd had for years and hugged him to her chest. "Who's Frost?"

Nikki frowned. "You heard that?"

"You're loud when you're mad." Lacey rubbed the end of the bunny's ear over her lips and hummed quietly, a sure sign she was ready to sleep.

"We don't know Frost's real name. But he's hurt a lot of women, and he's hurting a young lady now. My team and I have to find him before it gets worse."

"And the mall is always there." Lacey stopped humming long enough to reply.

"You said something to your dad about Rory going with us."

Her lips twitched. "I just wanted to see what he would say."

"Daddy? He said it was okay, but I'm not sure—"

"I like Rory," Lacey interrupted, her tone perking up. "I want him to go with us. But I want you to take me. So, if I have to wait, then I'll wait. But it's going to cost you a cool stuffed animal from the aquarium." She yawned and rubbed the bunny ear over her lips again.

"I can do that." Nikki pulled her into a hug, grateful that her daughter was still young enough to be placated by a stuffed animal. She wished her own guilt were that easy to squash. "Daddy's waiting on us, so let's get you ready to go."

After Tyler and Lacey left, Nikki showered and then called Rory. She hadn't had the chance to check in with him all day other than a few texts, and she was anxious to talk to him.

"I miss you," he said in a husky voice. "My sheets smell like you. Makes me think bad thoughts."

Nikki laughed, but heat flashed through her. Sex with Rory was unlike anything she'd experienced—it was much more than physical—she'd never felt emotionally close to anyone until Rory came into her life.

"Did you tell Mark about Annmarie?" she asked, changing the subject before he could say anything else distracting.

"Yeah," Rory said. "He was pretty upset. I guess they dated in ninth grade and stayed good friends for a while."

"That's right. Annmarie had the biggest crush on him forever." She closed her eyes, struggling to control her emotions, but the crack in her voice gave her sadness away.

"You doing all right? I know you compartmentalize and all that, but you're also a lot more of a softie than you let on. And this is pretty damn awful."

Nikki rubbed her face; she didn't want to fall apart even in front of Rory. He would worry and want to help, and there was nothing he could do. She needed to push down her guilt; it wouldn't help her get justice for Annmarie or find Darcy. And Nikki knew that doing that was the only way to ease her pain. She didn't know how to respond to Rory, but being on the phone with him was making her feel calmer at least.

"I wish I'd known her better," Rory said eventually. "Mark never stopped talking about her back then. She wasn't about the cliques and status like a lot of the girls in school. He was trying to get her back when everything happened."

Nikki grimaced. "Everything" meaning Nikki's parents' murders and Mark's wrongful arrest. "Really? I don't remember her saying anything about that."

"He told me she wrote to him in prison. He didn't say any more, but I could tell he was devastated."

Nikki struggled to hide her surprise. Annmarie had never mentioned staying in contact with Mark after the trial. How could Nikki have known so little of her best friend despite still seeing her nearly every day? She wondered how long Annmarie had continued to write to Mark. He might be one of the few people who could fill in the blanks in her life for Nikki. "Is he there, by chance? I'd love to talk to him about her."

"No, he's at Mom and Dad's. Why do you want to talk to him about her?"

"Because I need to."

An uncomfortable silence stretched between them until Rory broke it. "Does he need an alibi or something?" Sarcasm colored his deep voice. "I mean, you've been avoiding him since he got out of prison."

"You're kidding, right?" Nikki said almost in disbelief.

Rory was silent for a few seconds and then sighed. "I think that you're after a murderer," he said. "That you're looking for anyone in Annmarie's life who's suspicious. And I just told you that Mark was in contact with her. I know you look for ex-cons first and foremost, flag anyone who has a criminal record. He fits your profile."

Nikki was shocked. She hadn't been thinking that at all. "I'd like to think I'm a better agent than that," she said.

"Seems like ex-cons always get blamed to me," Rory replied.

"He's not an ex-con," Nikki snapped. "I'd never think about him like that and no one on my team would, either. His record was expunged." Nikki couldn't believe that she was having to defend herself like this. They'd had several conversations about Mark before, and Rory had always insisted he didn't hold any grudge against Nikki for the past.

"Look, maybe I'm overreacting. My mom was there when I told him, and when she heard you were working the case, she started talking about how you'd want someone to pay quickly. She said maybe you'd have blinders on, and she's got a point, Nikki. You don't have the best record with separating your personal and professional lives." Rory sighed, and Nikki heard the sound of a bottle cap snapping off. Rory always had a few beers after work, but she was starting to think he'd had a much larger dose of liquid courage tonight. "I just get tired of defending you to my parents. I know that's not your fault—at least, not entirely."

Nikki gritted her teeth and counted to ten. She didn't blame Mark's parents for hating her, and she tried very hard not to come between Rory and his family. He'd argued with her more than once about trying to talk to his parents, and deep down, she knew her pride was part of her issue. But the Todds owed her nothing, and it seemed wrong to push them to forgive her after losing so many years with their oldest son. She understood why they were doubting her, but it didn't hurt any less.

"You there?" Rory asked.

"Yeah." Nikki could already feel her anger turning to sorrow. "Mark knew the Annmarie that I knew, that's all. I wanted to talk about her because that's what people do when someone they care about dies."

"Shit," Rory said. He paused for a moment. "I'm sorry. I had a couple of shots—"

"I have to go," Nikki said. "I've got some work to finish, and I need to try to sleep. I'll talk to you tomorrow." She hung up before he could say anything else, hoping that some time apart would help them both calm down. She knew that she should have more patience with Rory; after all, he'd never resented her for mistaking Mark for her parents' killer. Instead, he'd offered her compassion from the moment they'd met. But right now, her emotions were basically a broken electrical wire, flipping around all over the place and starting fires.

Her phone dinged.

I'm sorry. That was stupid.

Nikki grabbed a tissue from the box on the end table and cleaned her face.

It was, but I probably overreacted. Right now, I'm all over the place.

He replied with an emoji and a phone number.

Call Mark. I'm sure he wants to talk about her too.

I will. Talk tomorrow.

Nikki set her phone aside and went into her office. She always kept it locked because she didn't want Lacey going in to poke around and seeing a crime scene photo or something worse. One of her walls looked a lot like Annmarie's Frost wall, but with far more details, including crime scene photos of all the victims.

Death photos always left Nikki unsettled, but seeing Frost's victims, Kim Hoff in particular, always gave her a sense of dread that she couldn't explain.

Like the others, Kim lay on her back, frozen solid. Her skin had an eerie bluish hue and the red velvet ribbon on her body looked striking against her nearly black hair, and her serene expression. Her hands were folded peacefully on her stomach. All of the others looked the same, and yet it was Kim who really looked like she could have been taken out of a coffin.

Nikki had initially thought the closed eyes might lead them to Frost's identity because Courtney found masking tape residue on the eyelids. He'd likely taped them shut until they were frozen enough not to slip back open in death. But the test had only revealed tape residue, no DNA or fingerprints.

Nikki was certain that Annmarie was another Frost victim, that the medical examiner wasn't going to be able to find anything on her body. If it was his work, he'd have cleaned her body with bleach and been exceptionally careful. The articles and maps in Annmarie's study, alongside any other evidence they could uncover in her apartment, were crucial. If Frost had killed her, Annmarie was likely the first victim to know what was about to happen, and Nikki wasn't going to rest until she found out why.

CHAPTER THIRTEEN

The next morning, Nikki stopped at the medical examiner's office before heading to Stillwater. Dr. Blanchard had emailed her late last night to tell her that Annmarie's autopsy was complete, and Nikki wanted to make sure that she spoke to the M.E. herself. The medical examiner's office in St. Paul handled the death investigations of multiple smaller counties, including Washington County. The building was new and well-ventilated, unlike some of the morgues Nikki had been inside over the years. Unfortunately, it was located in the massive medical complex in downtown St. Paul, so finding a parking spot during morning rush hour involved a lot of cursing and waiting. Nikki finally found a spot, but she still had a five-minute walk, and then she had to check in with the front desk to receive her visitor's badge.

"Dr. Blanchard is waiting outside the autopsy suite," the administrative guy said. "She's called twice to see if you're here."

Of course she had, because no matter how much extra time Nikki gave herself when she left the house, between dealing with school drop-off and traffic, she was always late.

She used the badge to buzz into the restricted area, where Blanchard waited, her index finger scrolling her phone with an impatient flick.

"I'm sorry," Nikki said breathlessly. "I left early this morning, I swear. There was a wreck on the I-10."

Blanchard was Minnesota's first African-American medical examiner, and Nikki had worked with her on several cases. She was meticulous and methodical, and she had a no-nonsense work ethic Nikki respected.

"It's fine," Blanchard said shortly. "Grab some protective gear and I'll meet you in the autopsy room."

Even if there were no bodies in sight, the morgue tended to have an odor that hung around on a person's clothes. Nikki quickly put on a paper suit and booties and hurried into the suite before she could talk herself out of seeing Annmarie's body again.

Nikki blinked at the sting of formaldehyde and joined Blanchard, who stood next to an empty steel table.

"Doug Larsen said Annmarie is your friend?" Blanchard's voice was unusually gentle.

"We grew up together, yes," Nikki replied, though she didn't want to seem too involved. She quickly changed the subject. "Tell me what you know." Nikki blurted the words quickly, trying to stay calm.

"Exact same injection point and needle size as Frost's victims," Blanchard said. "I'm waiting on tox, but I'm betting it will be the same drug as the others."

"Did she die Monday morning, like we thought?" Nikki asked.

"I believe so," Blanchard said. "She was still in rigor and there was very little lividity. Her stomach contents would suggest she last ate eggs and drank water just a few hours before she died."

Frost kept his victims alive for a while after he kidnapped them, so this could have been the last meal she had herself or something he forced her to eat.

"No sign of sexual assault?"

"No," Blanchard said. "No signs of any sexual activity in the last few months. Her fingernails were trimmed and cleaned. No real usable trace left on the body."

Nikki's legs felt weak—that was another similarity with Frost's other victims.

"She has an interesting tattoo on her hip." Blanchard's tone softened again. "If you'd rather look at a photo, I understand."

"No, I want to see her." Hands at her side, Nikki curled her fingers into a fist until her nails slightly dug into her palm. The pain helped her focus on the present.

Blanchard went over to the cold storage units, where the bodies were temporarily held before and after autopsy.

Nikki braced herself as Blanchard removed the gurney containing Annmarie's body. She had worked more murder cases than she could count, with victims in all states of decomposition, but there was always a shock when she saw the victim naked on the gurney, no more than a flesh and bone shell. But knowing the person made the experience nearly unbearable.

This isn't her anymore, Nikki reminded herself, her palm stinging from her nails digging in too deeply. *This is just her body.*

Her mother had said those words to Nikki when Grandma Jen died. As an adult, Nikki realized how much Valerie had masked her own pain from losing her mother to protect Nikki. *Death is nothing to be afraid of. Grandma's in a better place, watching over us still.*

But as Nikki understood the pain of losing her own mother, she felt a new appreciation for her. She'd tried hard to make Nikki's childhood safe and happy.

"Nicole?"

Nikki yanked her mind out of the past. "Go ahead."

"I should warn you, she has a lot of pre-mortem bruising on her arms and the bruising pattern on her right hand is strange. She's got a large, nearly solid bruise on the side of her hand, but the bruises on the top of her hand are indicative of fingers digging into the skin."

It took Nikki a moment to catch up. "Wait. That sounds like her hand was grabbed hard and squeezed. Can you tell what the angle is? I mean, would it be possible to tell if he reached up and snatched her hand, or if he just grabbed her hand tightly when he was forcing her somewhere?"

"All I can tell is that either scenario is possible." Blanchard lifted the part of the sheet near her left hip, revealing a small, faded heart with the name "Lyle" inside. "The red inside the heart looks unfinished. Do you want a few minutes alone with her?" Blanchard asked.

Nikki nodded.

Blanchard left the suite, but Nikki stood in overwhelmed silence. There were so many things she wanted to say to Annmarie, and now it was too late.

Finally, Nikki touched her friend's cold hand. "I'm sorry I failed you in life, Annie. I swear I won't fail you in death."

After leaving the morgue, Nikki held her tears all the way to the jeep. She gave into the grief for a few minutes, tears streaming down her face as memories of Annmarie pelted her. Finally, she reined in her emotions. The only way out of grief was through it, and Nikki had a job to do. They needed to find people of interest in Annmarie's life, and now they had a name to search. Annmarie had definitely had someone significant in her life called Lyle.

On the way to Stillwater, she checked in with Courtney, telling her what she'd found out and asking her for any news.

"What have you got? Anything good?"

"I don't know if good is the right word, but I do have information," Courtney replied. "So far, all the prints taken from Annmarie's office and apartment are hers. No foreign prints, which suggests she was as private as her neighbor said. We also found her prints on the scrap of material you found on both sides of the silk. I think she definitely tore that thing out. The bleach cleaner used was the same color-safe stuff used on other victims, and I wish I knew what it was, because that Burberry coat was clean as a whistle without a white spot on it."

Nikki was disappointed. She had hoped to find something at Annmarie's home. "What about the pickup truck Annmarie drove and Darcy Hoff's car? That should have arrived last night." Nikki crossed her fingers they would have Frost's prints on the exterior of the truck somewhere.

"Inside and outside both clean. I only found Annmarie's prints. We're still processing Darcy's car, but I have the report from the Eagan police. So far, I agree there's nothing useful. But we'll scour it down to the last thread."

"I know you will," Nikki said. "That's why I can do my job without worrying about the forensics team. You're a drill sergeant, and your people are terrified of you."

Courtney snorted. "There's a fine line between fear and respect, my friend. I just know how to walk it."

By now, Nikki knew the Washington County Government Center as well as she did her own FBI campus. Miller had secured an empty room in the sheriff's office, so Nikki parked next to a cruiser and headed inside, a pack of Pop-Tarts in hand. So much for starting the day off with an energizing breakfast. Nikki figured the Pop-Tarts had to be better for her than the massive, jelly-filled donut she'd almost bought instead. She shouldered her bag and nibbled on the frosted cinnamon tart.

Nikki nodded at the desk sergeant—she'd been here so many times in the past few months that everyone knew her.

Miller and Liam had already set up in the same room they'd been in just a few weeks ago when they'd worked together to solve a double homicide.

She hefted her bag onto the table. "Home sweet home, I guess."

Liam's eyes lit up when he saw the Pop-Tarts. Nikki and Courtney were fairly certain he had a hollow leg, because he could eat any time of day, no matter the situation, and he ate a lot. "You going to finish that?"

"Yes, but I'm a nice person." She slid a pack over to him, and then handed one to Miller. "Hope you like cinnamon."

"I'm human, aren't I? Are there people who don't like it?"

"My ex-husband," Nikki said.

"Is that why you divorced him?" Liam asked between bites, grinning.

"The exact reason."

All three of them laughed before the tension settled back into the room.

"I just came from Blanchard's office." Nikki filled everyone in on the autopsy results. "We need to find out who Lyle is. I did get the judge to sign off on a warrant for VPCloud's information. One of our agents in the Los Angeles office is going to serve it and oversee the search. Hopefully we'll have more information tonight. Annmarie's boss also sent me a copy of her references, so we have points of contact in the other states she lived in. We need to find out if there was anyone named Lyle she could have associated with in any of these states."

"Email me the list," Miller said. "I'll start going through it."

"Thanks." Nikki opened her phone and forwarded him the list. "Liam, where are the computer guys with her desktop?"

"Still working on it, but they should have access later today. And we didn't find her laptop anywhere in her apartment."

"It's probably in that bag she carried. She had it in the elevator footage." Plenty of people had external hard drives, and if Annmarie worked while she visited her father, she probably brought it along as backup.

Liam drummed his fingers on the table. "Well, if her laptop is issued through VPCloud, they might be able to track it."

Nikki shook her head. "She used her personal one."

"Why?" Liam asked in surprise.

"Her boss said she preferred her own computer because it was customized and she had control over the security. But I think it's strange too." Nikki rubbed the aching muscles in her shoulders. "How are the background checks for the security guys at The Pointe coming along?"

"Clean," Miller said. "And they're all alibied."

Nikki had expected as much. "We've officially taken over Darcy's missing person case. Until now, we've managed to keep the connection between Darcy and Annmarie out of the media, but with all the evidence we have that suggests Frost likely took both women, we need to work their cases as one. Check for a Lyle in Darcy's life too. Look for anyone with that name, and make sure you comb through every stitch of information we have for anyone who meets the description of Howie Doe."

"Lunds and Byerlys sent the customer list over. She's got several repeat customers," Liam said. "I started from the top, running background checks while Miller spoke to individual people. We're through the first month or so, and they all check out."

Miller wadded up his Pop-Tart wrapper. "I'm bringing in Deputy Reynolds to help us. Since Darcy didn't have a lot of friends, we should be able to finish with everyone on the list today."

"Can you tell who she delivered to first, Declan or Annmarie?" Nikki asked. "Was it a coincidence that Annmarie found Darcy or Darcy found Annmarie or did one of them seek the other out? Given Annmarie was researching Frost, I'd be betting she requested Darcy—maybe she wanted to find out more about her sister. But we can't rule anything out."

Miller scanned the list. "Going by this, there are three deliveries in February to Annmarie and none to Declan. His started the first week of March."

"She's an attractive girl," Liam said. "Declan might have seen her deliver to Annmarie and used the service as a way of talking to her?"

Nikki didn't respond. Liam was right, but it was conjecture. Yesterday, Nikki had asked him to coordinate with state and local law enforcement and make sure they were on high alert for Darcy. "Liam, any information from the state or local law enforcement?"

"They've all got the BOLO information. Since Eagan police haven't located her bag or the suitcase, I added those to the BOLO. And I sent it to the Wisconsin state guys too." Liam rubbed his temples. "Minnesota State Patrol had a couple of false tips, but so far, that's all we've got."

"Stay on them," Nikki said. "Make sure they understand we believe she could still be alive. We'll send them the composite sketch once it's done too. What about Annmarie and Darcy's financials?"

"Darcy just has a checking account and one credit card," Liam said. "Her paycheck was direct deposit, and she didn't spend a lot of money. She has a recurring payment of $400 to her father, presumably for rent. No activity on her bank or the credit card since she disappeared."

"What were her last purchases?"

"Uh …" Liam opened his laptop. "Let me double-check. She hasn't used the credit card in a couple of months, at Tires Plus. Last purchase on her bank card was the morning she disappeared. Looks like she stopped at a Holiday and filled up with gas."

"And the suitcase and toiletries from Walmart?"

"The transaction is for $101.78," Liam said. "Three days before she disappeared."

"You think there's any chance she really was going to take off?" Miller asked.

"Darcy wanted to make it on her own," Liam said. "Her mother said she loved a bargain and was frugal. Doesn't make sense to me that she'd leave her car and free food to start a new life."

"I agree," Nikki said. "What about Annmarie?"

"Even more unremarkable. She made good money, as you can imagine. Has a money market, savings and checking. As far as I can tell, there's no unusual spending."

"Just to clarify," Miller said. "You think Annmarie was targeted because of her connection to you or because she knew something about Frost?"

"Probably both," Nikki said. "I've been wondering if Annmarie started investigating Frost because of me. What if she figured out who Frost was? What if he killed her because she got it right?"

"Why did he leave the ribbon?"

"The ribbon is part of his signature," Liam said. "And I think Nikki's right. Maybe she was just close to finding him, and he killed her to protect his identity."

Miller crossed his arms over his chest and leaned back in his chair. "Which brings us back to the stuff on her office wall."

"I've been thinking about that," Liam said. "Obviously she was trying to track Frost, but Annmarie was a network security expert, right? If she knew who Frost was, she could have hacked into his cloud files or personal computer. His phone too. What if that's how he caught her?"

"I've been wondering the same thing," Nikki said. "This is as close as we've come to finding out Frost's real identity, and he knows it. That's why I'm planning on a press conference in the next few days. If we can get enough information to make him think he's backed into a corner, he might make the mistake that finally helps us catch him. That's why I'm working with a member of the media. I want to ensure specific questions are asked." She grinned at Liam.

"And she's giddy about it," Liam said dryly, his attention focused on his computer.

"Caitlin Newport," Miller guessed.

Nikki shrugged. "We need to control the narrative as much as possible. I never thought I'd say this, but I trust Caitlin."

Miller snickered. "And I never thought I'd hear you say that. But I agree. Just know I'm sure she'll remind you of how trustworthy she's been the next time she wants a big scoop."

"Oh, I know." Nikki chewed the last of her tart. "We'll have the composite from the CNA at the nursing home by morning. I'm going to schedule the conference for tomorrow afternoon."

"Holy shit." Liam stared at his laptop as though it had appeared out of nowhere. "I just got an email from our tech guys. They've been going over the closed-circuit videos from cameras near Annmarie's building. This one's from a dry cleaner across the street from The Pointe's parking garage entrance."

"Please tell me we have a good shot of Annmarie in the vehicle with him. A license plate number would be a godsend." Nikki's heart rate accelerated.

Liam turned his laptop around so that she could see it. "I wish, but no. It's cued up for you."

Nikki clicked the touchpad, and the video started. It was black and white and slightly grainy, but still good enough quality to see some details. "What am I looking for?"

"Just watch."

Two people emerged from the parking garage, walking quickly. Both had their heads down, but Nikki recognized Annmarie immediately. The man with her held her close, his hand resting on the back of her neck. At first glance, he could have been caressing her, but a sharp eye could tell by his posture that he had a tight grip on her.

"He's wearing a dark coat similar to the one the CNA at Heritage House described." Nikki could hardly get the words out. "It's got to be Howie Doe."

The man looked to be around six feet, in nondescript clothing. The ear flaps on his winter cap helped to hide his face. And then he looked up, probably scanning the area to make sure no one had noticed him taking Annmarie by force. In regular speed, his face was no more than a white flash, but their technicians had slowed the video down so they could watch frame by frame. The result was nearly as good as an eyewitness sketch.

"White male," Nikki murmured. "Trimmed beard. Sharp cheekbones—his face is fairly thin." She willed more details to come into focus. "Is this as clean as they could get the shot?"

Liam nodded. "It's not perfect, but it's a damn face. And it's not anyone we've interviewed, unless you recognize someone you've spoken to on your own?" He looked at Nikki for confirmation.

"No." Nikki felt out of breath from the adrenaline flowing through her system. "If it's the same guy the eyewitness at the nursing home saw, we'll share this footage at the press conference too."

"How do you think Frost is going to respond? If this is him and we release footage or a description that matches him, are you worried about what he might do to Darcy if he has her?" Miller asked.

"He's used to methodically planning things and feeling totally in control. Seeing his face on the news might push him to make another mistake," Nikki said. "That's our best shot at finding him while Darcy's still alive."

If she was still alive, Nikki thought. Dr. Blanchard believed that previous victims had been dead for several weeks before Frost decided it was time to get rid of the body.

Liam rubbed his temples. "Or to kill Darcy if he hasn't already, just to show us how much smarter he is than us?"

Nikki was silent for a moment. Liam and Miller were right, and her plan was risky, but she didn't have much choice in this. It was the strongest lead they'd ever had on Frost. "There's a risk of that happening whatever we do, but this way someone might recognize him. We have to try," she said. Liam and Miller nodded.

Nikki prayed that for Darcy's sake her gamble paid off.

CHAPTER FOURTEEN

Nikki wanted to speak with Declan about Darcy delivering his groceries, and she finally managed to reach him after her first two calls went to voicemail. Declan suggested meeting at a sandwich shop near Hewlett Packard, where he worked. Nikki would have preferred speaking to him at the office, because she'd learned a long time ago that people were the most honest when their employer was around, but her questions couldn't wait. If Frost had been in the building at all in the weeks leading up to Annmarie's murder, Declan might have seen him, too.

Liam and Miller were currently going through Darcy's delivery list, searching for any other connections to Annmarie or someone with the name "Lyle," but since Annmarie was dead and Darcy was missing, Declan's connection to both women couldn't be ignored.

Declan was already waiting for her when she arrived, eating his lunch. He sat hunched over a massive salad, already halfway through. "I'm sorry I didn't wait to order. I'm short on time. I'll flag the server down for you."

Nikki sat down and waved him off. "I'm short on time too, so don't bother." She'd initially planned to press him about not mentioning that Darcy Hoff also delivered his groceries since Engle's file mentioned interviewing him, but the security footage was more important. "We have an image taken from an adjacent security camera that shows Annmarie leaving with a man. I'd like you to take a look at it and see if you recognize him."

"Sure," Declan said. "I'll do my best."

Nikki cued the image up on her phone and showed it to him. Liam had sent her a close-up still from the man's face. "Have you seen this man around the building before?"

Declan leaned forward, studying the picture. "No, he's not someone I recognize."

"What about the name Howie Doe?"

"Doe as in 'John Doe?'" Declan shook his head. "I'd remember that name. I can have Caves check our guest logs. We keep them for several months."

"That would be great," Nikki said. "Please have him call me with any hits on the name."

She waited a moment, assessing Declan's demeanor. Just because he hadn't been the one in the photo with Annmarie didn't mean he wasn't involved. Nikki didn't believe that Frost worked with a partner, but she had to rule Declan out. He chewed quickly, glancing between his plate and Nikki, but he didn't appear flustered.

"One more thing." Nikki played her trump card without taking her eyes off Declan. "We know that Darcy Hoff delivered your groceries as well as Annmarie's. She's also missing. Why didn't you mention that?"

Declan looked at her in confusion. "The police asked me about her a few weeks ago. Is she still missing?"

"Yes," Nikki said. "And she was making a delivery to you before she disappeared." Nikki drummed her fingers on the table. "Two women you knew vanished, and you didn't think to tell us?"

"She didn't make the delivery," he said defensively. He dropped his fork. "The detective who came and talked to me said my call to Byerlys is what alerted them that she was missing."

"We know that Darcy didn't make it inside the building," Nikki said. "Why did you want her to deliver your groceries and not a random delivery driver?"

"She delivered to Annmarie." He shrugged. "I ran into Annmarie in the elevator a while ago and asked about her. Most stores don't let you pick the delivery driver, so I thought she might have been with a private service until Annmarie said Lunds and Byerlys let the customer choose. She suggested I request Darcy because she was reliable."

"You didn't tell us about that conversation yesterday," Nikki reminded him. The omission alone wasn't necessarily suspicious given that grocery delivery was so common, but Nikki wanted to see if she could get a reaction out of him. "You said that you and Annmarie never really had a conversation outside of the building meeting over security issues and that was the only real conversation you'd had with her."

He finished chewing a large bite of his food and then chased it down with water. "I honestly didn't think of it. It was two months ago, maybe more. And it was basically a question and answer. Not exactly a conversation."

"Did you have groceries delivered before then?"

"Sometimes," he said. "But I live alone, so I usually don't cook a lot. I've been trying to learn." Declan flushed. "I'm tired of takeout and boxed dinners."

Nikki nodded. "Had you spoken to her in passing when she delivered to Annmarie? You must have requested her for a reason... She's a pretty girl." Nikki smiled at Declan.

"No," Declan said. "I mean, pleasantries of course," he continued, panic entering his voice, but no more than it would for anyone if they were being grilled, Nikki thought. "Annmarie said that she was always on time and the groceries were well-packed, and she picked excellent fruits and vegetables."

"And Annmarie never said anything else to you about Darcy?" Nikki asked.

"I don't think so," he said. "Why are you so interested in this?" He looked confused. "It's not your case, is it? Detective Engle—I think that was her name—said they thought Darcy left town. She had problems, I guess."

"The Eagan police are wrong. She was taken by someone," Nikki said. She hoped this would shock Declan. He was involved in two serious crimes, but he didn't seem to realize that.

Declan sat back in his chair. "Oh my God. That poor girl…"

As much as Nikki wanted Declan to be a liar, she believed his reactions, and his story, were genuine. But she didn't want to let him off the hook just yet. "Declan, I really need you to think hard. Any little bit of information you can give me on either woman could be vital. It could help me get justice for Annmarie; it could help me find Darcy. If there's anything else you've forgotten, tell me now. If I find out you've held anything back from me, I won't be so friendly. I could have called you into the station at this point, but I haven't."

Declan shook his head. "I swear, I don't have anything to hide."

She watched him for a moment, giving him time to say anything that came to mind, but it didn't and eventually she let him be, the salad remaining untouched in front of him.

Nikki went back to Lunds and Byerlys to talk to the handful of employees the manager knew Darcy interacted with. They all said the same thing: Darcy was quiet and polite, and she focused on her shopping. No one remembered her hanging out in the break room or socializing in any real way unless she needed help finding an item. She left dejected and checked in with Liam, hoping he'd have news. But the delivery list was more of the same. No red flags, and they'd all been happy with Darcy's service.

She started the jeep with the intention of going back to the station, but Nikki couldn't shake the feeling that she needed to go back to Annmarie's. Before she could talk herself out of it, she made an illegal U-turn and headed towards Woodbury.

*

Nikki walked into the lobby at The Pointe and approached the security guard stationed next to a side door marked "private." She showed the guard her badge and asked to speak to Caves.

The guard nodded and unlocked the door. "He's in the control room. Straight back to your right."

Nikki thanked him and then hurried down the hall. Without the FBI techs and the rest of her team, the building was quiet, save for the bubbling fountain in the lobby and elevator music, something that hadn't been playing yesterday. She'd noticed a man in the lobby whistling as he checked his mailbox. It seemed that things had gone back to normal for everyone but Annmarie.

She knocked on the open control room door, and Caves, the head of security at Annmarie's building, waved her into the room.

"Agent Hunt, good to see you. Declan called me a few minutes ago," Caves said. "I'm checking our logs right now, but so far, no Howie Does are coming up."

Nikki thanked him and then explained that she needed to go through some things in Annmarie's apartment. She half-expected him to insist that Declan be aware of the request, but he nodded and went to his computer to create a temporary access code for her.

Nikki shouldered her bag and leaned against the corner of his desk. "You've worked here since the building opened, right?"

Caves nodded. "First person hired."

He seemed at ease around the computer, but online security was a specialized field. "Do you specialize in cybersecurity, or does property management hire outside help?"

"I didn't go to school for that, no," Caves said. "I've learned my way around most of our systems and can handle most issues. But the hack that upset Ms. Mason was definitely out of my league."

"And you never figured out who was behind the hack?" Nikki asked.

"The police investigated for weeks, but you know these guys just disappear into the internet universe. Finding them is harder than finding a needle in a haystack."

"And they multiply like cockroaches," Nikki said dryly. "Do you know what personal information was compromised?"

"That's the thing," Caves replied. "Our financial stuff is on a completely different network, and it wasn't touched. But the police said the hackers probably hadn't known that and were hoping to cash in."

Nikki nodded as though she agreed, but she couldn't help but wonder if the attack had been some kind of dry run for someone to break into the building. Had they intended to rob residents or had the attack been about someone specific, like Annmarie? Frost might have been trying to get into Annmarie's computer or digital cloud to see if she'd been keeping tabs on him.

Caves wrote down a six-digit code on a sticky note. "This is good for two hours, for both the elevator and her apartment. Would you like me to go with you, Agent Hunt?"

"I've taken up enough of your time," she said. "I won't be long."

"Call if you need anything."

Nikki thanked him for his time and went back into the lobby. She typed in the temporary code and then stepped into the elevator. By the time she reached the fourth floor where Annmarie's apartment was, Nikki felt queasy from nervous energy. Since she was alone, Nikki didn't have to censor her grief to make sure she remained professional in front of the team. But right now, she'd give anything not to be alone. Keeping it together was going to be a lot harder.

Her hand trembled as she keyed in the code and slowly opened the door. The smell of fingerprint dust was strong, but Nikki knew she wouldn't see any trace of Courtney's work. She prided herself on not leaving a big mess for someone else to clean up, especially in people's homes.

Nikki hadn't spent much time in the kitchen yesterday, so she perused the drawers and cabinets. Much of the apartment was sparse and modern, with contemporary furnishings, but looking through the cabinets, she recognized the Pfaltzgraff plates that Annmarie's mother had been so proud of and the collection of kitschy salt and pepper shakers that Howard had collected for as long as Nikki could remember.

Heart heavy, Nikki wondered who would take care of Annmarie's things. She hadn't been materialistic, and the old dishes and knickknacks likely weren't worth much, but the sentimental value was enormous. She made a mental note to see if Annmarie had a will on file with the state.

Nikki had already gone through much of the living room herself, so she bypassed it and went to the bedroom. She checked the dresser and nightstand for anything that might belong to a man, or better yet, a name or a picture of an old boyfriend. Now that she had the name Lyle to search for, she hoped that she'd find something new. But she came up empty and turned to the closet, noticing for the first time that Courtney had left the door open, something she never did. Courtney hated leaving someone's home different from the way they'd found it, even if the occupant was dead.

They'd gone through everything stored in the closet yesterday, but Nikki checked everything again, including the pockets of Annmarie's clothes. With a sigh, she realized she couldn't keep putting off the real reason she'd come here. Courtney had photographed the armoire and its contents yesterday, but Nikki had to step away. Annmarie hadn't put any things of her own in it, so the contents of the armoire hadn't changed since the night her parents had been murdered.

Nikki knew that Annmarie would want her to have the armoire and its contents, but she still wasn't sure she was ready to have them in her own home. It was just another reminder of her parents' deaths and more fodder for Lacey's relentless questions. But her mother would be furious that Nikki turned her back on the family heirlooms, so she took a deep breath and opened the door.

But immediately her blood seemed to turn to ice, her knees knocked together and then gave out at what she saw.

She rocked forward, rubbing her eyes.

This could not be real, she thought.

A picture lay on top of the antique quilts.

A picture that hadn't been there yesterday.

A picture of Nikki's mother in her casket, her folded hands resting on the red velvet ribbon that tied around the waist of her black dress.

And Nikki's world went black.

CHAPTER FIFTEEN

"She looks like a doll."

"Lovely dress and the red ribbon sets off her coloring. What a tragedy."

Nikki sat in the corner, watching people pay their respects to her parents and looking at her with pity in their eyes.

Annmarie squeezed her hand. "We'll be able to go home soon. Are you hungry? You look so pale. I think you should eat something. There are snacks in the room across the hall."

"I can't eat," Nikki answered. "This is my fault. They're dead because of me."

"I know." Annmarie was no longer the sixteen-year-old Nikki remembered. She was Nikki's age, wearing the same clothes and coat from the crime scene, her face tinged blue. "And now I am too."

Nikki forced her heavy eyelids open, the grief weighing so heavy on her chest that she gasped for air. How had she wound up on the floor? She'd come back to Annmarie's building, talked to Caves and then …

The picture.

She slowly sat up, cradling her sore elbow. The picture lay where Frost had left it. Nikki felt dizzy from shock, but she shifted to all fours in an effort to stand without falling again.

Her phone blared through the silence, and she hurriedly dug it out of her jeans pocket, relieved to see that she'd only lost a few minutes.

She didn't give Liam a chance to talk. "Liam. I'm at Annmarie's," she said quickly. "Get here now and get Courtney here to process Annmarie's apartment again. Make sure she doesn't bring any techs. I want this kept as quiet as possible. Frost's been here."

"What?" Liam said incredulously.

"Someone's been here and left a picture in the armoire. I'll tell you when you get here."

She ended the call and got to her feet. She walked shakily down the hall to the front door and hit the intercom button for security, careful to cover her hand with her sleeve.

"Caves, I need you to go through all of the security footage for the building in the last twenty-four hours right now. Someone's been here. Can you lock down the building and make sure no one else leaves or enters?"

Caves agreed, but his shock was evident, and Nikki could barely hear him as she tried to shake the image of her mother in the casket out of her mind.

"Let me pull up yesterday," he said. "Here you are leaving yesterday afternoon. Your forensic people left later. I'll keep skimming through, but, Agent Hunt, the thing is, Declan's temp code expired yesterday. No one could enter the apartment without it."

"Would Annmarie's last code still work?"

Caves groaned. "As long as it wasn't deactivated, yes. I was going to do that today and hadn't gotten around to it. Let me run her code through our system and see if it's been used."

Nikki wanted to lean against the wall, but she didn't want to touch anything she hadn't already contaminated.

"Shit," Caves said. "Someone used it to access the elevator around eleven last night, and then accessed her door a minute later."

"Look at the security video during that time, please. I'll stay on the line while you search."

"I'm cuing it up now. It's a man. He's keeping his head down, like he knows where the cameras are."

Because he did. He probably knew the entire layout of the building, Nikki thought.

"Are there cameras over individual doors?" she asked.

"No, just the hallway. He gets off the elevator, head down the same way. He walks off frame in the direction of her apartment. Looks like he returns about three minutes later, but he didn't go back down the elevator. He used the emergency exit at the end of the hall."

"Can anyone open that door?"

"No, it's code-operated like everything else. But the code to get out of the door is posted. He must have gone down the back stairwell to avoid the rest of the cameras. Agent Hunt, I'm so sorry. That's on me. I should have deactivated her code yesterday."

"Take a screenshot and email it to me ASAP. You have my card, right?"

"I do."

"My team is on their way. Please allow them access but stop anyone else from entering or leaving the building. Is anyone home at the moment?"

"No," he replied. "I'll alert my officer in the lobby to give your team full access to the building."

Nikki hung up, her heart racing. The picture flashed through her mind on repeat as she stood beside the door, her mind unraveling.

Frost was connected to her.

The realization took over, and she couldn't move because of the shock.

Bile rose in the back of Nikki's throat.

Frost had killed countless women, and every single one of them had been positioned the same way. Positioned to look like Nikki's mother.

And after all this time he wanted Nikki to know that.

She had always felt a strange sense of dread when she'd seen their bodies. There was something so familiar about them that she'd never been able to put her finger on. It had kept her up at night, entered her dreams—the hands placed so purposefully…

She'd always known the red ribbon meant something specific to Frost too, and at times she'd experienced a nagging feeling that she was missing something obvious about it.

Now she knew why.

The red ribbon is about Mom.

She couldn't believe it.

Had Frost taken this picture? She had never seen it before. Had he been in the same building with Nikki at some point during her parents' funeral?

Nikki's phone dinged with the sound for her email, and she hastily opened it and clicked on the image that Caves had attached.

There he was, standing in the elevator, in his peacoat, his hands in his pockets and his head down. He wore a newsboy-style cap, but she could tell he had dark hair. Nikki brought the phone closer to her face. She could see some kind of pattern peeking out from in between the lapels of the coat. Could that be the scarf that cost more than Theresa's monthly salary?

Did Nikki know who this was? Was he someone in her own life?

Liam had texted while she was talking with Caves to let her know he should be there in twenty minutes or so, with Courtney not far behind.

As much as she never wanted to see it again, the picture of her mother beckoned Nikki. At least she'd had the presence of mind not to touch it without gloves. She found a pair in her purse and went back to the bedroom. Her stomach rolled with every step, and her mouth was so dry her lips felt sticky.

She took photos of the closet, armoire and picture before she touched it, because Nikki knew she wouldn't be able to recall anything but what the picture looked like.

She tried to slip on the gloves, but her hands were shaking too much. Nikki had spent years trying to remember exactly what her mother looked like in her casket, which had been placed next to her father's in the funeral home, but the images of her body lying in a pool of her own blood had always superseded everything else.

Nikki and her aunt had picked out the black, long-sleeved dress because it was high-necked and would cover bruises better. The red ribbon had been Aunt Mary's idea, because her mother loved red and she would have hated to be buried without a little pop of color. She didn't have a lot of facial injuries to cover, so her mother looked like she was sleeping.

Like a porcelain doll.

Bile burned her esophagus again, and Nikki rushed to the bathroom, spitting into the sink.

Nikki didn't remember anyone taking pictures at the funeral, and this had been taken from beside the casket, as though the person were looking down at her.

Frost had known her mother. It was her death he was paying homage to with his victims. But why?

The questions ran through her mind so quickly she felt dizzy. She stumbled to the bathroom and splashed cold water on her face and rinsed out her mouth, staring at her reflection, trying to get her head straight before the team arrived.

Something about the security picture nagged at Nikki. She dried her face and opened the image again.

Liam was likely a few minutes out yet, so Nikki called down to security again and asked Caves to email her the actual video clips from the security cameras. She stood in the living room looking down at the gardens before the files arrived a couple of minutes later, attached in the order they'd been taken.

Nikki watched the videos in order: first, the lobby feed showing the man in the peacoat strolling in confidently, his head down, pretending to be focused on his phone. The video from inside the elevator came next. The man still kept his head down, but he slipped his cell phone in his coat pocket. He seemed to freeze, and then he turned his coat pockets inside out before moving to the inside pocket. Nikki could see the end of the picture in that pocket, but the man was clearly looking for something.

She pushed down her emotions, trying to focus and forget what she had just found out. She imagined herself in Frost's position; what might he have been looking for?

"Gloves?" Nikki's heart pounded against her chest as she clicked the final video from the hallway feed. He made sure to keep his head down until his back was turned to the camera, but his hands were in his pockets as he walked stiffly away.

A loud bang echoed down the hallway, and Nikki almost dropped her phone, which had vibrated with a text from Liam telling her to open the deadbolt.

Her agony over the picture temporarily forgotten, she raced down the hall. Nikki unlocked the deadbolt and then yanked the door open. Liam and Courtney both looked shocked, and Liam rested his hands on her shoulders.

"Why are you so out of breath? What happened?"

Nikki was breathing hard from the adrenaline rush, but she managed to get the words out, telling them about the picture left in the armoire. She handed Liam her unlocked phone. "The picture's on my camera roll."

Courtney peered around his shoulder, her face pale. "Oh my God, Nikki."

"I'll be okay," Nikki responded. "Especially since the bastard forgot to bring his gloves this time."

Courtney practically shoved Liam out of the way. "How do you know?"

"The security videos. He got cocky. Did you leave Annmarie's bedroom door open?"

"No," Courtney said. "I remember specifically closing it because it was the last thing I did before I left."

"Then don't waste your time with the keypad or the front doorknobs. Fingerprint the bedroom door, the closet door, and the armoire."

"The knob's iron, but the chemicals might strip the wood."

"I don't care."

"How could he possibly—" Liam started.

"He had to have taken the picture," Nikki replied impatiently. "At the funeral."

Liam was looking at her with concern, and Nikki knew that once her adrenaline wore off, a very dark reality would set in. She was going to ride the high for as long as she could.

She pointed to her phone. "Please just watch." Liam was silent as he did, the creases between his eyes growing deeper with each video.

"I'm connected to Frost. He was in my life in some capacity when this picture was taken. His murders are about Mom or me, or maybe both of us. This photo proves it."

Both Liam and Courtney looked as sick as she felt.

"Once he realized he didn't have the gloves, why go ahead with his plan?" Courtney asked. "He could have left, and we would have never known."

"Because it's personal. I'm in his head now. We're going to catch him this time."

Nikki glanced up at Liam to confirm he agreed, but he stared past her, his eyebrows knitted together.

"What is it?" Nikki asked.

"I was just thinking about us going to that North Woods cabin to save Bailey Banks. You remember that, right?"

That had been during the missing girls case that had brought Nikki back to Stillwater. "Of course I do."

"Didn't you say that your family vacationed up there a few times? Do you remember what resort?"

"The last several years, we went to Satko's near Deer River. We went somewhere else when I was young, but I don't know the name of it." An involuntary shiver shot down Nikki's spine. "Why?"

Liam opened his phone and typed something in before turning it so that she could see the map. He pointed to the area around Grand Rapids, Minnesota. "Deer River's right here, not far from Grand Rapids. If I remember my map key correctly, that's around a hundred miles from where the first victim was found."

"That's a huge distance." Nikki wasn't sure where he was headed with this, but the roots of her hair were beginning to dampen with sweat.

"But that's not the only resort you stayed at when you went to the North Woods," Liam said.

"Fill me in here," Courtney said. "What are you getting at?"

"Two years ago, victim three was found in an area Nikki associates with fond memories," Liam said gravely. "Did Annmarie ever go with you on those trips?"

Realization dawned on Nikki. "Yes."

Liam nodded, looking more alarmed by the minute. "We provided extra security and background checks for the Super Bowl that year. You volunteered, didn't you?"

"You still resent that I went to the game and you didn't?" She tried to laugh, but her throat felt glued together.

He shook his head. "Last year, near First Avenue, victim five. You're a Prince fan, right?"

"Annmarie and I went to his concert in high school." Nikki's legs threatened to buckle. "He performed there again in 2007. I was in town for a conference. It was the closest I'd come to Stillwater since I graduated high school." She stood in shock.

"And you attended?"

She nodded. "He was delayed. I had to leave before he came on. But yes, I was at First Avenue that night."

"Maybe it's a coincidence," Courtney said.

"It's not," Liam said. "It's more evidence that Nikki knows Frost."

Nikki leaned against the wall for support. "We have to change our lens."

"What?" Liam and Courtney spoke in unison.

"Something I learned in early psychology classes," Nikki said. "We all look at the world through the lens created by our experiences. In order to really understand someone's issues, you have to figure out what shaped their lens. We've been approaching this as though Frost's issues were solely about him, but they aren't. They're somehow tied to me. That's why he chose locations that I had ties to."

"But you don't have any connections to the first two, do you?" Courtney asked.

"Not that I know of, but my mother might have. But if that theory is right, for him to know about Mom's past, then he had to have been close to her at some point."

"Michigan and Wisconsin," Liam said quietly. "Maybe your mother had ties there that you aren't aware of."

A fresh wave of fear and disgust rolled through Nikki. "Maybe I don't know him. Maybe he knows more about my own family history than I do, and he's been trying to tell me."

CHAPTER SIXTEEN

An hour later, the team had re-dusted the entirety of Annmarie's apartment, including the hallway, the doors the security footage showed Frost using, and the elevator. There were no fingerprints. Nikki wasn't surprised that Frost had been smart enough to use something to cover his hands, but she couldn't help but feel disappointed. And she was starting to feel angry at herself: how had her connection to Frost been so obvious and yet so hard to see?

Nikki debated calling her bureau chief, but she didn't want to lose control of the case. As long as she didn't hamper the investigation, Nikki wasn't about to take a back seat. The only thing keeping her going right now was the thought of putting cuffs on Frost and ensuring he rotted in a cell.

Nikki still hadn't seen the picture of her mother again. Courtney had bagged it immediately, and Nikki could see the uncharacteristic anger in her movements as she'd been working. "There's a timestamp on it," she said. "It looks like it was taken with a basic but decent camera. Printed out on Kodak paper."

"It must have been a small camera, because he was able to stand and take the picture without anyone noticing," Nikki said.

"How do you know that?" Courtney asked gently. "You said yourself that day is a blur."

"I don't know for sure," Nikki admitted. "I know some people take pictures at funerals, but I can't see anyone noticing that and not saying something. My parents' murders were a sensational news story at the time, and anyone who saw that might have thought he was a reporter or something."

"Maybe Annmarie saw him," Liam mused, coming over too. "Maybe that's how she figured this all out. She could have demanded to know what he was doing. Or maybe she said nothing at the time but she remembered recently. The position of Frost's victims' bodies is well known—maybe they jogged her memory."

"And then what? If that's all there was, then why would he have tracked her down and killed her?" Nikki's voice cracked. "I keep trying to remember everyone at the funeral, but my mind's blank. We didn't have a lot of extended family, either. I should call the funeral home. Maybe someone there remembers seeing something. What time is it?" She grabbed her phone, noticing a missed call and a message. "The sketch artist should be doing the composite right now. We'll have plenty to throw at Frost at the press conference. What time is it scheduled for tomorrow?"

"10 a.m.," Liam said. "But hear me out on something." Liam could tell just how eager Nikki was to leave. "We now know that Frost's motivations somehow revolve around you. But we also know he's getting bolder. He killed Annmarie, but he must have panicked—hence why some of the scene differed from his previous murders. And now coming here again. This picture was clearly left to get a major response from you specifically. Seeing you talk about him on television is exactly what he wants. Let me do the press conference."

"That's a good idea," Courtney said. "You don't have to stand up there and act like this whole thing isn't killing you, and you won't have to field questions about your parents and all the other stuff. Plus, the bureau chief might not like seeing you up there talking about developments involving your past."

Nikki wanted to argue. She wanted to be the one to stare into the camera and tell Frost his days were numbered. But Liam and Courtney were right. It would kill Frost that Nikki didn't see him as important enough to give the conference herself. And right now, she wasn't sure that she would be able to stop from responding with emotion—something else Frost desperately wanted. Nikki wasn't sure how she was connected to Frost, but she knew from everything he'd been doing over the last few years that he liked to be in control.

"Remember the conversation we had after talking to the Hoffs?" Liam asked quietly. "We agreed that you would take a back seat if this case continued to get more personal. Not that I'm asking you to step down. The bureau chief's at a counterterrorism conference in DC, but if things keep going down this road—"

"You're right," Nikki said. "You both are taking a risk by trusting me, and I don't want Frost to get off because of my ego." Her throat ached as the picture of her mother in the coffin flashed in her head. "Liam will do the press conference announcing that we have solid security footage matching a suspect identified by an eyewitness, assuming the video stills match Howie Doe from the nursing home. We'll obviously keep the nursing home and Theresa's name out of it, and not knowing who might be able to identify him will agitate him."

Liam nodded in agreement. "Can we get Miller to put a unit at the nursing home? If Frost somehow figured out Theresa is the eyewitness who helped with the sketch, she's going to be in serious danger. Let me see the videos again."

"Good point." Nikki unlocked her phone and handed it to him. "Talk to Miller and make sure there's a unit at Heritage House at all times, at least for the next few days."

Courtney had been listening in silence, her expression getting more concerned by the second. "What's Frost's end game?" she asked quietly. "Is he just proving that he's smarter? Or does he intend for you to be his final victim?"

"I'm not sure, but I promise you, if anyone dies, it's going to be Frost, not me," Nikki said firmly.

"I'll get my comments for the press conference typed up so you can approve them before we go live," Liam said.

"Don't forget about the name Lyle that Annmarie had tattooed on her hip. Name him as a person of interest."

"I got it." He gave Nikki's phone back to her. "Looks like you have a message from Tyler."

Too tired to seek privacy, Nikki listened to the message. Lacey's little voice came through the speaker loud enough for the others to hear.

"Hi, Mommy. I just wanted to say I'm sorry for being mad about the mall. It'll be there forever, right?" She giggled, but Nikki could hear the sadness in her voice. "I guess I'm going to be with Granny and Pa tomorrow, so… call me. I love you."

Nikki rested her forehead in her hands.

"Listen," Liam said. "You're exhausted. I'm sure you haven't eaten since those Pop-Tarts this morning. Why don't you call Lacey and make plans to go to the mall in the morning? I'll schedule the press conference, and then you can catch up with us whenever you're finished with Lacey."

Nikki shook her head. "Darcy is out there. We have some actual leads."

"If Frost's been following you this long, he might know about Lacey," Courtney said gently. "You need to sit down with Tyler and let him know what's going on."

Nikki felt weak all over again. "He might not. He can't possibly know everything about my life, and Tyler's usually the one taking Lacey places." Nikki knew how foolish she sounded. Frost had to have seen her with Lacey.

"Every cop in the state is looking for Darcy," Liam reminded her. "And pretty soon everyone will be looking for Frost."

Courtney grabbed Nikki's hands. "You need this, Nik. Rest tonight, and take Lace to the mall and ride all the rides. Eat some junk. It will do your heart and your head good."

Nikki's throat ached from fighting tears. She wrapped her arms around her friend. "You're right. Thank you both."

"I'll walk you to the jeep," Liam said. "And text us when you get home."

She could only nod, exhausted from the day's events and overwhelmed by their kindness.

"I told Caitlin she could have a front row seat and have first crack at questions at the press conference."

"Believe me, she'll be there." Liam rolled his eyes. "She'd kill me if she wasn't. Now, let's get you home."

On the drive to Stillwater, Nikki still debated taking Lacey to the mall tomorrow. While Liam handling the press conference would anger Frost, she could also be putting Lacey at risk. Fortunately, she didn't have to make the decision alone.

She called Tyler, crossing her fingers and hoping Lacey didn't answer.

"Hang on," Tyler said when he answered. "Lacey, finish your bath and then you can talk to Mom. Don't skip parts, either. She really wants to talk to you tonight."

"I'm sorry," Nikki said to Tyler once he'd finished with Lacey. "There was a major development in the case. That's actually what I need to talk to you about." Without telling him about the picture or other specifics, she told him about the theory that Frost was making choices based on some perceived connection to Nikki's past and their intention with the press conference. "It's a good strategic move, but I wanted to know what you thought about taking her to the mall under the circumstances."

Tyler was silent for a moment before telling Lacey to get out and that he'd be in the hall talking to Nikki. "I know you can't give details, but you really think Frost's motives revolve around your past?"

"Yes," Nikki said flatly. "I keep telling myself that he's had opportunities to hurt Lacey or me and didn't, and my gut tells me that's not his plan." Six women were dead and one missing, and it felt wrong to even discuss something as frivolous as going to the mall. Even though the trip was for Lacey, Nikki's face burned at the thought of the Hoffs learning she'd been shopping instead of working.

"He's not going to expect you to be at the mall," Tyler said. "It opens at ten, so if he sees it and gets upset you aren't involved, he's still not going to know where to find you."

"True," Nikki said. "The few hours with Lacey will do me a world of good, and I'm not going to let her out of my sight. Rory might come along, too, and he'll be just as watchful." She waited for Tyler to make a comment about Rory.

"She's safer with one of us than anywhere else," Tyler said, and then went quiet. "And she wants to do something with you, so yes fine, take her to the mall during the press conference. I'll tell her it's a compromise so it's only going to be a few hours."

"And then she'll be out of town with your parents," Nikki said, grateful Lacey was young enough that school would be okay with her missing a few days. "Safely away from Stillwater, thankfully. You're okay with it, then?"

"Yes," Tyler said. "I know you'll keep her safe."

"I really appreciate that," Nikki said. "And thanks for being okay with Rory going with us."

"I'm not exactly thrilled about it, but she really likes him, and a second pair of eyes is always good."

"We'll pick Lacey up around 9:30 a.m. Can you put her on?"

Lacey's high-pitched squeal nearly cracked the jeep's windows, but Nikki relished the sound of her voice. Listening to her daughter talk about all the rides she wanted to check out and how excited she was helped distract Nikki from thinking about the last few hours. She felt her shoulders relax a little, her grip on the wheel loosening.

"Mommy, is Rory coming with us?"

Nikki grinned at the excitement in her voice. "As long as you want him to."

"Duh." Lacey giggled. "'Member he said he'd go on the big and fast rides since you're too chicken?"

"I'm not too chicken," she retorted. "I just don't enjoy them, and not to burst your bubble, little missy, but you may be too small for some of the rides."

"I know, but my friend at school said there are lots of other ones. And you know what else she said today?" Lacey launched into a tangent about her friend's obviously false claims about butterflies and moths until Tyler told her it was time for bed.

"I'll pick you up around 9:30 tomorrow," Nikki said. "Make sure you have all your things for the weekend at Grandma and Grandpa's."

"I need to wear tennis shoes," Lacey said solemnly. "There's lots of walking at the mall, and my boots hurt my feet. Bye, Mommy. See you tomorrow."

Nikki heard her muffled excitement as Lacey gave the phone to her dad. She reminded Tyler of the pickup time tomorrow.

"You know she isn't going to let me forget," Tyler laughed. "You sound exhausted. How are you doing?"

"You know how these big cases take their toll."

Tyler snickered. "I know how you put on blinders and only think about the case and not your body's basic needs like sleep and food."

"There's that too." Nikki turned onto the rural road that would lead her to Rory's and, if she kept driving, the house she'd grown up in. The beautiful farmhouse had already been tainted in Nikki's memory since she was a little girl, but a new question tormented her. If Frost had known her mother, had he been there too?

"You guys have fun. Try to enjoy yourself for a few hours and not think about murder, okay?"

Nikki had no clue how to manage that, but she promised to try. "Drive safe to the conference, Ty. Text me when you arrive so I know you made it. I'll let you know when I drop Lacey at your parents' too." She wanted to thank him for being understanding about Rory when she knew how hard it was for him, but the horror of the last few hours was beginning to catch up to her, and she wasn't going to be able to hold it together much longer.

She said goodbye to him just as she pulled into Rory's driveway. She parked next to his big, white pickup truck and then opened the garage door with the code he'd given her. She didn't mind parking outside, but Rory kept talking about getting a shed to hold all of the equipment in his garage, including the snowmobile, so Nikki could park in the garage, but he'd been too busy to get around to it.

She hung up her coat and left her wet shoes downstairs and went in search of Rory, feeling more fatigued with every step. She knew that he'd worked late tonight, so she wasn't surprised to hear the shower running. Nikki stripped her clothes off and put them in the basket she kept at his place. The bathroom door was open, steam pouring into the bedroom. The sight of Rory's muscular silhouette against the frosted shower door glass sent a wave of need through her.

"Can I join you?"

"Shit." He opened the door wide enough for her to step in. "I didn't hear you come home."

Nikki stepped silently into the shower and shut the door. The hot water pelted her skin as she drew Rory close and pulled his face to hers in a heated kiss. He responded with as much urgency as Nikki felt, his hands on her thighs as he lifted her up and pressed her against the shower wall. She moaned and wrapped her legs around him, letting him take control. Her hands tangled in his wet hair, his mouth leaving a trail of hot kisses along her collarbone.

They stayed in the shower until the water started to cool. Nikki's legs were still shaky when they got out of the shower, her system still flooded with satisfaction. She reached for a towel, but Rory's hands snaked around her waist, pulling her back against his chest, and they started all over again.

Finally spent, they collapsed on the bed, and Rory snuggled her close. "Christ, that was intense. I wasn't sure if I'd even get to talk to you tonight, let alone do that." He kissed her forehead. "You must have had a good day."

And that was all it took for the dam to break, and she felt tears begin to form.

"What's wrong?" He shifted so he could look into her eyes. "Did I say something I shouldn't have?"

Nikki hated for anyone to see her cry, but she felt safe with Rory. Wordlessly, she shook her head and reached for the tissues on the nightstand. He held her close until she was cried out.

"Nicole." He stroked her hair. "What happened to you today?"

She wadded up another tissue and attempted to dry her eyes. "I saw my mom."

Nikki told Rory about the picture, trying not to reveal any more sensitive information. "All I can see is her dark hair against the white satin lining in the casket and how pale she looked. I remember when I touched her hand, she was so stiff, it was almost as bad as finding her body." She leaned against Rory and tried to focus on the steady rise and fall of his chest. "And I remember being so angry that she looked like she was just sleeping, but she was still gone. I wanted to shake her."

He hugged her tightly. "I don't know what to say… I'm sorry, Nikki. You're certain the picture means he's doing all of this because of something in the past that connects both of you?"

Nikki hadn't told him about Frost's signature trifecta, only that after seeing the photo, she knew Frost was inspired by it, that he was connected to her in some way. That his killings were about him, about her family. Personal. "I can't give you details, but yes, I'm absolutely certain."

"But why wait so long to make a move?"

Nikki scrubbed the tears off her face and sat up. "What do you mean?"

"You're the expert, obviously, but if he's doing all this because of something that happened so long ago, why did he just start killing in the last several years?"

A jolt of electricity ran through her; it was something she hadn't even considered. "That's a good question." Before Rory could respond, she had her phone out, calling Liam.

He answered groggily. "You are supposed to be resting. You can send me the press conference information in the morning. Or later in the morning, since it's like 1 a.m."

"I know, but listen to me," Nikki said. "We need to look again at the states Annmarie lived in since she left Minnesota after graduation. If Frost's obsession started in 1993 when Mom was murdered, there's a good chance he was killing much sooner."

"If he was leaving them in cold areas, the only climates that work are Colorado and Washington State," Liam said. "He wouldn't have left a frozen woman in California or Nevada."

"No, but he could have done trial runs while he figured out exactly what he wanted to do," Nikki reminded him. "He could still leave them laid out like that without the cold. Maybe it took him a while to realize he wanted to preserve them. Or maybe he came back here and started killing because he followed Annmarie."

"But why follow her and not you, if this is about your mother?"

"I don't know, and we might be wrong. But he wouldn't be the first killer to practice, and since we know when Annmarie lived in each state, it's worth checking on. Check burglaries or reports of stalking too. Many killers start off with smaller offences. And we know that there's no sexual angle, so we can narrow the searches down by a significant amount."

Liam sighed. "It's still a long shot, but we have to take it. I'll contact the other state bureau offices for help before I do the press conference. Now go to sleep and stop worrying about things. Enjoy the morning with Lacey."

"Wait," Nikki said. "Are you calling Simon Funeral Home tomorrow? They handled everything to do with my mother's funeral. I doubt the director is still alive, but maybe someone will remember something."

"Yes. I'm calling them in the morning. Go to sleep."

Nikki put her phone back on the charger and settled back into Rory. She told him about the plan for tomorrow, and she could tell how pleased he was to get to spend more time with Lacey.

Rory fell asleep quickly, but Nikki lay awake, unable to stop thinking about the picture and its implications. She knew Frost's actions weren't her fault, but that didn't stop the guilt from weighing heavily on her. If she'd known Frost when she was younger, had she wronged him in some way? Her memories of life in Stillwater after the murders were hazy at best. Had burying all of that pain instead of dealing with it caused her to miss something that might have saved Annmarie or any of the others?

There had to be a way to narrow down potential suspects, but how? So much time had passed since the murders that she doubted the funeral home would have any useful information. Nikki tried to remember specifics from the visitation and funeral, but she could only come up with a sea of blurry faces and no names. Aunt Mary had dealt with most of the guests so that Nikki didn't have to endure everyone's questions about that night. Nikki could still remember her aunt standing next to her like a small watchdog, ready to bite anyone who upset Nikki. If Aunt Mary were still here, she'd probably be able to tell Nikki every person who came through the doors that day.

Nikki's eyes flew open. How could she have forgotten about the guest registry? Aunt Mary had done her best to make sure everyone signed so they could send thank-you cards. Whoever took the picture may not have signed it, but the registry was their best opportunity to find a name.

Nikki rolled over and changed her alarm for thirty minutes earlier. She and Rory had a stop to make before picking up Lacey.

CHAPTER SEVENTEEN

Thursday

Nikki woke to the sound of Rory making breakfast—she hadn't slept much, haunted by the events of the past two days. She rolled over and grabbed her phone, relieved to find the sketch artist's composite in her email. He apologized for not letting her know last night, but Theresa confirmed that the man in the stills from outside the parking garage and in the elevator was the same one she'd seen at the nursing home once she had finished describing him for the sketch.

Her fingers hovered over the attachment icon. She knew that she could just send this to Liam without looking at it. For a few hours, she could pretend that Frost didn't exist and just enjoy life. But she couldn't shut that part of her brain off. And there was every chance she might recognize Frost. Nikki clicked the icon, and the sketch loaded.

She gasped at the detail of the composite. A handsome man with dark eyes stared back at her. He wore the same newsie-style hat he'd had on the day he took Annmarie, but there were tufts of dark hair sticking out from under it. He appeared to be a little darker skinned than Nikki realized, but then she remembered that Theresa had described him as having an olive skin tone, similar to an Italian. His cheekbones were defined so much it looked as though they were almost too big for his face, but that somehow worked for him. The artist had drawn him slightly smirking, as though he knew something no one else did.

Nikki stared at the drawing for several minutes, noting the square jaw and full lips. The man had a familiarity about him, but she didn't recognize him. Had he been in her life without her even knowing it?

"Breakfast," Rory called from the kitchen.

Nikki sent the image to Liam and threw on her robe just as Rory came in with two plates of bacon, eggs and toast. Between delicious bites of salty bacon, she explained to him that they needed to stop at her house before picking Lacey up. "I want to go through the guest registry from Mom and Dad's funeral. I know exactly where it's at, so it will only take a few minutes, but you know how traffic is in the morning, so we need to hurry."

They finished eating and quickly showered and dressed before heading to Nikki's house. Traffic was as bad as she'd expected, but they were only running a few minutes late when they reached her place in Highland Park. Nikki ran inside and went straight to the locked cabinet in her office. The guest book was in a box full of her parents' things, but Nikki couldn't allow herself to get caught up in the memories right now. Riffling through it, Nikki found the book quickly and hurried back out to the jeep. She was surprised to see Rory sitting in the driver's seat.

"I figured you'd want to look at that thing right away," he said.

"Thank you." Nikki got into the passenger seat and slipped her seatbelt on, the leather-bound book feeling heavy on her lap. She'd been so focused on finding names that she hadn't allowed herself to think about what it would feel like to actually look at the pages.

"You okay?" Rory asked as he pulled out of her neighborhood. "If this is too much, you could have Liam or someone—"

"No… I should do it. I'll be able to see if there's an unusual name in there." She took a deep breath and opened the book, bypassing the pages with the Bible verses and her parents' obituaries. She wouldn't be able to get through every name before they picked up Lacey, but she could at least skim it and look for any that stood out.

She recognized the names of people who were all closer to her parents' ages at the time, so Nikki could mentally cross those off quickly. Annmarie's mother had signed the book for their family, but with Stillwater being such a large school, dozens of Nikki's peers had attended. She found a pencil in the console and started placing dots next to the names she wanted checked. Her hopes started to sink as she realized only around two hundred people out of the three hundred plus who'd attended the services had signed the book.

"Turn here." Nikki pointed to Tyler's street. "His townhouse is halfway down on the right. One of the house numbers is off the sign, but his blue truck should be in the driveway."

"I see it." Rory pulled in behind the blue truck, and before Nikki could get out of the jeep after putting the guest book into the side of the door, Lacey burst out of the house. Nikki swept her daughter into her arms and hugged her tightly. It never ceased to amaze her how Lacey's presence brought a slice of calm to Nikki.

Tyler waved to them from the front door. She'd hoped he might bring her out to the jeep so that she could introduce Rory, but she understood that he wasn't ready for that.

"Did you pack your entire room?" Nikki asked as she took Lacey's stuffed-to-the-gills backpack off and tossed it into the back of the jeep.

"No," Lacey huffed, climbing into the booster seat. "Only the essentials. Hi, Rory. You remember what you said about the rides, right?"

"Yep." He grinned at her in the mirror.

He kept Lacey entertained while Nikki finished with the registry. She took pictures of each page and emailed them to Chief Miller and Liam, asking them to divvy up the names and track each person down. Miller would probably know who still lived in the area, but the FBI's database could find everyone else faster than the county sheriff's system.

*

The Mall of America in Bloomington had taken some economic hits in recent years, but on the rare occasions that Nikki visited, the place was packed, and today was more of the same. She shivered as they drove through the east parking garage in search of a place to park. Parking garages had always set her on edge, making her feel slightly claustrophobic, especially after she and Annmarie had gotten lost in one in downtown Minneapolis after going to a concert the summer before Nikki's life went to hell. The night had been hot and sticky, and cell phones were only for the very wealthy at the time. Getting lost had been funny until some creepy guys had emerged seemingly out of nowhere. Although Annmarie had frozen in fear, Nikki had the presence of mind to grab her and run before anything could happen. They laughed about it when they finally found Annmarie's car, but they both hated parking garages after that.

It was sad and ironic that Annmarie had likely been snatched in the parking garage at The Pointe. If Frost had known Annmarie well at all, he could have been aware of her fear. Had the parking garage been the easiest place for him to attack, or had he done it out of spite?

Rory finally found a spot and they headed inside. As much as she looked forward to spending time with Lacey, she couldn't stop thinking about the impending press conference. Liam had let her know they were running late because of technical issues, but Miller was heading to the podium to explain the reason for the press conference and introduce him.

Nikki fumbled with her phone, trying to find the local news feed. She'd come prepared with her wireless headphones, but her connection was lousy. As they passed through the downstairs welcome area where the restrooms and mall maps were kept, she noticed Miller on the television mounted on the wall.

"Hey, Bug." She knelt down and helped Lacey out of her coat. "My team is doing a big press conference for me this morning, and it's on the television. Why don't you go on with Rory to the theme park and I'll catch up." She pointed straight ahead as she addressed Rory. "It's in the middle. You can't miss it."

He rolled his eyes. "I might live in the country, but I have been to the Mall of America once or twice."

"You promise you'll catch up and not end up working forever?" Lacey asked.

"Cross my heart." Nikki made an 'x' over her heart with her index finger.

"Okay." Lacey grabbed Rory's hand. "First things first: the barnyard hayride. It's a little-kid thing, but I still want to do it. Then we can work our way up to the bigger rides."

He laughed. "Yes, ma'am."

Nikki realized she should have asked him if he minded taking her, but judging by the way his eyes lit up, she knew he was fine with watching Lacey for a bit. She handed him cash for the park pass and then bent down to kiss Lacey on her chubby cheeks. She grumbled and wiped it off, already pulling Rory toward the escalators.

By the time Nikki reached the television, Miller had already introduced Liam. The mall was too noisy to actually hear the TV, but the closed captioning had been turned on.

Nikki felt a little surge of pride seeing Liam addressing the media. He looked dapper in his dark shirt and gray tie. Caitlin had no doubt dressed him for the occasion.

This morning, she'd emailed Liam the statement she'd drafted, and he appeared to be following it to the letter. After reminding the public of Frost's previous crimes, he told the reporters that Frost was responsible for the murder of Annmarie Mason and the kidnapping of Darcy Hoff. Hopefully Caitlin had read the email containing her questions that Nikki had sent on the drive to the mall.

Hands shot in the air, but Liam held up his index finger and reminded them that he'd answer questions at the end. He explained the eyewitness statement in vague enough terms that the nursing home employees wouldn't be caught in the crosshairs. Nikki experienced a brief moment of panic before remembering that she'd spoken to Lynn this morning, who promised to ensure that Howard didn't accidentally turn on his TV.

Liam followed the eyewitness account with the elevator still shot, as well as the images of Frost taking Annmarie out of the parking garage and briefly turning his head.

"We have solid evidence that Frost has ties to Stillwater going back twenty years or more, and we believe that Annmarie Mason might have known him for a significant amount of time," Liam said. "We believe Darcy Hoff is still alive, and we're asking the public for their help. If you recognize this man, please call the FBI hotline that's on your screen. If anyone in the community has information about a man by the name of Lyle with a connection to Annmarie Mason, we want to know. I'll take questions now."

The closed captions didn't identify each reporter, but the expected questions followed about Nikki's whereabouts and whether or not she believed Annmarie was murdered because of connection to her.

"Agent Hunt is following an important lead," Liam said. "She asked me to give this in her stead. Annmarie and Agent Hunt did go to the same high school, but they haven't spoken in years."

Liam had given the perfect answer, intimating that Frost wasn't quite important enough for Nikki's presence, and he'd managed to downplay the question about her connection to Annmarie.

"Have you found any ties between the first five victims and the two new ones?" Caitlin had asked the question exactly how Nikki wanted it presented.

"We have, but it's too sensitive to be discussed."

"Do you know why he chooses his specific victims?" Caitlin followed up.

"We can't share those details. Suffice it to say, we believe that we've figured out his motivation for the murders, and that will help us find him. One final point of note: we believe that Frost is in possession of a stolen Wilcraft." Liam reminded the reporters what the vehicle was and showed a picture of Kimberly Hoff and her father ready to take it out for the first time. "If you have knowledge about any of the information shared today, please call the hotline. Thank you."

Nikki exhaled, feeling warmed with pride. Liam had done an excellent job. Nikki had promised him that if things backfired, she would take full responsibility, but she felt it was important that they told Frost how close they were—or that he at least believed they were getting close—because the escalated stress could very well drive him to make the mistake that would finally help Nikki and her team catch him.

She fired a quick text of appreciation off to Liam and then headed off to find Rory and Lacey.

She finally spotted them riding the log chute. They waved to her from the car, and she took pictures when they came out of the cavernous mountain. Lacey threw her hands in the air and squealed when the car dropped several feet as the ride's grand finale.

"Mommy." Lacey ran to her and pulled her hand. "You have to go on that ride with us. It was so much fun."

"If you say so." Nikki had never been a fan of roller coasters and even though the log ride was geared toward younger kids, there were still plenty of twists and drops. But she wanted to make Lacey happy, so they rode together before going to the next ride.

The morning passed in a blur of yelling kids, sticky fingers and turning stomachs. Nikki rode more than she'd planned, but she eventually tapped out and just enjoyed seeing Lacey having so much fun with Rory. He was like a big kid himself, going excitedly from ride to ride and helping Lacey eat all the sugary stuff that she wasn't supposed to.

"I'm going to grab something to drink at Grub." Nikki gestured to the small food shack. "Why don't you guys do the Ghost Blasters thing without me?"

Lacey's hair had come out of her ponytail, and her cheeks were flushed pink. "But the Ghost Blasters thing has laser guns, Mom. You could kick butt."

"Yeah," Rory said. "I want to see how good of a shot you are. And then we can all eat." He ruffled Lacey's messy hair. "Except you, because you've had a pound of sweets."

She stared up at him. "Don't worry about that. Mommy says I have a hollow leg like Liam."

"How is that possible? He's a mini-giant, and you're pint-sized."

"Not in spirit." Lacey grabbed both their hands and pulled them over to the ride. The line wasn't horribly long, but Nikki still felt claustrophobic with all the kids pushing and yelling and worrying about getting the best car.

Ghost Blasters looked like a small storefront from the outside, but once they were settled in the cars, the double doors opened. Nikki had watched videos of Disney's Haunted Mansion, and this ride seemed like a smaller version of that, laser guns included. Nikki's eyes took a few seconds to adjust to the dark room and ultraviolet lights. She wrapped her arm around Lacey and showed her how to point the laser at the ghosts that randomly popped out at them.

"Jesus." Rory jumped as a fat Slimer-looking ghost came out of nowhere. "I wasn't expecting that."

By the time the ride ended, Lacey had become pretty good with the laser gun. When she got a little older—and bigger—they could play laser tag.

The car exited the house, and Nikki squinted at the natural light.

Rory shaded his eyes with his hand. "Dang, that's bright."

Lacey had been sitting between them, but she hopped out of the car, practically vibrating from sugar and adrenaline. "Mommy, there's the Ferris wheel. Can we do that before we eat, please? The line doesn't look too long."

"Yes, go ahead." Still squinting, Nikki checked to make sure none of them had left anything inside the cars. "You and Rory go stand in line while I go to the bathroom," she said, taking Rory's hand as she climbed out of the car.

Standing, she glanced around Rory to make sure Lacey hadn't gotten ahead of them. Her insides stilled. She couldn't see Lacey anywhere.

"Lacey?" she called, starting to feel panicked.

Rory must have heard the worry in her voice, because he swiveled around and scanned the crowd. "She was just here."

A fear unlike anything Nikki had ever experienced immediately took hold of her. Images of the child kidnappings and murders that she'd worked in her career exploded in her memory.

Rory took her shoulders. "Stay right here in case she comes back." He dodged the crowd, frantically looking around and calling her name.

A little voice in the back of Nikki's head told her that she should be the one doing this, but her feet wouldn't move. Thanks to her job, nightmares of losing Lacey kept her up some nights. Now it was coming true, and Nikki was useless.

A hand touched her arm.

Nikki realized it was the woman who'd been sitting behind them with two rowdy boys. "I think he found her." She pointed toward the Ferris wheel, and Nikki searched for Rory's tall form and red hoodie.

He broke through a crowd, Lacey on his hip. He was saying something to her, his expression serious, and Lacey nodded like she understood.

Nikki's legs unlocked, and she ran toward them without even thanking the woman. She pulled Lacey into her arms and held her tightly. "Don't you ever do that again."

"Sorry, Mommy." Lacey's voice was muffled against Nikki's hair. "I just got excited. But the man said I shouldn't get so far away from you and Rory. I was coming back when Rory found me."

Nikki shifted so she could look into her daughter's eyes. "What man?"

Lacey shrugged. "He was by the Ferris wheel. Look what he gave me." She held up a white carnation. "Isn't it pretty?"

Nikki didn't even see the flower. She only saw the red velvet ribbon wrapped around the stem. A rush of adrenaline unlike anything Nikki had ever experienced rendered her speechless for a few short moments. Her maternal instincts made her want to grab Lacey and run, but she couldn't just let Frost walk away after bringing her daughter into this. She'd known the mall trip had been risky. Why hadn't Nikki listened to her gut?

"Rory, take her to the food place and wait for me." Some of the color had returned to his face, but she could feel the tension rolling off him. "Lacey, did you see which way the man went?"

"No. This place is huge, Mom."

"Okay, that's fine. Give me the flower."

Lacey's eyes widened, her body tensing in Nikki's arms. "Why? It's mine."

"I just want to make sure I find the right person to thank." She kissed Lacey and handed her to Rory, taking the flower before Lacey could argue anymore, and sprinted through the crowd, already breathless. She searched the bodies around her, looking for anyone resembling the man in the peacoat. She reached the Ferris wheel quickly, but there was no sign of him. Nikki turned to the ride operator. "Did you notice a man with this flower?"

The teenaged boy shrugged. "Sorry."

Nikki scanned the area for a security guard, finally spotting one near the end of the amusement park. She raced over to him.

"I need you to close the exits."

The stocky guard adjusted his belt. "Lady, I don't know what you're talking about."

Nikki stuck her badge in his face. "Special Agent Hunt with the FBI. I've reason to believe that a suspect in a murder investigation is here. Tell your security team to close the exits and get the police here. Radio everyone to look for a man in a dark peacoat and newsboy-style hat."

CHAPTER EIGHTEEN

Nikki found Rory and Lacey sitting at a table in the food court. Rory sat with his back against a wall. He looked pale and upset, repeatedly scanning the crowd for any sign of trouble, and Nikki could tell by his white-knuckle grip on the back of Lacey's chair that he was shaken.

The sight of her daughter brought the fear back that she'd managed to suppress on the way back from security, and her knees weakened. But she had to keep it together, for Lacey and for Rory, who had never been through anything like this before. What if Frost had taken Lacey?

Nikki's breathing accelerated at the thought, and she struggled to contain her emotions. Lacey would pick up on her distress, and Nikki needed her to be calm in order to remember as much about the man as possible. She should have known better than to bring Lacey to the mall, but she'd underestimated how desperate Frost was for Nikki's attention.

Fresh chills went down Nikki's spine as she thought about how much both she and Lacey resembled her mother. Since Frost's previous victims had few physical traits in common, Nikki had always believed his victims were chosen at random and that the murders revolved around the presentation of the bodies. But now that she knew about her mother's picture and how long Frost had been skulking around their lives, Nikki couldn't stop thinking that he'd started killing because of her. Her name had been in the national news before she returned to Minnesota because she'd caught the Ivy League killer, who'd been working his way through the elite schools, killing women. What if Frost had seen her on the news and realized that he could be part of Nikki's life in some twisted way?

She forced a smile as she reached the table. "Sorry I took so long," she apologized and Rory looked around at her.

"Any luck?" Rory seemed relieved when she sat down, his grip on Lacey's chair easing.

Nikki shook her head. "Security is closing the exits, but he's probably long gone." The security guard had found a plastic bag for Nikki to put the flower in, and she carefully set it down on top of her bag.

"Mommy, why are you mad about the flower?" The sadness in Lacey's eyes sent a wave of fury through Nikki. She was supposed to keep Lacey safe, and she'd failed even though she'd stayed so close to her.

"I just want to talk to him." Nikki didn't want to worry Lacey, but it was hard to hide her concern. "What did he look like?" she asked Lacey.

Lacey's nose crinkled. "Like a man."

"Was he tall like Rory?" she said, trying to jog Lacey's memory. She smiled at her daughter.

"I think so," Lacey replied.

"Did he have light or dark hair?"

Lacey drained her bottle of chocolate milk. "He was wearing a hat. Like that weird one Grandpa wears."

Rory caught her eye. She'd shown him the stills and the sketch of Frost before they left this morning. Nikki nodded subtly. Fear flashed in his eyes, but the set of his jaw gave away his anger.

Nikki quickly shook her head. She appreciated how much Rory cared, but she didn't want to upset her daughter any more than necessary, and she wanted to make sure he kept his anger in check.

"What exactly did he say to you, Bug?" Nikki put her chin in her hand, her elbow casually resting on the table, trying to act like this was a normal conversation.

"Well, he asked me where my parents were. That's when I realized you weren't behind me. I was going to come back, but then he pulled the flower out of his coat."

"Do you remember if he had on gloves?"

"Yeah, he did. Maybe he was cold." She took a huge bite of a chocolate chip cookie Nikki had bought her earlier in the day.

"Did he say anything else?"

Lacey started picking the chips out of her cookie and eating them separately. "Who's Valerie?"

This time, Nikki couldn't stop the full body tremor. "He asked you about Valerie?"

"No, he said that I looked just like Valerie. I thought he knew you, that's why I took the flower. You've always told me to be careful of strangers but… he said you'd understand."

Nikki could tell by both Lacey and Rory's faces that she wasn't doing a very good job of hiding her rage. Part of her wanted to blurt out exactly who the man was, but she knew that would terrify Lacey.

"Mommy, who's Valerie?"

Rory's hand slipped over hers and squeezed.

Nikki took a deep breath and tried to keep herself steady. "Valerie was my mother, honey."

"Oh. You said she died a long time ago, with your daddy."

A knot formed in Nikki's throat. "Yes, she did."

"Do I look like her?"

"I think you look like your mom," Rory said absentmindedly. "And she looks like her mom."

Lacey's eyes widened. "You knew her mom?"

Rory nodded, moving closer towards Lacey. "Your mom and my older brother were buddies."

"Did you and Mommy date then?" she asked in wonder.

"Nah," he said, smiling. "I was the younger brother who tagged along. She didn't give me a second glance."

"Mom," Lacey said. "I bet Rory was just as pretty then as he is now. Why didn't you like him?"

Nikki had to chuckle at Rory's red face. "He's four years younger than me. It's not a big deal now, but when you're sixteen, you can't date a twelve-year-old."

"Oh." Lacey paused. "I guess it makes sense that I would look like her, then," she said. "Remember that picture you showed me of you from when you were my age? You were sitting in her lap. She was pretty. Is she why we have pale skin and dark hair?"

"I think so. She once told me her ancestors were Irish, and that's why we are so pale." Nikki was still trying to make sense of what Lacey had told her. She hadn't looked at her parents' childhood photos in years, but she remembered Tyler pointing out how much Lacey's baby pictures looked like her grandmother's when she was that age. Nikki still saw more of her own mother in Lacey than herself; she had the same twinkle in her eye and the same quick smile and big heart. Nikki's hair hadn't been curly as a child, but Lacey's was, and Valerie's had been.

"Why did they die?"

Lacey's question snapped Nikki out of her memory. Nikki had only told Lacey that her own parents had died a long time ago. She was too young to hear the details. "A car accident."

"How old were you?"

The lump in Nikki's throat doubled, and she felt the tears trying to build. "Sixteen."

"That's really sad," Lacey said in a small voice. "I don't know what I would do if something happened to you."

Nikki scooted close to Lacey, wrapping her arms around her. "Nothing's going to happen to me, Bug."

"Better not," Lacey said and went back to her cookie.

Nikki planted a kiss on the top of her head. "I need to go talk to security again. You stay with Rory, okay? Don't leave his side."

"Okay, but is the man in trouble? He was nice to me. But Rory said it's really wrong for someone to give a little girl a flower like that because he's a stranger to me."

"I couldn't have said it any better myself."

Nikki located the security guard she'd spoken to earlier standing with another security guard and two uniformed Bloomington police officers. She made sure to glance at the officers' ID badges.

"Tracy, any luck?"

Tracy turned to Nikki, her hands on her security belt. "No, ma'am. We're going through our security videos, and we've positioned guards at the exits. We also have two plainclothes special operations officers looking around. Is there anything else you'd like me to do?"

Nikki knew that the Mall of America's large security team wasn't typical mall security, and they'd been trained in various procedures. They also had a large K-9 unit. She hadn't touched the red ribbon around the stem, and Lacey had been too obsessed with smelling the flower to mess with the ribbon much. Hopefully Frost's sent was still on the velvet. "Your K-9s can do regular scent searching, right?"

"Absolutely," Tracy said. "If you have something for them to sniff, they'll track it. I'll have a dog brought to this level." She touched the small radio on her chest and requested the animal be brought to their location. The dogs were a fairly common site at the mall, as they were usually on the lookout for explosive devices.

"Agent Hunt, who do you believe this man is?" the older, female officer asked.

"A strange man who gave a little girl a flower should be questioned, period," Nikki said. "But as I said, he's a suspect in a murder investigation."

"I know who it is," her partner said. "I saw the press conference. You think it was Frost, don't you?"

"Yes." Nikki handed her a business card. "If you do see him, don't approach. Call me. I'm going to alert all of the local authorities and bring in agents to search the mall in case he's hiding somewhere. It's a big place, and it wouldn't be hard."

"No, it wouldn't," the officer said. "We can bring in backup to assist in the search."

"Please do that ASAP," Nikki said. "If you'll excuse me, I need to call my partner."

She walked over to the restrooms, positioning herself against the wall so no one could sneak up on her, and then called Liam.

"Christ," he said when she'd finished telling him what had happened. "Is Lacey freaked out?"

"I don't think so," Nikki said. "We're trying to downplay it as much as possible. The mall security is going through video, but it's going to take a little while. We have some uniforms searching the mall for him in case he's hiding somewhere, but we can't have too many because the crowds will start to ask questions, and there's a lot of space to get through."

"How long has it been since he gave it to her?"

Nikki checked the time on her phone. "Forty-four minutes. He's probably gone. He no doubt did his research—knew where to sneak out without being seen, where to walk away from the security cameras, where to exit the mall."

"He also had to have followed you," Liam said. "Tyler's the only one who knew you would be there, right?"

"And his parents. Oh God, it's past noon. I need to call them and tell them we'll be late."

"You sure Lacey's safe going with Tyler's parents?"

"Honestly, I don't know. But I need to talk to Tyler and figure out what to do."

"I can be there in half an hour or so."

"No, I need you and Miller to keep going through the people in the guest registry. Did you check with the funeral home? The picture was definitely taken in the same room the viewing was held in, and if anyone was still around, they might remember some odd guy that took the picture."

"It's changed hands. The last Simon descendant sold it to the current owners. No one who worked there in 1993 is still there."

"It was a long shot." Nikki tried to cover her disappointment. "Have you contacted the other bureaus looking for similar crimes?"

"In all four states. They said it would take a couple of days to go through all the cold cases." Liam paused. "Do you think he did this because of the press conference?"

"Perhaps. But he had to be following me to know we were here, and we arrived right before the press conference started." Nikki hadn't noticed anyone, but she'd also been preoccupied with Lacey and Rory, the day they were having, the distraction, the moment of relief. "If Darcy's still alive, he must be keeping her somewhere he feels is secure."

The security guard Nikki had been speaking to earlier waved at her.

"I have to go. I'll call if anything changes." She jogged back to the guard. "Did you guys find something?"

"Security's got him on video by the Ferris wheel and then he heads down central parkway. He managed to blend into the crowd, but we have him exiting the mall at the taxi and shuttle drop-off. He turns left and walks off."

"Did someone pick him up?"

"Not that we can see," the guard said. "But he could have walked out of frame and got into a vehicle. You still want the dog?"

"No, he's long gone by this point. Call your plainclothes guys off too." She turned to the Bloomington police officer. "There's a BOLO out on Frost. Please let your people know he could still be in the area."

"We're on it," Rogers said. "We notified other districts as well."

"Thank you," Nikki said. "Let them know that if they find anyone matching his description, bring them in for questioning and then call me right away."

Rogers nodded. "We'll do everything we can to help."

Nikki thanked her again and then turned her attention back to the security guard. "Tracy, any chance I could take a look at those videos?"

CHAPTER NINETEEN

Lacey's anxiety subsided quickly, mostly due to Rory's ability to keep her entertained, but she'd started begging to go to Build-a-Bear. Nikki had promised she could make a new bear, and she was torn between keeping Lacey occupied and making sure she was safe. Rory was on high alert and would stick to her like glue, but he wasn't a trained police officer, and even though he'd left the mall, Nikki could tell he was still leery of Frost reappearing, and she didn't blame him.

"What should we do?" he asked her while Lacey was preoccupied with a game on his phone, his voice low. "I want to keep her mind off it, but if he makes an appearance, I don't know if I will be able to stop myself from kicking his ass."

"Swear money, please." Lacey stuck out her hand and grinned. Rory didn't cuss a lot, but he'd slipped around Lacey shortly after they met, so she'd convinced him that giving her money every time he swore would help him kick the habit.

Rory laughed and handed her a dollar. "You don't miss anything, do you?"

"Nope. Are we going to Build-a-Bear?"

"Give me two minutes."

Nikki walked over to Officer Rogers, who had agreed to stick around in case Frost reappeared. She explained the situation with Lacey to Rogers.

"I don't want her leaving the mall without me," Nikki said. "But I don't want her scared and worried either. Would you mind keeping an eye on them while they go to a couple of stores?"

"Sure," Rogers said. "I'll tail them without letting her see me."

Nikki sighed in relief. "Thank you so much."

"No problem. My boys are older now, but I remember what it was like to be on the job with a little one. We need all the help we can get."

"That's an understatement." Nikki glanced back at Rory and Lacey, who was clearly getting impatient. "I'll go tell them before she bursts."

Lacey was on her feet as soon as Nikki said they could go, and she quickly gathered up their trash. She stopped and looked at Nikki. "Can I walk over to the trash can?"

Nikki's heart broke at the worry in her daughter's voice. The trash can was less than ten feet away, and Lacey shouldn't have to ask if she could throw away her trash. "Of course."

When Lacey was out of earshot, Nikki addressed Rory. "Officer Rogers is going to follow you guys. She'll hang behind so Lacey won't notice, but she'll be close just in case."

"Good deal," Rory said.

"Listen, I just want to say I'm sorry you got dragged into all of this, but I'm so grateful that you're willing to help out with her. Let me give you some cash—"

He waved her off. "It's my treat, really."

Nikki impulsively kissed him, something she'd avoided doing in front of Lacey. Though Lacey saw her, she didn't react, almost as though it were a normal occurrence. Knowing that Lacey was comfortable with Rory and that she could trust him made Nikki's job a little easier.

Lacey grabbed his hand and they headed off just as Tracy returned. "My boss said to bring you down to the security office. You can watch the videos there. I'll walk you down."

The security office was located in the basement, and the camera room was impressive, with dozens of monitors providing real-time video of the mall.

"How do you guys keep it all straight?"

"It's easier than you think," Tracy said. "We assign specific areas to officers, and one focuses on the camera while others walk that area of the mall. We have a different team dealing with the exterior cameras." She pointed to the stocky black woman walking toward them. "This is our head of security, Ashley Stack. Ash, this is Special Agent Nikki Hunt with the FBI."

Ashley shook her hand, and Nikki noticed the various pins on her uniform. "You're an Air Force veteran. Thank you for your service."

"I appreciate that, Agent Hunt," Ashley said. "Tracy brought me up to speed earlier. I'm sorry we weren't able to stop the man from leaving the mall."

Nikki shook her head. "You would never have been able to. He's too smart. He wouldn't have given the flower to my daughter if he wasn't certain he would be able to make a quick getaway."

Anger flashed in Ashley's eyes. "Is your daughter all right?"

"She is, thank you. She's with my friend right now. Do you mind if I look at the videos? I just want to see if there's any decent images of his face to send to the media."

Ashley walked over to one of the monitor stations and accessed the feed. "We've got them cued up."

Nikki's stomach dropped as she watched the first video. It had been taken from a camera mounted discreetly near the Ferris wheel. Frost walked briskly into the frame from the opposite side of the theme park, the Nickelodeon store and Burberry. Between the camera angle and the hat, Nikki couldn't make out his face.

"Smart of him to have a couple of bags," Ashley said. "Looks like a regular dad looking for his kid."

"Yes, it is." Annmarie's coat had been Burberry too. Nikki wondered if Frost had chosen that as a cheap shot at Nikki. "Did you look at the video from those stores?"

"He bought a puzzle at the Nickelodeon store and a cashmere scarf from Burberry. Guess he has money to burn."

"Did he pay cash or use a card?"

"I'm not sure," Ashley said. "We haven't had the chance to look at those videos. Our first priority was making sure he wasn't a threat to customers and no longer on the property."

Nikki nodded, watching as Frost moved through the throng, eventually stopping near the Ferris wheel. She felt sick when her daughter appeared, her little feet moving fast as she made a beeline for the ride entrance. Lacey glanced back and seemed to realize they weren't behind her. She rolled her eyes dramatically and started walking back the way she came.

"You've got quite the spitfire there," Ashley commented.

"You have no idea."

Nikki went rigid when Frost stepped in front of Lacey. She looked up at him in surprise, and then nodded about whatever he was saying. Then he pulled the flower out of his left inside coat pocket. Nikki recognized the excitement on Lacey's face as she carefully took the carnation. As Lacey was thanking him and turned to run, Frost reached out and caught the sleeve of her sweater. Nikki saw a flash of fear on Lacey's face, and then she nodded and pulled away, running out of frame.

"He's wearing gloves. And none of the other videos show his face, but let's go to the Burberry security feed." Ashley pulled up the morning's security videos.

"He had to have followed me to the mall," Nikki said. "We got here around ten, if that helps."

"It does." Four camera angles appeared on the screen. "Burberry's cameras catch the entire store, so if he was in the shop, there's no way he can hide."

The three of them watched the videos in silence for what seemed like an eternity.

"There." Tracey pointed to the camera that covered the accessories section of the floor. "He's looking at scarves. No gloves here, either."

Nikki hoped that he'd tried on some of the scarves and that somehow those scarves would still be in the store instead of in someone's bag. But Frost only touched the one he decided to purchase.

"Where's the camera for the cash register?" Nikki asked.

"Hang on."

A new video started playing, this time from a camera mounted directly over the cash register. Ashley sped the recording up until Frost appeared, the hat blocking his entire face.

He appeared to be making small talk with the clerk. Nikki held her breath as he pulled out his wallet.

"That's a six-hundred-and-fifty-dollar scarf," Tracy said. "Nobody carries that much cash around nowadays."

Tracy turned out to be right. Frost had paid with a credit card.

"Timestamp." Nikki's voice shook.

"11:27 a.m." Ashley paused the video. "I'll call Burberry."

Nikki paced while Ashley made her phone call. She texted Rory to check in, and he quickly replied with a photo of Lacey and a white bear wearing sparkly butterfly wings.

A few minutes later, Ashley returned. "The clerk actually remembered this guy because he was so charming. She'd been disappointed when he gave her a credit card with his wife's name on it."

"What name was it?"

"Annmarie Mason," Ashley said. "That name sounds familiar."

Nikki's entire body reverberated with anger. "Because she's dead. He killed her and took the card." Frost had been shopping at Burberry before the press conference aired. He'd probably used Annmarie's card as another way to stick it to Nikki. Surely he'd known that bringing Lacey into it would only increase Nikki's determination to catch him, and he was too smart not to expect her to go through the security videos. Had that been his intention all along, or had he approached Lacey as a reaction to the press conference? How could he have followed them through all of the traffic without Nikki noticing?

"Didn't the girl ask to see ID for the credit card? You can't tell me they aren't trained to do that at Burberry."

"Oh, they are," Ashley said. "But he charmed her apparently."

Nikki continued to stare at the video. Ashley had paused it as Frost started to turn around to leave the store. "Can you hit play again?"

"Sure."

Frost turned and looked up until he saw the camera. Then he looked like he smiled.

CHAPTER TWENTY

Before she went back upstairs, Nikki emailed copies of the footage to Liam, who immediately called her. "What game is he playing? Does he want to be caught?"

"He still thinks he's invincible," Nikki said. "He wants us to know he's not worried about being caught."

"He wants you to know," Liam corrected her. "Between the smirk and Lacey, he's basically waving a red flag at the bull. He's counting on you coming for him."

"I know." Nikki had accepted that fact as soon as she calmed down from seeing Frost smirk at the camera. "He'll get his wish soon enough. I just hope we get there in time for Darcy."

"Don't do that," Liam said. "You have to make rational decisions, and I get it if you can't with Lacey being threatened. God knows I couldn't. But he knows how to get to you, and he's ready for you to come after him. That's what he's been working up to all along."

"I won't let that happen," Nikki assured him. "Are you making any headway with the guest registry?"

"Miller's talking to the attendees who still live in the area, and so far, no luck. I've made a lot of calls, but I'm mostly leaving messages. And at the moment there are no unsolved cases with any real similarities in any of the other states that Annmarie lived in. But maybe Frost didn't follow her. They might have reconnected when she returned to Minnesota—if they did at all."

Nikki stopped at the soda machine and ran her card through the reader. "Two dollars for water," she muttered.

"That's cheap for such a touristy place," Liam said. "Where are you headed now?"

"I have to take Lacey to Tyler's parents." She tossed the cap into the recycling bin and took a long drink. "Even though I'm uncomfortable leaving her."

"Where's Tyler?"

"He's out of town at a conference. Tyler's parents live about forty-five minutes north of here, and they have good security, but so does the Mall of America. How can I just drop Lacey off there after this? I'd be putting her grandparents in danger too."

Liam sighed. "I can't tell you what to do, boss. But we're ready to step in however we need to. Lacey's got to be your number one priority right now."

Nikki thanked him and promised an update as soon as she figured out her next move. She was lucky to have such a loyal team, and she made a mental note to do something special for Liam and Courtney when things finally settled down.

"Agent Hunt." Tracy practically ran toward her. "I just got a call from our K-9 unit. Before we called them off, one of the dogs tracked the scent to a red jeep in the east parking ramp."

"That's my jeep." Nikki's heart lodged in her throat.

"They brought in the bomb dog, just in case," Tracy said. "The vehicle's clear, but they found a magnet attached under the front fender."

"A magnet? As in the kind that are used to attach GPS trackers?"

"Looks like it," Tracy said. "Our lead K-9 handler is a retired army mechanic, and he's certain that's what it was used for, but the tracker itself is gone."

"I need to see it." Nikki turned toward the elevator. "Tell your people I'm on my way."

"Don't go that way," Tracy said. "The back way is a lot faster."

Nikki sent Rory a text that she would be a little longer and then followed Tracy through a maze of basement hallways that seemed to lead to nowhere, but they reached the east parking garage in only a few minutes. Nikki's anxiety ticked up when she saw the security and dogs surrounding her vehicle.

One of the Belgian Malinois eyed Nikki and then barked. The handler, a petite woman with short blond hair, turned and then spoke in German to the dog. It immediately stopped barking.

"Agent Hunt, I'm Jan Gray. My dog's the one who found the magnet."

Nikki shook her outstretched hand. "Thank you. Does the rest of the vehicle check out? Is it safe?"

Gray nodded. "My dog and another checked it over thoroughly. No sign of anything else planted." She handed Nikki a plastic bag with the magnet, which was flecked with road dirt. "Someone's been tracking you."

"The higher-tech tracking systems report in real time, right?" Nikki asked.

"Yep, and that also means police can figure out who put the device on, or at least where the signal's going to. That's probably why whoever approached your child today came straight to this vehicle."

Nikki wanted to scream. She should have thought about a tracking device as soon as she realized Frost had been in the mall. Instead, she'd nearly served her daughter to him on a silver platter.

Gray crouched in front of the jeep, and the big dog immediately nosed into her space. She patted him and spoke in German again. "It was right here, under the front fender."

"I can't thank you enough for everything your team did for us today," Nikki said to Tracy and Gray.

"I wish we could have done more," Gray said. "But it seems like he was two steps ahead of us.

"You have no idea," Nikki replied.

*

Nikki texted Rory that she'd pick them up at the front entrance in a few minutes and tried to regain calm as she drove back through the garage.

Rory and Lacey waited outside; she clutched her new bear, and he was carrying a massive bag of candy.

"It's not all for her." Rory looked at her sheepishly. "I have a sweet tooth, and I don't know if you remember but—"

"Mark can eat a pound of candy and still want more." Nikki smiled. "We were all jealous of his metabolism."

"Look at Henrietta." Lacey held up the white bear decked out in butterfly attire.

"She's beautiful. How'd you come up with the name?"

Lacey shrugged. "I heard it on TV, I think."

Nikki ushered her into the booster seat and made sure her seatbelt was secure. She shut the door and turned to Rory. "Frost put a GPS tracker on my jeep. The K-9 found the magnet, but the tracker is gone. He must have taken it off today."

Rory's eyes flashed with anger. "You okay?"

Nikki nodded. "Can you drive, though? I need to figure out what our next steps are, and I'm not sure I trust myself behind the wheel right now." She settled into the passenger seat, hoping the distraction of Lacey's happy voice would settle her nerves, but the little girl passed out before they made it out of the mall complex.

Nikki took the magnet out of her pocket. The serial number had been filed off, and getting prints was unlikely, even with Courtney's magic. The magnet felt heavy and wrong in her hand, mirroring her anxiety. Before finding the GPS, she'd been certain Frost's actions were at least partially related to the press conference, but now she had to consider the idea that he'd been planning to approach Lacey for a while and decided the mall was the perfect place to do so without making a scene. It was feasible that he wasn't even aware of the press conference when he smirked at Burberry's security camera. That would mean he didn't know about the eyewitness or composite sketch.

She explained her theory to Rory. "He's cocky, but making sure his photo was taken today when he knew I'd scour the security videos is risky, even for his massive ego. It didn't make sense until now."

"But if his picture's in the system, doesn't the FBI have the ability for facial recognition?"

"To an extent," Nikki said. "But my guess is that he knows he isn't in the system. He doesn't have a record, so he still thinks he's in control." She opened her phone and pulled up the still photo. "I bet he's not smirking now."

If Lacey hadn't been put in danger, today would have been a home run for Nikki and the team. Nikki wished she could have seen Frost's smirk melt away when he heard about the press conference and realized his enormous mistake.

Right now, she had a more pressing issue. "If Frost's been planning this for a while, then he could have a tracking device on Tyler's truck, which means he could know where her grandparents live. I'm not sure she's safe with them. I have to call Tyler and see if he can come home."

She dreaded telling Tyler what happened at the mall, and she really didn't want to ask him to drive back from the conference, but what choice did she have?

"Is it safe for her to be at home with him, though?" Rory asked quietly. "Even if there's no device on his truck, Frost's got to know where he lives."

"He works in white-collar crime, but he's perfectly capable of keeping them both safe. And we will have security in the neighbor-hood."

Nikki glanced back at her sleeping daughter, completely torn. Even though Liam could handle things, especially with Miller's help, it was Nikki's job to lead the team. But Lacey needed her mom.

"He's never hurt kids, right?" Rory asked. "Maybe he doesn't intend to do anything to her. He just used her to get to you."

Nikki shook her head. "Remember what he told her? He specifically mentioned that she looked like my mother. If the obsession revolves around Mom, I can't ignore that."

"You also look like your mom."

"I know, but I can take care of myself," Nikki said impatiently.

Rory looked like he wanted to argue. "Is there any sort of protective custody or an escort you could ask to help out?"

"Probably, but I really don't like the idea of leaving her with strangers, no matter how competent they may be."

"Well, I have an idea, but you probably won't like it."

Nikki didn't like the sound of that, but desperate times really did call for desperate measures. "What is it?"

"You know the state offered Mark a huge monetary settlement before he could sue for wrongful imprisonment?" Nikki had been surprised when the Todds took the deal. It was lucrative, but Mark could have gotten more if he'd taken the case to court. He'd said he just wanted it to be over so his parents, who were both in their mid-seventies, could enjoy their remaining years. "He bought a house in a gated community for Mom and Dad, and he's staying with them for now."

Nikki stared at Rory. "Lacey's never met your parents. Or Mark."

"I know," he said. "I'm not suggesting leaving her there without one of us. I can take a few days off and spend time with her there. Mom's been wanting me to do a few things around there, anyway. Lacey could help."

"I don't know," Nikki said. "It's a lot to ask of your parents, especially considering I'm part of the reason Mark spent twenty years in prison for something he didn't do."

She knew that Rory's parents didn't want him dating her, and Nikki didn't feel like she had any right to force her presence in their lives. It was a point of contention between them. Rory was certain his parents would come around with effort, but Nikki didn't want to put them in that position. She wanted them to focus on being with Mark.

"That won't matter in this situation. I've told them all about Lacey, and they've been nagging me for grandkids for years. Mom will be thrilled."

"I saw your mother at Lunds the other day, and she saw me and walked away."

"She did? You never mentioned it."

"There's no point," Nikki said. "I don't blame her. Look, if you want to take a few days off, why not just keep her at your house? If you're there, she'd be safe."

"You're kidding, right?" Rory asked testily. "You think he hasn't tracked you to my place by now? Do you really want her there without you when he probably knows where I live?"

"There has to be another way."

"I'm not asking you to deal with them, Nicole."

Nikki glanced back at Lacey to make sure she was still asleep. "Keep your voice down, please. You think we'll just be able to stroll in and ask them to babysit? That they'll be happy to do me a favor? That's ridiculous."

"If I tell them it's to keep her safe, they'll agree to it."

"No," Nikki said. "I don't want—"

"You don't want what," he interrupted. "I know you want to protect her. Surely that's going to triumph over your pride."

Nikki glared at him. "You have no right to say something like that."

"Maybe not, but I'm going to say it anyway." His voice was hard. "I was there today. I saw the terror in your eyes when you couldn't find her and then when you realized who it was, you went full steam ahead trying to find him."

"What else was I supposed to do?" Nikki demanded, her anger flaring.

"That's not what I'm saying. I'm saying that this thing with Frost... Look, I don't know what his connection is to you, but I know that you're going to move heaven and earth to find out and put him in prison because that's what you do. You get tunnel vision, and any other time, that's fine. But you can't let what he did today narrow that tunnel even more. It puts Lacey in danger, and I'm guessing it makes you pretty vulnerable too. Isn't compartmentalizing supposed to be crucial to your job? You haven't been able to do that since you found Annmarie, which is understandable. But you've got to step back here and make a decision that isn't emotional. If this were anyone else in this situation, if their kid was threatened, what would you tell them to do?"

Nikki wanted to scream at him, because he was right. She had to put her own issues aside and make sure Lacey was safe. "I'll call Liam and tell him I have to stay with Lacey until Tyler comes home."

Rory snorted. "You'll go crazy. And they need you."

"I can still help from the house," she said. "I just won't be on the ground."

"How long can you keep that up? For God's sake, Nikki. Swallow your pride."

"My pride has jack to do with this," she hissed. "And I'll thank you not to use my daughter as a negotiating tactic in the future."

"What's that supposed to mean?"

"Come on." Nikki rolled her eyes. "Don't play mind games with me, Rory. You won't win."

His jaw went rigid, the muscles in his arm tense. "I'm done with this conversation."

"Good." Nikki pulled out her phone. "I'm going to call Tyler and his parents."

Tyler was predictably livid about Frost, but after he'd calmed down and been assured that Lacey was fine, he agreed with Rory that Frost knew where all three of them lived. "I'll come home. Your team needs you."

"It's two days," she said. "We'll figure it out."

Tyler sighed. "Nik, I know you. You won't feel safe unless one of us is with Lacey, and frankly, neither will I."

He was right. As much as she trusted Rory, her ex-husband was still a trained FBI agent. "I'm so sorry, Tyler. This isn't fair to you at all."

"It's not your fault."

"Who else is there to blame?"

"That bastard Frost, period. You have enough guilt on your shoulders. Don't put this on them too." Tyler's words hit home. He knew her so well and she was blaming herself. "I'll call Mom and Dad and tell them change of plans." He continued, "You didn't mention what happened at the mall, right?"

"God, no." His parents had made snarky comments about Nikki choosing to stay in major crimes after Lacey was born. She didn't need to hear them brag about being right.

"Good. Have Lace call when she wakes up. She knows you have to work, so tell her Grandma and Grandpa are sick or something."

"Thank you for being so understanding, Ty. We'll plan on you picking her up in the morning."

She glanced at Rory after the call was finished. He watched the road in stony silence.

"Tyler didn't freak out," she told him. "He's coming home."

"I gathered as much," Rory replied.

The trauma of the last few days had settled into Nikki's bones, and she didn't have the energy to keep arguing with him. "I know I've put off discussing your parents, and you're not completely wrong about my pride. But these last few days have been hellish, and you're the last person I want to fight with. Can we table things for a few more days? I know you want what's best for Lacey, and that's the most important thing to me."

He sighed, his shoulders beginning to inch down. "Okay."

"Thank you."

They were silent for a few minutes and then Rory cleared his throat. "So, do you want to drop me off at home and then take her back to your place?"

"Oh, okay." Her cheeks burned. She'd assumed he wanted both of them to stay at his place. "If that's what you want."

"I'm not saying that. But you're stressed out and upset, and your place has a badass security system. You guys are safer there."

"Where are we?" came a tired voice from the back seat.

"We're almost to my house," Rory said. "Your mom has to drop me off before you two can go home."

"What about Grandma and Grandpa's?"

"Change of plans," Nikki said brightly. "You're staying with me tonight, and then Daddy's picking you up in the morning."

"Yes." Lacey raised her fists in triumph. "But won't Grandma and Grandpa be upset?"

"They both have colds and feel yucky," Nikki said. "We'll reschedule once they feel better."

Lacey frowned. "Are you going to find the bad man?"

"My team and I will," Nikki said firmly. "Don't worry about that."

"Rory, why can't you stay with us tonight?" Lacey asked excitedly. "We can play games while Mom does her job from home."

He glanced at her in the rearview mirror. "I don't know, Lace. There are a lot of things going on right now."

"Please," she whined. "It'll be so much fun. And Mommy was supposed to be with you tonight, anyway."

"And she'll spend all of her time talking about you," Rory said.

"Well, yeah, I'm awesome," Lacey said matter-of-factly. "But you can spend time together and with me all at once if we stay at our house. Come on, people."

Nikki smiled despite the wall of tension between her and Rory. "It's up to Rory. He's welcome."

"Please, please, please." Lacey's high-pitched squeal made Nikki's ears ring. "For me?"

Rory glanced over at her, and Nikki nodded. Lacey deserved a good night, and Nikki really didn't want to be alone right now.

He grinned at Lacey in the rearview mirror. "Guess I need to stop and get some clothes."

CHAPTER TWENTY-ONE

Lacey's happy chatter helped alleviate some of the awkwardness between Nikki and Rory. Nikki hadn't expected Lacey to be hungry since she'd eaten so much junk food, but she insisted she was starving, so they grabbed some Taco Bell on the way to Nikki's house. Lacey's bag was empty by the time Nikki pulled into the garage.

"You sure you don't have a tapeworm?" Rory stared at her in amazement.

"What's that?"

Rory grinned. "It's this little parasite that looks like a worm that people can pick up and it hangs out in their gut, stealing food."

Lacey considered this for a few seconds and then shook her head. "That's dumber than the urban legend about the spider eggs hatching in the girl's arm."

"No, it isn't," Rory said. "Tapeworms are real."

"Prove it." She hugged her new bear and climbed out of the jeep.

"Fine, if it's okay with your mom."

Nikki wasn't sure her five-year-old daughter should be learning about tapeworms, but she'd never been the squeamish type, and Nikki needed to touch base with the team; she was finding it hard to pretend everything was fine to her daughter. She was certain that Lacey would eventually notice how distracted and agitated she was. "Fair warning, Lace," she said, unlocking the inside door. "It's gross."

"Cool. I'll go find the iPad." Lacey raced off.

"I hate to do this, but I've got to talk to Liam and Courtney."

Rory nodded. "Go ahead. I'll keep her entertained."

She left Rory to it and headed into her office, careful that she could still hear Lacey and Rory if anything happened. They had a few minutes before the Zoom call was supposed to start, so Nikki decided to catch up with Courtney. She told her what happened at the mall and the ride home.

"Am I wrong in not going to his parents—if they'd even have us?" Nikki asked as she sat down in her office and turned on her laptop. "It's not like Lacey wouldn't pick up on the tension."

"Oh, she would, and then she'd just outright ask what the problem was," Courtney chuckled. "I don't think you're wrong, really. It's kind of an impossible situation."

"But am I not putting Lacey first by having her here instead of somewhere Frost won't find her?"

"If you left her with someone other than you or Tyler, then I'd say yes. But Tyler's coming home, right?"

"Yes, but it's not fair to him." Nikki sagged into the chair. "I think part of the reason it makes me angry when Rory brings it up is because, deep down, I know he's partially right. I don't think his parents should have to deal with me if they don't want to, but I also don't want to face them."

"I get that," Courtney said. "Have you told him that specifically? If you're open about everything, he might be more understanding. Not that he hasn't been given the situation, but you know what I mean."

"You're probably right. But spilling my guts isn't exactly my strongest trait."

"I know, but I think you'll feel better if you do. And you should talk to him about today because I know you were scared to death. I'm sure he was too."

"Well, it's over now."

"Stop." Courtney sounded exasperated. "You're doing it again. Yes, Lacey is safe, but we know Frost is a threat to her. That is terrifying, and just because you're an FBI agent doesn't mean you can't have a few minutes to freak out like a regular mom. How long did it take you to switch into all-out cop mode after you knew she was safe?"

A fresh wave of anger crashed through Nikki. "You mean after I saw that ribbon? Probably about two seconds."

"And you had to spend the rest of the time trying to find him."

"Mostly," Nikki said. "After I told the guard to call the police, I went back to Lacey and Rory for a few minutes. We talked about exactly what Frost had said to her. Courtney, he told her she looked like Valerie."

"Jesus. When you finally catch this guy, I want two minutes alone with him."

"I'd agree if you weren't essentially half his size," Nikki said. "But it's been nagging at me, and not just because it has to do with Mom. It's something else, and it's driving me nuts that I can't put my finger on it."

"Stop trying to think about it and it will come to you," Courtney advised. "I can help with that, actually. After you left The Pointe last night, I started thinking about the security videos. You know how the head of security said Frost had to have taken the emergency exit stairs since he didn't go down the elevator?"

"Yes."

"It took some convincing, but I talked Caves into letting me take that door."

"You what?"

"Think about it," Courtney said. "When Frost gets to that point, he's home free. He managed to keep from leaving prints even though he didn't bring gloves, and he was probably euphoric after leaving that picture."

"And then he's not cautious when he touches the door?"

"That's my hope. Caves said the camera mounted over that door has been offline a couple of days and they didn't realize it. Declan came home, so we talked to him for a couple of minutes. With only he and Annmarie living on the floor, he didn't think there should be many prints on the door. He's lived there a few years and only used it once. Anyway, I have the door, and I found something."

Nikki's heart lurched into her throat. "A fingerprint?"

"Nope," Courtney said. "But I found a smudge toward the inside end of the handle. It's small, but I'm trying to extract DNA without destroying the sample. That's why I took the door."

"You're sure it's recent?"

"Yes," Courtney said. "It's pretty easy to distinguish between a new print and, say, one that's a week old. It also helps that the door isn't used much."

"How much can you fast-track it?"

"As much as I want," she said. "We have a murdered woman, a missing girl, and he threatened a child today. I'll push it through as quickly as physically possible."

Nikki told herself not to get too excited because Frost might not even be in the DNA database, but she was grateful to Courtney for being so good at her job. "Will you be able to run familial DNA?"

"I hope so. We might be able to catch him the same way they did the Golden State Killer." After decades, the notorious serial killer had been caught in 2018 after detectives had the idea to comb DNA databases and family trees on sites like Ancestry and 23andme to identify potential suspects. Eventually, the genetic genealogy led to an arrest.

Nikki still wasn't sure how she felt about the FBI being able to use the DNA sites to track down offenders, but nothing was off the table with Frost. "That takes time, though," she reminded Courtney. "Darcy Hoff doesn't have it."

Just then, Liam sent both of them the Zoom link. Nikki ended the call with Courtney and they both joined the meeting.

"Are you in a hotel?" Courtney peered into her camera. She was still in the lab, her hair held back by a red headband, her black glasses halfway down her nose.

"Easier than driving back and forth," Liam said.

Nikki spotted a Coach bag sitting next to the television. "Caitlin's with you?"

"I was just about to go to the lobby and get some coffee." Caitlin appeared, leaning over Liam's shoulder, smiling. "Are you and Lacey okay after what happened today?"

"She's fine," Nikki said. "For once I'm thankful for her short attention span."

"What about you?" Caitlin asked.

"I'll be fine once we have this bastard. We have to catch him, and soon. Liam, did you tell her about last night?"

"Not all of it," he said. "I wasn't sure if you wanted her to know."

"I appreciate that, but she might be able to help us out."

"Frost left a picture of Nikki's mother lying in her casket," Liam said.

Caitlin paled. "He did what? Oh my God, Nikki."

"I'm okay," she said. "But I think we all know Frost is somehow tied to my past and my mother, including the locations where he left his victims. So far, we haven't found anything in Michigan and Wisconsin with connections to my family but—"

"That's actually not true," Caitlin said.

"What?"

"You don't remember?"

"Remember what?" Nikki asked, confused.

"A few months before the second woman was found, you were scheduled to be the guest speaker at a forensic psychology event held at the University of Madison. But the event was cancelled because of a bad snowstorm."

Liam stared at her. "How did you know to look into that? I never told you about the connection."

"I didn't," Caitlin said. "I was covering the story. Local woman with a tragic past returns home as a decorated FBI agent. I was really bummed about the event being cancelled."

Nikki had a vague memory of a cancelled conference in Wisconsin, but that was it. "Did they reschedule?"

"Nope. You don't have any family or history in Michigan?"

"Not that I know of, but Howard Mason said some things that made me wonder if I knew everything about my mother's past. He was confused so we have to take them with a grain of salt, but he talked about Mom going out of state to take a college prep course or something one summer, and she never attended college."

Caitlin chewed the inside of her cheek, a look in her eyes that Nikki immediately recognized.

"You want to dig into my mother's past?"

"At least in Michigan," she said. "You guys have your hands full with tangible leads on Frost, and I know the police are stretched thin. I have contacts in Ann Arbor. What summer would that have been?"

"Howard didn't say, and I'm not sure it would be reliable if he did."

"When did your mom go to high school?"

Nikki had to think about it for a minute. "She was born in 1955, so she would have been a freshman in 1969."

"What was her maiden name?"

"Nolan."

"I'll call my contacts but it'll probably take a little while to get the information. I'll do everything I can to have it tomorrow." Nikki watched as Caitlin discreetly kissed Liam's cheek. "I'm going to let you guys talk. Nikki, if you need anything, I'm around."

Nikki was still acclimating to the idea of Caitlin being an actual friend, but the intimacy between her and Liam was sweet to see, especially after all the madness of the last few hours. "Thanks. And thanks for the help."

As soon as Caitlin left, Courtney grinned like she'd caught Liam in the cookie jar. "Quite cozy there, aren't you?"

"Shut up," he said, shaking his head. "Did you tell her about the door?"

"Yep," Courtney replied. "I'm going to be here all night, but I'm going to get the damned sample."

"I can't believe you talked that place into letting you take the door," Nikki said.

Courtney grinned. "I have a gift."

Liam snorted. "Yeah, the gift of being a royal pain in the ass. She wouldn't take no for an answer. I think she just wore Caves out."

"Declan got home after I left?" Nikki asked.

"Said he'd been on a date. He was totally cooperative."

"I don't think he's involved." Nikki held up the dirty, bagged magnet. "This is what Frost used to attach the GPS tracker to my jeep. I'll have a tech come get it and bring it to the lab." Nikki explained her theory that Frost hadn't seen the press conference before he'd smirked at the camera but had been planning to approach either Nikki or Lacey—or both—and seized his opportunity at the mall.

"I've been thinking the same thing. There's no way he saw the press conference before he smirked into that security camera," Liam said, practically giddy.

"Exactly," Nikki said. "He's probably reeling right about now. You got that image added to the BOLO, right?"

"And faxed it to every department in the metro area, along with the state police," he confirmed. "So far, no one's found similar murders outside of the ones we know about."

"No luck with the guest registry?"

"Not so far," Liam said. "Miller's hoping to shake locals' memories, but he's not optimistic."

"Where's Miller tonight?" Courtney asked.

"His daughters had a big dance recital. One of his deputies is finishing up the last of the registry contacts." Liam rubbed his temples, and Nikki noticed the circles under his eyes for the first time. He'd been running on even less sleep than Nikki, and she knew he'd been holding off on using his vacation time until Frost made his move this year. Nikki intended to make Liam take a few days off after Frost was behind bars.

"What about VPCloud?"

Liam sighed. "Mostly a big, fat disappointment. Annmarie's cloud space was strictly for work and personal records. Nothing of use to us. But her boss did give us the names of a couple of employees who were friendly with Annmarie when she worked in the California office. I left them both messages."

"When you hear from them, ask if you can email them that photo. Annmarie's only been back here five years or so. Frost can't look all that different.'"

Liam scribbled something into his notebook. "That brings me to the useful information. I also talked to Annmarie's prior employers in Colorado and Washington State. Nothing from Washington, but the woman she worked for in Colorado had some interesting information. Annmarie moved there first after leaving that technical firm in Indianapolis. By the time she left, she'd moved up the ladder and was making nice money, good benefits, all of that. The place in Colorado was a start-up at the time, and the hiring manager didn't understand why Annmarie would leave a steady job for the risk, especially since she'd have to move so far. Annmarie sold them on her excitement for getting in on the ground floor and a new adventure, the usual."

"Where's this going?" Nikki asked.

"I'm getting to it. Since it was a start-up, the staff was small and spent a lot of time together. Annmarie not as much as the others, but she and the hiring manager were friendly. One night over drinks, Annmarie admitted she'd left Indianapolis because of an ex who kept stalking her. They'd been together for nearly fourteen years, and he couldn't let go. Annmarie clammed up after that, but the hiring manager said that when she left, it was kind of abrupt. And she always wondered if the ex had somehow found her."

"Wait, what year did she start that Colorado job?" Courtney asked.

Liam checked his notes. "2007."

"1993," Nikki said softly. "They had to have started dating that year. Annmarie would have been sixteen."

"Did she have a boyfriend back then?"

"Not before the murders." Shame nagged at Nikki. "I have no idea about after."

"You and Miller went to high school together, right?" Courtney asked. "Did you guys run in the same circles?"

"Not really. For a small town, Stillwater High School is huge because there are so many rural communities. I knew who he was, but we didn't hang out. I don't think Annmarie knew him either. Funnily enough, she dated Mark when we were in high school. They'd broken up about a year before everything happened."

"I did a search for 'Lyle' and Stillwater High School," Liam said. "There were only a couple of them, and they were both more than ten years older than you guys. There could be more, but the records might not all be updated."

"Miller's part of the alumni board," she reminded him. "Have him do some digging."

"Have you talked to Mark since Annmarie died?" Courtney asked.

"No, but Rory told him what's going on. I guess he took it hard. Annmarie stayed in touch with him in prison." Nikki rolled her eyes to the ceiling. "I need to talk to him about their communications. I completely let that go over my head."

Because she didn't want to face Mark or his parents unless she absolutely had to.

"But Mark didn't go to the funeral, right?" Liam said.

"He was already in jail."

"You need to talk to someone who was there." Liam ran his hand through his red hair, a sure sign he was about to say something he knew wouldn't go over well.

"Mark's parents sat in the back and weren't there very long." Nikki beat him to the punch. "His mother told me they'd only come out of respect for my parents. She was so angry with me for thinking Mark did it, even though everything pointed to him. Or so we thought." Nikki sighed. "I don't think they would remember anyone."

Courtney cleared her throat. "Yeah, but there is someone who was probably with you during the funeral, right?"

Nikki recoiled. "You're talking about John, aren't you?" Her ex-boyfriend, her parents' real killer, was finally in prison thanks to Nikki and her team. The thought of seeing him made her skin crawl.

They nodded.

"He was by your side during all that, and since he was the one who actually killed them, he had to have been a nervous wreck."

"On high alert," Liam said. "If anyone's going to remember someone taking a picture of your mother in the casket, it'll be him."

Nikki knew that he was right, and she couldn't let her personal hatred of John derail the investigation. Darcy Hoff might still be alive. "I'll see if I can get into the prison to talk with him."

Nikki ended the call and then joined Rory and Lacey in the living room, where they were engaged in a heated game of Chutes and Ladders.

"Mom, I'm winning," she said excitedly. "And Rory isn't letting me win like you and Daddy do."

"No way," he said. "A competition is a competition."

Nikki laughed and sat down next to Lacey, snuggling her close and soaking in everything about her. Courtney was right. Today had been terrifying, and Nikki never wanted to go through anything like it again.

Rory made an amazing comeback to win the game, and Lacey decided his prize should be the dishes, so he took care of them while Nikki helped Lacey with her bath.

"Were you scared today?" Lacey asked while Nikki washed her hair.

"In a way that I've never been before," Nikki said. "I'm going to keep a leash on you from now on."

Lacey giggled and splashed bubbles at her. "They don't make leashes for kids, silly."

Nikki decided not to burst her bubble. "Well, they should. Don't ever take off like that again, please."

"I'm sorry," Lacey said. "I was excited."

"I know." Nikki rinsed the shampoo out of her thick hair. "But it's a lesson learned, right?"

"I guess."

Lacey hated towels, and running through the house half-naked after the bath was one of her favorite things, but Nikki reminded her that she couldn't do that in front of Rory.

"I know that." She rolled her eyes. "Where's he gonna sleep?"

Nikki felt the heat rushing over her face. "We'll figure it out."

She helped Lacey dry off and get into her pajamas, and Lacey did her version of brushing her teeth, which consisted of about three passes with the toothbrush. Nikki normally made her brush longer, but she was too tired tonight. Lacey was too. Her eyes were drooping as she climbed into bed. Nikki doubted she'd even get through a page of the book they were currently reading before she fell asleep.

"How did that man know what your mommy looked like?" she asked sleepily.

"I'm not sure," Nikki said. "But my team and I will figure it out."

"Your team? I thought they were for bad guys. Was he a bad guy, Mommy?"

Nikki brushed the hair off her daughter's face, torn between scaring the hell out of her and telling her something scary enough to remember if Frost approached her again. "That's why we're trying to find out who he is."

As expected, Lacey was asleep before Nikki read more than a handful of sentences.

She found Rory on the couch cradling a beer, lost in thought. "She's out."

"How does she not have stomach aches all the time?"

"I don't know." Nikki laughed. "She asked where you were going to sleep. I told her we'd figure it out."

He laid his arm on the back of the couch. "I wondered about that. I can sleep in the guest room if you need me to."

"I don't want you to sleep in the guest room. And I doubt I'll be getting much sleep anyway." Nikki crossed her arms over her chest, trying to think of the right words. "Listen, about your parents. You're not wrong. Part of the issue is being too scared to face them."

"You don't need to be afraid of that."

"Surely they both want to lay into me at the least, especially your mother."

"Her bark is worse than her bite," Rory said.

"Maybe."

"What are you going to do tomorrow?" he asked.

"Something I never wanted to do." She told him about the decision to talk to John about that day.

Rory scowled. "I guess you should, but damn, that's the last person you need to be dealing with right now."

"I'll manage. The team is following all of our other leads, but there are some things only I can do with my connection to Frost. I have to figure out who he is. I must know him…" She tried to relax, knowing she should be relieved that they'd reached some kind of an understanding for the night, but she had so many unanswered questions, and though she didn't want to worry Rory, they were still at risk. "Would Mark be available tomorrow too? I want to ask him if he remembers what Annmarie talked about when she wrote him in prison. I think she must have known Frost when we were in high school. If she wrote to Mark, maybe he was like a secret confidante or something."

"He'll make the time," Rory said. "I can call him, but I did give you his number."

"Sorry," she said, glad that they were both over the argument. "I'd honestly forgotten. I'll call him in the morning." She gave him a lingering kiss. "Thank you for staying."

Rory headed to bed, but Nikki went back to her office, the events of the past several days floating like jigsaw puzzle pieces in her head. How did they fit? Frost had essentially welcomed a statewide manhunt with his camera stunt. Clearly, he believed he had the upper hand, but what exactly was his end game?

Flashing blue on the desk startled her, and she stretched to grab her phone before it stopped flashing. "Tyler, why are you calling so late?"

"Nikki, I am so sorry."

"For what? Have you been drinking?"

"No. I mean yes, but that doesn't have anything to do with it. I saw the press conference. I've seen him before." Tyler's emphasis on the pronoun sent a chill down Nikki's spine.

"Hold on." She slipped out of the office and padded down the hall to check on Lacey. "What are you talking about?" Nikki whispered.

"Six years ago… actually, it was more like seven… that guy came to our house in Virginia and asked to talk to you."

Nikki must have misunderstood him. "Did you just say the man we've identified as Frost—"

"Yes," Tyler said. "You were pregnant with Lacey, and we'd just made the decision about your taking the job here. So much was going on, but things were good. And then this guy comes knocking on the door, saying he's extended family."

Nikki's mouth was too dry to speak, so she waited for Tyler to continue.

"I thought he was joking at first, but then he had this picture. Nik, I didn't want you to see it. I don't know how to describe it without destroying you."

"He had a picture of my mother, didn't he?"

"How did you know?" he said, surprised.

"Because he left it for me to find at Annmarie's last night." Nikki couldn't believe what she was hearing. "How could you not tell me this?" She felt herself getting angry, even though she knew she shouldn't.

"Because you were doing so well. You were pregnant and actually excited about coming back to Minnesota. My parents were going to get to see their grandchild, and I couldn't bring myself to tell you about the guy. He said he'd been at the funeral and decided to wait to approach you. He'd never got the chance and had tracked you down here. I told him…" Tyler's voice shook so much that Nikki could barely understand him. "I told him he had the wrong house."

Nikki felt like he'd physically struck her. Her whole adult life, through the ups and downs in college and therapy and work, Tyler had been the one person she'd never worried about betraying her. "How could you not tell me?"

"I wanted your life to be full with just me and the baby. I thought he would only bring you sadness, and I didn't even know if he was telling the truth."

Extended family? What did that mean? Was Frost related to her? Nikki felt overwhelmed with questions, her heart in her throat. "Six women are dead," she said almost to herself. "Including Annmarie. He's taken Darcy Hoff, and he approached Lacey."

"Honest to God, Nik, I'd completely forgotten about the guy until I saw him on the news. I would have said something if I'd ever come close to putting two and two together."

"Did he give you his name?"

"No," Tyler said. "I had one of the Alexandria police follow him for a bit, but nothing came of it. We moved and I thought that would be the end of him."

Instead, it had been the beginning of a nightmare. Frost had killed his first victim within weeks of Nikki's arrival in Minnesota. And that was just the beginning.

CHAPTER TWENTY-TWO

Friday

Nikki had finally dozed off on the couch shortly before sunrise. She'd spent the rest of the night restless, trying to think of who Frost might be and how she might have known him. Every harmless noise sent her on high alert. She'd texted Courtney, knowing she'd still be awake, and told her about what Tyler said.

Predictably, Courtney had texted back right away. Talking to her about Tyler helped ease some of Nikki's anger at him. She'd probably been too hard on him, but the events of the day had overwhelmed her, and his confession sent her over the proverbial cliff.

Extended family members kept running through her head, even during her few moments of sleep. Before this week, Nikki would have told Tyler the guy was either mistaken or a creep with an agenda, because she didn't have any extended family members. Now she wondered just how many family secrets were waiting to burst out of the closet and derail life.

She knew Tyler was being honest about not thinking much of the visitor, and she should call and apologize for snapping. He'd take it in stride as usual, because he still loved her, and he was a good person. He'd been so afraid of losing her long before she realized she wanted a divorce, and his insecurity used to irritate Nikki. But as it turned out, Tyler's instincts had been right, and if Lacey hadn't come along, they would have divorced sooner.

She'd met Tyler at the FBI Academy when they were both new recruits from Minnesota. For years, until she met Courtney, Tyler and her therapist had been the only two people she trusted with her innermost feelings. He knew how much it hurt not to have any blood relatives left, how much she wished that Lacey could have known her grandparents. Were there more members of her family out there? Where did Frost fit into the picture?

Nikki tried to step back and look at things from a cop's point of view. Frost's taking the picture of her mother in the casket had been a desperate attempt to preserve something that he'd cherished or had been coveting. What had Valerie's death done to him? Had he latched on to Annmarie as a way to stay in Nikki's life, to keep an eye on her?

Whoever he was, Frost had to know things about her family that Nikki didn't.

Why hadn't he just approached Nikki himself all those years ago?

She couldn't stop thinking about how they might be related. She'd looked at the smirking image from the Burberry camera dozens of times by now, and she was fairly certain Frost was around her age, maybe a few years older. Her parents had a large circle of friends and only a few relatives, and Nikki had only really known Aunt Mary. Howard's words came back to her, and her stomach did a fresh turn. Did she have a sibling?

"That's ridiculous," Nikki said to the empty room. But then she remembered Howard's ramblings. Mom and Dad had started dating during her senior year in high school, and she loved Dad. Would she have cheated?

Rory had told her that Mark was still operating on prison-time, so he was up at dawn and ready to sleep by seven. Nikki found her phone and scrolled through texts until she found Mark's number. She gnawed her lower lip, nervous about speaking to him even though she knew he'd welcome her call.

"Hello?" The surprise in Mark's voice eased some of her tension, but she still felt tongue-tied.

She cleared her throat. "It's Nikki. I hope I didn't wake you, but Rory said you're an early riser." She remembered Rory saying that Mark was still operating on his prison schedule.

"Yeah, I was just making a pot of coffee," Mark replied.

"Me too." She dumped a few scoops of ground coffee into the filter and then realized she wasn't sure how many she'd put in so far. "Trying to, at least."

"I'm really sorry about Annmarie," Mark said, sadness coloring his tone. "She was a nice person."

"Thanks," Nikki said thickly, trying to think of a way to cut to the chase without hurting Mark's feelings "Listen, if you want to get together and talk about her sometime, that would be great. I know it would do me some good. But I'm actually calling to pick your brain because Rory said that she wrote you in prison."

"She did. Not for long, though. She wrote to me about you sometimes, never spoke badly of you," Mark said. Somehow, he seemed to know she needed reassurance on that. He had always been empathetic, kind. "She loved you."

Nikki blinked back the rising moisture in her eyes, overwhelmed by Mark's compassion. She filled the carafe and dumped the water in the reservoir, giving up on making the coffee taste right. Caffeine was the whole point. "Actually, I called to ask you about those letters. I'm not trying to dig into anything personal to you, but I'm certain she knew the person who killed her, and I think she met him around that time. I'm trying to piece together her past."

"I can't say the letters were real personal on her part. She just talked about basic life stuff. I just loved getting them because she wrote them by hand, on this pretty stationery. Made me feel like part of the real world, I guess."

Nikki hated to hear the wistful sadness in his voice. Mark had lost so much of his life because of what had happened, and Nikki would always regret her part in things, even if she believed she'd been right at the time. "I can understand that. She had beautiful cursive. I was always envious actually."

"Yeah." Mark chuckled. "Meanwhile, my best handwriting is barely legible."

"Same," Nikki said. "I always write too fast. Seems like I'm always in a hurry."

"Well, you have a pretty packed life," Mark acknowledged. "Being a single mom and an FBI agent can't be easy to balance."

"I wouldn't be able to do it without help from Lacey's dad, that's for sure."

There was an awkward pause, and Nikki plunged ahead before she lost her nerve.

"Did she mention boyfriends?"

"No, although I remember she got one dude's name tattooed on her. You know she was always scared of needles, so it was a big deal, and I do remember her telling me about that."

"Lyle, right?"

"Maybe," Mark said. "Rings a bell."

"Can you think of anything personal she did tell you? Did she talk about where she was living and why? Why did she move from Indianapolis to Colorado? Then to Washington and California?"

"Not really. She never said anything specific about that."

"What about my family?"

"You mean your parents? I guess, but just that she missed them or whatever."

"Actually, I meant Mom specifically. This is going to sound kind of bizarre, but did she mention knowing things about my mom or extended family that I didn't?"

"Erm, no," Mark said. "That would have been weird, especially given what happened to me. We mainly steered clear of that particular topic. I don't remember her saying anything about them, and eventually she did stop writing. I think she just got too busy.

In the last few she sent me, she'd just come back to take care of her dad, and I could tell it was tough on her."

"Thanks anyway," Nikki said. "I'm just trying to cover every possible base. If you remember anything more, please give me a call."

"No problem." He cleared his throat. "Thanks for asking me, even though I couldn't be any help. Still means a lot."

Nikki swallowed her brewing emotions. "Of course. Hopefully we can get together before too long." She put down the phone, glad that the conversation had gone well even if it hadn't been helpful.

The coffee finished brewing and, sure enough, Nikki had made it strong enough to walk on its own. She found a bigger mug and added cream and sugar, her mind already moving to the next thing on today's agenda. She scanned the local news, pleased to see that pictures of Darcy and Frost remained front and center on every site. Seeing Darcy's face reminded Nikki that they were no closer to finding her, and the girl's time was running out—if it hadn't already. Frost must have a safe place to hide, and he must have been prepared to go to it when he looked into that camera at Burberry. Is that where he was keeping Darcy, if she were still alive?

"She has to be," Nikki said to the empty kitchen. "We've just got to keep looking for her."

Rory soon joined her in the kitchen, looking harried. "Just got a call from one of my foremen. A whole bunch of back-ordered materials that weren't supposed to show up until next week are now sitting around the job site, and no one knows what to do with them." He looked at her apologetically. "You're going to have to take me to Stillwater. I thought I could take today off, but since Tyler's getting Lacey and you're going to be working, I'd better go in."

"I figured as much," Nikki said. "Lacey's in her pajamas already. I'll get her shoes and pack a bag. Tyler should be here before long."

She'd just finished tying Lacey's shoes when she heard the sound of Tyler using his security code.

Rory paused, Pop-Tart in hand and his coat half on. "Should I go in the other room?"

Nikki shook her head. She had assumed that since she'd hung up on him, Tyler would have the good sense to at least knock. Since he chose not to do that, he'd have to deal with meeting Rory.

"Daddy." Lacey ran to open the door.

"Hey, baby. I missed you." Tyler swept Lacey into his arms.

Nikki could feel the tension in the room thickening as Tyler realized she and Lacey weren't alone.

He managed to mask his surprise quickly, but Nikki had seen the irritation on his face.

Tyler put Lacey down and stuck his hands in his coat pockets. "I didn't realize you had company."

Rory stuck the Pop-Tart in his coat pocket and held out his hand. "Rory Todd. Good to finally meet you."

Tyler hesitated and then shook Rory's hand. Nikki was struck by the difference in the two men. Tyler had been a wrestler in college, and even though he was thicker around the middle, he still had the same stocky, solid build. He kept his hair short and neat, just as the FBI preferred. Rory was at least two inches taller, lean, and his dark curls stuck out from underneath his skullcap.

"Thanks for helping with Lace yesterday," Tyler said. "I'm glad you were there."

"Me too." Rory crouched down in front of Lacey. "I hope you had fun."

"I did." She beamed, throwing her arms around Rory's neck. "And don't worry, I hid the candy really good," she whispered loudly.

Rory ruffled her hair. "I'll see you later. I'll be in the kitchen," he said to Nikki. He nodded to Tyler and left the room.

Nikki could tell that Tyler wanted to talk, but she wasn't ready, and they weren't going to discuss things in front of Lacey. She cradled her daughter's little face in her hands and kissed her nose.

"Be extra good for Daddy. No talking or answering the door for strangers."

"I know." Lacey slung her backpack over her shoulder. "Let's go, Dad."

Nikki dropped Rory off at his place so he could get his truck and then headed to the sheriff's station to meet Liam and Miller. She struggled with her decision all the way to the station. What if Lacey still wasn't safe? And Tyler? Frost surely knew about Rory too. Would he target him? Nikki's work experience told her that Frost wouldn't go after someone capable of defending himself, but he'd surprised her before.

"Sorry I'm late," she said. "Have any tips come in since the press conference?"

Liam tossed a paperclipped pile of pages together. "So far, the usual people looking for attention, although one woman insisted Frost killed her cat. Fortunately, the Minneapolis police confirmed that she calls about that regularly, so we haven't wasted any time on her."

"Great." Nikki sat down, trying to convince herself that she wasn't exhausted. She'd told Liam about Tyler's confession first thing this morning. "I assume you told him that Frost visited my house in Virginia."

Miller scowled. "I still can't believe he never thought to tell you."

Nikki held up her hand before Liam could chime in. "He didn't realize the man was a danger at the time. I didn't think I had extended family, so he assumed the man was either mistaken or a creep."

Liam dragged his hands across his face. "You called Quantico already, right?"

"Yes, on the way here. I sent them all the images and information and asked them to search Virginia and Maryland for murders matching any part of Frost's signature. They're also going to use facial recognition software to expedite searching arrest records for a match. He's probably not in the system, but he could have some misdemeanor on record."

Miller flipped through his notebook. "Not a single person on the guest registry remembers someone taking a picture at the funeral or visitation, but there have to be quite a few who didn't sign."

"Especially if they were our age, which we know Frost is—or at least close to it. What about the Stillwater alumni?"

Miller shook his head. "I sent the picture to the vice president, and he's going through the alumni, but he's only got access to people who've updated the alumni association. He's going to look at the graduating classes between 1985 and 1995 for anyone with 'Lyle' in their name. It's not very common, but that's a lot of names to go through."

"What about current high school faculty?" Nikki asked. "There's got to be a few people from the nineties still working in the system."

"That's the first thing I did yesterday when I got the images," Miller said. "No one could remember, but they see a lot of kids. There are a couple of retired teachers I want to talk to, and I've got a call with the high school guidance counselor in a little bit. He worked at the high school in the eighties and nineties."

"Good thinking," Nikki said. "Courtney's still running tests on the door and I dropped the magnet off at the lab this morning, but it's so dirty I don't expect any real prints." Nikki looked between the two men. They both looked as exhausted as she felt. "I know we keep coming up empty and it's frustrating, but we are getting closer. Liam, go back to Lunds and Byerlys with Frost's picture and talk to the employees again. If anyone recognizes him, we might be able to get a warrant." She tried to ignore the butterflies beginning to war in her stomach. "I'm going to talk to John Banks."

CHAPTER TWENTY-THREE

Nikki couldn't help but enjoy the poetic justice of John Banks being incarcerated in Oak Heights. Her parents' murderer had to serve his time at the same prison where Mark Todd had served twenty years for the same crime he hadn't committed. Mark had been well-liked among both the inmates and the guards, and she'd heard through the rumor mill that John didn't have many friends in prison. Considering the way he'd destroyed her life, Nikki hadn't lost any sleep over his suffering.

Nikki checked in at the visitors' entrance, stowing her gun and personal belongings in a locker. The last time she'd seen John Banks, she'd shot him in the leg and carted him off in handcuffs, so he wasn't willing to see her without some concessions. John had agreed to the interview only if Nikki sat face to face with him in the common room instead of talking on the phone with the glass separating them. That was going to be the only time he had the upper hand today. Nikki had only agreed because she didn't have time to waste.

Nikki tucked the file she'd brought along under her arm, and a guard led her to the room where John waited. He sat alone at a table against the wall, looking out of the window. His blond hair had already been graying when Nikki had last seen him, but it looked like the gray had definitely overtaken the dirty blond now. He still wore his wedding ring, but Nikki knew that his wife was divorcing him. She hoped their son was still doing well after everything that had happened.

"Would you mind waiting here?" Nikki asked the guard who'd escorted her.

"No problem," the guy replied. "I'll be here if you need me."

Nikki could tell by the man's derisive glance into the room that John wasn't a favorite.

Nikki thanked him and then walked towards John. He quickly stood and pulled out a chair for her, but Nikki shook her head. "I'll stand. This isn't a social call."

"Nik, it's so good to see you," he started, flashing her the same smile that had charmed so many for so long.

"Agent Hunt," she corrected him. "I need to ask you some questions about my parents' funeral. Specifically, who you remember attending." She was thankful that her voice didn't reveal how hard it was for her to be civil to him.

"Yeah, okay," he said, placing his hands on the table in front of them. "But how are you doing? Have you talked to Amy recently?" he asked.

"I'm fine, and not lately, but I hear your ex-wife is doing well." Nikki opened the file and laid out the different images of Frost. "Do you recognize this man?"

John barely glanced at them. "No. Who is he?"

"A murderer like you," she said. "Look carefully at each image, not just the one facing the camera." Nikki thought she'd kept the edge out of her voice, but John excelled at reading people's emotions. That skill had helped him manipulate people for decades.

He studied her now. "There's something else you're pissed at him for. What?"

"Irrelevant. Look at the pictures."

Predictable anger flashed through John's eyes. Sociopaths didn't like being challenged. "Not yet, Agent Hunt. I'm bored in here. How's Mark Todd enjoying his freedom? You and his little brother still hot and heavy?"

"Mark is doing well, and my personal life is none of your business." She ignored his jab about Rory, refusing to let him get to her. "Please look at the pictures."

John tapped his fingers on the table. "I don't need to. I saw the press conference yesterday. Why didn't you give it?"

Nikki ignored his question and shoved the still from the Burberry store at him. "Look at this one. It wasn't on the news."

"Why are you treating me like a common criminal?"

Nikki rolled her eyes. "Don't worry, John, you're special. You're a murderer and a serial rapist who spent twenty years living the high life while someone else paid for his crimes."

"That wasn't entirely my fault, though, was it?" he asked, deadpan.

Nikki wasn't sure which emotion was stronger—her shock or her anger. Her stomach felt sour, her throat burned, and her head seemed ready to explode from keeping her emotions in check. "You really don't think you can manipulate me at this point, do you?" She leaned forward. "I interviewed the Night Stalker and the Green River Killer when I was still in the FBI Academy. Ridgeway hadn't been incarcerated for more than a few months and was still trying to play games. I've gone head-to-head with some of the most pathological, violent criminals in recent history. Your pathetic attempts aren't going to work with me."

His face had started to turn red. "Who else can tell you about your parents' funeral, Nicole? I was there."

"Your memories aren't crucial to this case. They're just filling in a few blanks." Her muscles ached from fighting to hide her emotions.

John crossed his arms over his chest. "Nikki, please. I can't take it in here. They all hate me. I'm constantly being threatened—"

"I don't care. Unless you can give me this man's real name, you have zero chance at a quid pro quo."

"God, you're still a cold bitch." The mask had fallen off, and John looked no different than the dozens of killers Nikki had put behind bars.

She smiled. "Thank you. Now, I could probably negotiate some changes for you, at least with the guards, but you have to help me first."

His jaw set, John looked at the pictures again. "Swear on my kid's life, I don't recognize him."

"Fine," Nikki said. As much as she hated John, he did love his son. But he'd also use him to gain any possible advantage. "Do you remember seeing anyone at the funeral home who seemed out of place? He would have hung out on the fringes, not really socializing with anyone."

"I was with you every time I went to the funeral home," he said. "I sat next to you during the service."

She knew he was trying to hurt her, but she wasn't going to show him he'd succeeded. "Did you see anyone with a camera? Hanging out by the caskets too long?"

"Your ability to dissociate is admirable. It must be so hard to sound nonchalant about your parents' coffins."

"That's not what dissociate means," she said, determined not to rise to the bait. "Answer the question."

"No, I didn't notice any creeps ogling the casket. Why?"

Nikki ignored him and asked her next question. "You remember Annmarie Mason, right?"

"Of course. Haven't seen her in years, though. Why?"

"In the weeks and months following the funeral, do you remember if Annmarie dated anyone? Do you remember if she had a boyfriend when she graduated?"

He snickered. "Weren't you her best friend?"

"Until you murdered my parents in cold blood, yes," Nikki said evenly. She was losing her patience. "I can tell you're not capable of providing any useful information." She put the pictures back in the file and went to leave.

"You're just going to go?" John asked. "I thought you wanted information."

"You don't appear to have any. Unlike you, I don't have loads of free time, so I have to prioritize. You just put yourself at the bottom of my list."

She turned away from his cocky face and started for the door.

"Jesus, fine. Annmarie dated an older guy senior year. I didn't know his name, but I heard he's the reason she chose Mankato State."

Nikki sighed with relief. She regained her composure and turned toward John.

"What else do you remember about him? Could he have grown up to look like the man in these photos?"

"Hell, maybe. I don't remember much about his face, and I only saw him at a few parties. Just that he stuttered. Not real bad, but it seemed to be worse if there were a lot of people around. I remember thinking a hottie like Annmarie shouldn't be with someone so backward and antisocial."

"Do you remember him from high school?" John was a few years older than Nikki, and that had been part of his appeal when she was a teenager.

"He was older than me," John said. "He was a graduate assistant at Mankato State."

"When?" Nikki asked, trying not to react to John's information.

He shrugged. "I think that was around '96, '97. It was winter break, people were home. I ran into her at a party." John stopped talking, and Nikki waited for a moment to see if he had anything to add. But what he'd said gave her plenty to go on, and she believed the details he was giving her were real.

"Thanks for your time," Nikki replied.

John stood. "Nikki, please think about helping me get transferred. It would help you too. Send me up north. Then I'm in the frozen tundra and nowhere near you."

"No." Nikki didn't stop walking this time. "Enjoy your time here, John."

After retrieving her belongings, Nikki practically ran outside. She took a few cleansing breaths, trying to shake the scummy aftertaste of seeing John. She'd managed to let most of his taunts roll off her back, but his comment about sitting next to her still stung. She'd never allowed herself to think about the fact that she'd cried on his shoulder after the murders, that he'd kept a close eye on her during the services. She'd been so grateful at the time.

The satisfaction that must have given John burned like acid. But the crushed look when he realized she was going to leave helped soothe some of the pain. He could never suffer enough for what he'd done to so many lives, but Nikki wasn't going to spend the rest of hers letting anger eat away at her happiness. She needed to start living in the present. But right now, the past had to be untangled.

Nikki was certain that what John had said could help her finally track Frost down. She got into the jeep and called Liam at the sheriff's station, where he and Miller would be going through tips that had come in since the press conference.

"How are the tips going?" she asked.

"Not well," Liam answered. "We've already ruled out dozens. A few more came in this morning, so Miller and I were headed to check them out."

"Ask Miller if a deputy can help him. I need you to do something else for me. According to John, Annmarie was dating an older guy in 1996 or 1997. The guy was a grad assistant at Mankato State. If we can find him through the college, we could have Frost's real name."

"Talk about a needle in a haystack. Any idea what he was getting his graduate degree in?" Liam asked.

"Unfortunately not." Nikki started the engine. "See if you can get a warrant for Mankato State's registrar from 1992 to 1999. We want to know who was in grad school during that time, and we're looking for the name Lyle."

"That's going to take a little while," Liam replied. "I don't know how willing the judge is going to be to sign the warrant based on information given from a convicted felon."

"Darcy Hoff's life is at stake," Nikki said. "Just make the case the best you can. While you're waiting for the warrant, check with the Mankato State alumni network. He's probably not given his information, but it's worth checking. Look at LinkedIn, any place where he could have a profile. You're looking for Lyle, born around 1971. Annmarie was in the tech field, so he could have been as well. Let me know if you hit on something."

"Where will you be?" Liam asked.

"Caitlin wanted to go over the information she dug up, so I'm meeting her for lunch. But I'm headed to Heritage House right now."

"To talk to Howard again? You think that's a good idea after what happened last time?"

Nikki looked out of the window of the jeep, watching as the wind gushed around the trees in the distance.

"It's not Howard I'm going to talk to."

CHAPTER TWENTY-FOUR

Nikki didn't recognize the girl sitting at Heritage House's front desk, but the girl apparently recognized her. She looked up from the charts spread over the desk.

"I'll get Lynn, Agent Hunt."

"Actually, there's no need to bother. I just need to speak with Mr. Hardin for a bit. Is he available?" Hardin had been the responding officer when Nikki found her parents, but more importantly, he was around her mother's age, had lived in Stillwater all his life, and he had a cop's memory. That made him one of the few people who might recognize Frost. She'd already endured meeting with her parents' murderer, so dealing with Hardin would be easy.

"He should be," the girl said. "He's in the rehab wing of the building, room five."

"Thank you." Nikki quickly signed in. "How's Mr. Mason doing?"

"He's his usual self," the girl replied. "I guess it's a blessing he doesn't realize Annmarie hasn't come back to see him."

Nikki thanked her and followed the signs for the rehab unit. Room five's door was open, and she could see Hardin lying with his bandaged knee propped up, a remote in his hand. He looked smaller than she remembered—not just his physical size but his overall stature. He was no longer intimidating. She hadn't seen him since Mark's release, and he'd barely spoken to Nikki then. She wrestled with her feelings toward Hardin. Part of her remembered the compassion he'd treated her with all those years ago, but she was still angry that he'd let his personal issues with Mark override his sworn duty as a law enforcement officer.

She rapped on the door.

"Got a minute?" she said.

He looked stunned to see her, but he nodded. "Sure, have a seat."

"How's the knee?" She took the padded chair in the far corner of the room, near the window. A couple of pink and yellow flowering plants sat on a nearby table, and Nikki saw a set of colored pencils and thick stock paper on the nightstand. She'd never taken Hardin for the artistic type, but at least he had something to do while he was stuck in here.

"Healing…" he said, looking awkward. His face was thinner, and Nikki could see skin sagging on his arms.

"Looks like you've lost some weight," Nikki said. "That's good."

"Helps with the rehab, but I got a lot more to lose." He eyed her. "Why are you here?"

She appreciated his need to get down to business and dispense with polite chit-chat.

"Did you hear about Annmarie Mason?"

"I did," he said. "I'm sorry. Looks like you're closing in on Frost, though."

"Maybe," Nikki replied. "But he's still several steps ahead of us. What did you know of Annmarie? Have you seen her recently?"

"Once," he said. "Old Howard don't even know she's gone, does he?"

Nikki shook her head. "It feels wrong, but there's no point in telling him since he'd just get upset and then forget. That's if he even recognizes her name."

"I'd do the same thing if I were in your shoes. As for what I know about Annmarie, it's not much. She worked in computer engineering, came back to visit her dad. That's about it."

"Did you see the press conference with Agent Wilson?" Nikki asked.

Hardin nodded. "He did a good job, but I was surprised not to see you there."

Nikki chewed the inside of her cheek, trying to decide how much she could trust Hardin. He had to understand the context of her questions in order to answer them honestly. "Look, you probably resent me, but you were a good cop most of the time. I know you had good intentions, that you didn't mean to put the wrong man behind bars. And you were there when everything happened. To my parents, I mean—"

"I don't resent you," Hardin interrupted, and Nikki looked at him, surprised. "I did for a while, but then I had to admit it was all my own doing. I never knew John did it, but I was never sure about Mark, either. It always felt like something didn't add up, like his being there was too easy. But I was too proud to do the right thing."

Nikki knew that she might end up regretting what she was about to say, but she believed Hardin. "Someone took a picture of Mom in her casket on the day of her funeral," Nikki said. "It was left for me the other day."

Hardin sat up straight, a look of absolute disgust on his face. "They did what?"

"Do you remember what she looked like in the casket?" Nikki asked softly. "I'd forgotten."

"She was a beautiful woman," Hardin said. "And a kind one. Your parents are that case for me." She knew what he meant. The case that imprinted in your head because it was so gruesome and sad. "I remember thinking how she looked like a doll lying there."

"Did you notice anyone who shouldn't have been there? Or anyone hanging around by my parents' caskets?" Nikki asked.

"Shoot, Nicole, I haven't thought about that day for a long time. Not really… there were so many people there…" Hardin said. "I'm sorry I can't be more helpful. Honestly."

Nikki got to her feet. "It was a long shot. You know how it is."

He nodded. "There's one person your mom was close to who might know."

"Nadine isn't doing very well, and she's visiting family," Nikki said. Nadine had been her neighbor growing up, and she'd been one of the first people Nikki had reconnected with when she returned to Stillwater.

"Not her." Hardin looked almost apologetic. "I'm talking about Ruth Todd."

Nikki slid into the booth across from Caitlin. The Main Café was a downtown Stillwater staple, and ironically, the last time Nikki had eaten here, she and Caitlin had had a heated exchange. She shrugged her coat off and stuffed it next to her. "Sorry I'm running late."

"No biggie." Caitlin eyed her. "What's got you all riled up?"

Three months ago, Nikki hadn't trusted Caitlin as far as she could throw her, but Nikki had gotten to know her better in recent weeks. Caitlin did want to help, but she was still a journalist. "Before I say anything, I need to hear that you won't include any of this in any sort of report or documentary. It could jeopardize the case against Frost."

Caitlin sighed. "You really think I'd do that now?"

"I just need to hear you say it."

"All right. I promise it stays right here between us. Now, why do you look ready to explode?"

"I saw John Banks this morning, and then Hardin. I came straight here from Heritage House."

"Holy crap," Caitlin said. "Talk about a bad morning. Was it worth it?"

"Maybe," Nikki said. "We're tracking down some information." She yanked the menu open, but she couldn't focus on the words.

"Lacey's with her dad, right?" Caitlin asked.

Nikki nodded. "He's keeping her home from school a few days. She'll be safe at his place."

"That has to ease your mind a little bit." Caitlin dumped three packets of sugar into her iced tea. "How are you doing with everything else?"

"My treasure trove of dark family secrets? Peachy."

Caitlin rolled her eyes. "Come on, I'm trying to be a friend here."

"I'm sorry," Nikki said. "Honestly, I feel like I'm on a roller coaster that keeps breaking down." Without thinking, she told Caitlin about Tyler's information. "That was years ago. How long has he been watching me? What if I'd answered the door instead of Tyler? Would those women still be alive?"

"Maybe, but you could be dead," Caitlin said matter-of-factly.

"Or he would have been satisfied by having some kind of connection with me."

Caitlin leaned forward, resting her elbows on the table. "You're the psychologist, Nikki. You know better than that. Frost is compelled to hurt women, and even if his trigger has something to do with your mother or family history, that doesn't mean you could have kept him from killing."

"I know." Nikki sighed. "Guilt is my go-to emotion."

"Same, but I think it was you who told me that we do the best we can in the moment, and we can't feel bad about those decisions."

"You're right." Nikki closed the menu. "I've never been good at taking my own advice."

The bubbly server arrived, and Nikki ordered a cheeseburger and fries. She was tempted to throw in a chocolate shake but decided against it. "Water's fine."

"I'll have the Caesar salad." Caitlin handed their menus to the server. She laughed at the snide look on Nikki's face. "Stop looking at me like that. I had four Eggo waffles for breakfast, I swear to God."

"Now that sounds like my daughter."

Caitlin laughed, digging around in the big designer work bag she lugged around. "Was Hardin civil?"

"He was," Nikki said. "He also suggested I talk to a close friend of Mom's. Close former friend, I guess."

"Who?"

"Ruth Todd."

"Ouch. What are you going to do?"

"I should call her, but I know she doesn't want to talk to me."

Caitlin stirred her iced tea. "Probably not, but if it's about a missing person, I think she'd do what she could to help."

Nikki agreed with her, but she still wasn't sure how to approach Ruth. "I don't have her phone number."

Caitlin picked up her phone and typed. Seconds later, Nikki's phone dinged. "Now you do."

"Thanks." Nikki decided to change the subject. "Did you find out anything from your Michigan contacts?"

"I did." Caitlin set a red folder and a legal pad on the table. She slipped on a pair of reading glasses. "Maybe what I dug up will help you decide if talking to Ruth is necessary."

"I'm all ears."

"Well, Nolan is a common name, but I did find your mom's birth record. Her mother is listed as Jennifer Nolan." Caitlin took a document out of the file and slid it over to Nikki. "This is a copy of your mom's birth certificate. 'Father' wasn't named, and your mother wasn't given a surname at birth."

"Mom's maiden name was Nolan, though. I've seen my parents' marriage license. Why wouldn't it be on the birth certificate?"

"Because your mother was adopted by Roger Nolan."

"No, he was her birth father," Nikki insisted.

"I don't think so," Caitlin said. "Your grandmother married Roger Nolan in 1944. Mary Sue Nolan was born a year later. According to tax records, the Nolans moved to Minnesota in 1952.

They divorced in November 1954. Your mother was born when they were separated, so I checked her birth certificate."

Nikki wasn't following her. "Are you saying that Grandma Jenny had an affair, and that's why Mom doesn't have a last name on the birth certificate?"

"Maybe, or maybe they were separated. Either way, your Grandma Jenny remarried Roger two years after your mother was born, and he legally adopted her. But they divorced for good in 1972."

"So Frost could be related to my mother through her birth father? That could be his connection to me?"

"It's possible," Caitlin said. "I also tracked down your great-grandparents. Jennifer's parents lived at the same Michigan address until 1978, which is the same year your great-grandfather died. The property was sold. Your great-grandmother passed four years later."

"I have a vague memory of Grandma Jenny talking about her mother," Nikki said. "When she died of a stroke, Mom and I were both devastated. But at least she went before my mother did; she never had to suffer the loss of her child, see my mother murdered."

Their food arrived, but Nikki wasn't sure how much she'd be able to eat.

"So Frost could be a long-lost relative on my mother's biological father's side, but how could he have known?"

"He could have done the research just like I did," Caitlin said. "The internet makes it easy, if you have the knowledge and patience."

"Did you cross-reference my mom's name and Grandma Jenny's with the birth records here and in Michigan?"

Caitlin cocked her head. "I didn't find any other births."

Nikki held up her hands, feeling hopeless. "I have no idea about anything anymore."

"That's okay," Caitlin assured her. "It helps narrow things down a bit."

Nikki ate a few of her fries. "That doesn't help Darcy Hoff."

"Not yet, but it may eventually. Did your aunt get married or have any kids? I didn't find any records."

"She never married," Nikki said. "She did have her share of female live-in social companions, as she called them. We all knew there was more to it, but no one said anything."

"So she was a lesbian?"

Nikki nodded. "For some reason, I feel like she couldn't have children, so I assume she tried to at some point and found that out. I know for certain that she and my mother had a huge falling out before my mother died. As far as I know, they never reconciled."

Liam's name flashed on Nikki's screen. She answered immediately.

"Hey, I'm with your girlfriend. Did you get in touch with Mankato State?"

"Yep," Liam replied excitedly.

Nikki nearly dropped her phone onto her half-eaten cheeseburger; she could tell he'd found something significant out before he even said it. "What?"

Caitlin's eyes lit up. "What is it?" she hissed.

Nikki ignored her. "Liam?"

"I found Lyle. He was a grad student at Mankato State and the time frame is right. But his full name is Oliver Lyle Riley. He owns property about thirty miles northeast of Stillwater."

CHAPTER TWENTY-FIVE

Nikki dropped her stuff on the floor of the task force room. She'd thrown twenty dollars on the table of the restaurant and promised to keep Caitlin in the loop and then raced over to the Washington County Police station as fast as she dared to drive. The name Oliver Riley repeated in her head; she couldn't believe they had him, but she didn't recognize the name either. She was still out of breath from running through the parking lot when she saw Liam. "Tell me everything," she said as she sat down at the table in the center of the room with Liam and Miller.

"Mankato State faculty records told me his name and address, and before you ask, I didn't need a warrant because I talked to the associate dean of science and engineering." Liam chugged an energy drink. "Information technology falls under that umbrella. Anyway, the current dean of that program was an adjunct professor in the nineties. He recognized him right away," Liam said. "Great student, brilliant, moody. Not a lot of friends, but no one ever had an issue with him. All the female students had crushes on him, apparently." He rolled his eyes. "But he had a very pretty girlfriend."

"Did you show him Annmarie's high school photo?"

"Yep. He verified that she was Oliver's girlfriend." Liam pointed the clicker at the smartboard, and a driver's license appeared. "Last renewed in Virginia seven years ago." The still of Frost from the Burberry store appeared next to the driver's license, followed by the composite sketch. Oliver had aged some in the last several years, but the images clearly showed the same person.

Nikki felt like her chest was about to explode. Frost's cocky smirk was coming back to haunt him.

Miller leaned back in his chair near the end of the table. "I can't believe we have him. It's too easy. There's got to be a catch."

"We have to assume there's a trap of some sort set." Nikki could understand where he was coming from, but they'd only identified him because Nikki had spoken to John. Frost couldn't have any idea about that.

"I've got aerial photos of his property," Liam said as the images of Oliver were replaced by the aerial photos. "It's an older, ranch-style home on about an acre. It's fairly secluded."

Nikki stepped closer to the board. "I know this is rural, but is there a street view?"

"I think so."

Nikki heard a click as the picture changed, and they were looking at the house from the highway. The image had been taken during the summer, and the grass needed mowing. The house sat back at least a hundred feet from the road, and the driveway had needed new blacktop when the picture was taken.

As she studied the picture, Nikki was hit with a crushing wave of déjà vu. "Who owned this place before Oliver Riley?"

"Give me a minute," Liam said.

His typing sounded like an anvil being struck in Nikki's head. She felt clammy, like she'd just come down from a high fever. She kept staring at the willow tree in the front yard. It was overgrown, but it would have been a lovely place for a little girl around Lacey's age to play. Nikki shivered, gooseflesh breaking out on her arms.

"Last owner was Michael Smith, who sold it to Oliver four years ago."

"Interesting timing," Miller said. "Annmarie had already moved back to care for her father. Frost followed her here."

"Did Smith own it in the early eighties?" Nikki asked.

"No, that would be one…" Liam paused. "Jennifer Nolan."

Icy fear shot through Nikki. "That's Grandma Jenny's old house."
Miller sat up straight. "Wait, what?"

"I knew it looked familiar. Grandma Jenny died there, of a stroke.
I was twelve, I think. Her wake was at this house. It looked a lot
prettier then. She had flowers all around the outside. I remember lots
of daisies." Nikki knew she was probably rambling, but she couldn't
help it. "Frost knew my family came from Michigan. He owns my
grandmother's old house. He took a picture of my mother—" She
rested her elbows on the table, her head in her palms. They were
missing some vital piece of information, she knew it. They didn't have
enough to pinpoint Frost's interest in Nikki's family, but they did have
a lead on Darcy's possible whereabouts. She could be in that house.

Nikki's ears buzzed from the adrenaline rushing through her
veins. They only had one shot at storming in and finding her. If they
failed, Frost would know that they knew his name and disappear.

"We have to move quickly and quietly on this," Nikki said. "I
know you both think he might be expecting us, but that doesn't
change anything. It will take too long to mobilize the FBI TAC team.
How quickly can you get the county's tactical unit ready to deploy?"

"Couple of hours," Miller said. "There's only a few houses on
that road, so we should have plenty of cover."

Nikki nodded. "Call your team, then."

Miller grabbed his coffee and stepped into the hall, his phone
cradled against his ear.

"We have to be prepared for anything," Liam said. "Including
Frost making a run for it."

"We will." As much as she wanted to go in guns blazing, they
had to have a plan and execute it to perfection if they wanted to
catch Frost without anyone getting killed. He'd proven how easily
he could blend in, and he appeared to be at ease in just about any
circumstance. Seeing his picture from the Burberry store matched
with an eyewitness composite might have him out of sync, but
someone like Frost was most dangerous when backed into a corner.

"We'll iron out the details when Miller comes back, but we'll have him post units on the nearest roads that Frost could use if he is able to flee. I'll have the tactical team create a wide perimeter around the house. I just need to make sure someone with a good shot has a clear view of the front door."

Liam narrowed his eyes. "Why just the front door?"

"Because that's where I'm going to knock first."

Liam stared at her over his open laptop. "You aren't seriously going to just walk up and knock, are you? Even with a vest, at that range, you're done if he shoots at you."

"He won't," Nikki said. "There are too many things he's aching to tell me first."

Liam looked confused.

Miller returned. "They'll be ready to roll in two hours."

Liam scowled. "Tell the chief what you just told me."

"I'm going to knock on the door, and I need a good shot backing me up."

Miller's dark eyebrows knitted together. "Are you sure that's a good idea?"

"Positive. If anyone else approaches him, we're going to have a standoff."

"You could let the tactical team make the breach like they're trained to do." Liam's face had gone red.

Nikki ignored him. "I'll keep him occupied while the team closes in."

"Nikki, you're way too close to this." Liam held his ground. "Frost has got to be paranoid. He's unpredictable, and you know those two things don't mix well."

But Nikki wasn't having any of it. "Yes, I am," she finally exploded. "This connects to my family somehow, and he brought my child into it. You're damned right I'm close to this thing. But I'm still capable of making the right decision."

Liam threw his hands up in the air and turned to Miller. "Sheriff, what do you think?"

Miller drummed his fingers on the table, his gaze on Nikki. "I think you're walking a fine line, agent. But since I know you're going to that house one way or another, I guess the best thing we can do is back you up."

Liam sighed, red-faced. "Two things: TAC checks the area before you go in, and I walk up with you. Or it's a no-go."

"A no-go?" Nikki asked in amazement. Had all of the energy drinks fried his brain? "I realize you've been shouldering the load lately, and I appreciate that. But I am your boss, not the other way around. It's my call."

Liam rested his hands on the back of his neck, every ounce of visible flesh pink with frustration. "Agent Hunt, I'm not against you. I'm not trying to undermine you. I'm just trying to help keep everyone safe. And I'm trying to keep the case from being compromised."

Nikki rubbed her temples, willing the forming headache to dissipate. "Fine. You can hang behind me a few feet, so you're in Frost's sight when he opens the door, but not right in front of him. I want the opportunity to speak with him before he's taken in. I think that's what he wants too."

"Deal," Liam said. "But if I think it's too dangerous, it's my call to fall back. Agreed?"

Nikki could tell by the set of his jaw that he wasn't going to back down, and he had every right to hold his ground. She had to keep her cool and remember Liam was on her side. "Agreed."

"I'll talk to the TAC commander and iron out their end of it." Miller exited, leaving Liam and Nikki in an awkward standoff.

Liam broke the silence. "After you left the restaurant, Caitlin called and told me about your family ties to Michigan."

"Good. Saves me from repeating it."

"Frost is either a flesh-and-blood relative, or he's been obsessed with your family for a long time. Either way he's playing us," Liam said. "There's a catch. There has to be."

"I know," Nikki said. "We have to be ready for anything, just like you said. But we have to try and save Darcy."

CHAPTER TWENTY-SIX

Nikki scanned the house in front of her as she and Liam pulled into the long driveway. A single interior light had been turned on, along with a porch light. Nikki could just make out Miller in place along the north end of the house, shrouded by a large evergreen tree.

A memory taunted Nikki, hanging out on the very edges of her consciousness. It was wintertime, and they were decorating outside. Grandma Jenny always put lights in that bush. Nikki had been playing in the snow under the willow tree.

She hadn't been alone.

He'd sat on top of her, pushing her face into the snow. It had been a joke at first, but he kept pushing her head down. Nikki had wet her pants from fright. Her mother had yanked the boy off her, screaming words Nikki didn't understand.

Grandma Jenny said he was wicked, just like his louse of a father. Nikki struggled to see his face, but her memory was too fuzzy.

Her mother took her inside to get cleaned up while Aunt Mary and Grandma Jenny finished putting the lights on the big pine tree on the corner of the house.

Where had the blood come from?

Nikki screwed her eyes shut tighter, willing the images to make sense. A woman crying for help.

"Hey, you with me?" Nikki jumped at the sound of Liam's voice.

"Sorry. Just remembering this place when I was little. Bits and pieces that don't make any sense, you know how it is." The heavy Kevlar Nikki wore under her coat was making her overheat. She took her gun out of the center console, double-checking to make sure the magazine was loaded. "Let's go."

Nikki went first, trying to focus on her peripheral vision and what was right in front of her. Someone had put ice melt on the concrete steps.

Her heart banged against her chest. What did Frost do inside that house? What sort of miserable trap had he laid for her? She felt lightheaded, but she promised herself that she wasn't blacking out this time.

"Stay at the bottom of the stoop," Nikki whispered to Liam.

She stepped slowly toward the door, her hand inside her open coat, ready to draw her weapon.

"The door is open a little bit."

For a split second, Nikki was back at the farmhouse, slowly pushing open the broken front door just minutes before she found her dead mother.

"Wait," Liam said. "This feels like a trap. Get back. We need to bring the K-9 and check for a bomb wire near the door. If you walk in, you could trip it."

She could hear a television coming from somewhere in the house. Since when was *The Price is Right* on at night?

"No, it isn't." Nikki gritted her teeth, remembering their earlier conversation. "He's not going to bring us here just to kill us, because he hasn't had his big reveal. He's working up to something that puts him alone in the spotlight, and I don't think this is it. But it's your call, like we discussed." She waited for Liam's decision, the seconds ticking loudly by.

"Go in and stay low," he whispered.

Nikki pushed the door open with her foot and shined her flashlight into the dark front room. Nikki glanced down the hallway to her right and counted two doors. Single bathroom, one bedroom. Two places for Frost to lie in wait. Even if he didn't know they had identified him, he'd have been prepared for that to happen—noticed them sneaking up on the house. She was sure of it. "Oliver, this is Special Agent Nikki Hunt. The house is surrounded by the Washington County Sheriff's tactical team," she said loudly into the open door.

"It could still be a trap."

Nikki inched forward, scanning the doorways for any sign of a tripwire.

A low moan came from the direction of the kitchen. Nikki remembered with a jolt that Grandma Jenny's room had been off the kitchen.

"Do you hear that?" Nikki asked Liam, who was still standing behind her. "There's a bedroom off the kitchen. That's where the TV is."

"Sounds like a woman," he murmured.

Nikki eased down the hall and scanned the kitchen to make sure it was clear before racing across the room. She could tell the television was in the small bedroom just off the kitchen—she remembered that it had been Grandma Jenny's room.

"Oh my God," Liam gasped, coming up behind Nikki.

Darcy Hoff lay on her side in the bed, her eyes closed. She wore different clothes than the ones she'd had on when she was taken, and Nikki could see bruises on her arm, as she moved towards her slowly, checking everything in the vicinity to make sure no one else was there. Her skin had an unhealthy look, as though she had gone a while without seeing the sun. But her chest rose and fell in a ragged pattern. She was alive.

As soon as Nikki saw her breathe, she hurried to Darcy's side and looked at her wrists for the telltale needle marks. "She's been drugged," she confirmed. "Darcy, it's Agent Hunt. Try to open your eyes."

Darcy moaned and tried to move her chapped lips.

"It's all right," Nikki said as she smoothed the stray hairs off Darcy's forehead. "Help is coming. You're going to be okay."

*

The tactical team helped Liam and Miller search the house while Nikki stayed with Darcy. Her breathing appeared to be even, and despite her wan coloring, she didn't seem to be in distress. Darcy stirred a couple of times, as though she were trying to break free of the sedation, but Nikki quietly assured her things were okay and that she'd be with her parents soon.

Frost might still be out there, but Darcy was alive. Nikki found her phone in her back pocket and called Irene Hoff.

"Hello?" a voice answered the phone after a couple of rings.

"Irene, this is Agent Hunt," Nikki said.

"Please tell me you have news." Irene sounded desperate.

A lump formed in Nikki's throat. "I'll do you one better. I have your daughter in front of me, and she's alive," Nikki replied.

Irene started sobbing, shouting the news to Ernie. She must have put Nikki on speaker, because she could hear both of them trying to talk through their tears.

"He kept her sedated," Nikki said. "She's not awake right now, but she's doing okay. The paramedics should be here soon, and we'll get her to Lakeview Hospital in Stillwater. It's the closest."

"When will she wake up enough to talk to us?" Ernie asked.

"The paramedics might be able to administer flumazenil, which helps people come around faster after conscious sedation and anesthesia. I'm not sure if they carry that, but if not, the hospital will." She heard the sirens approaching. "They're arriving now. We'll meet you at the hospital."

"Thank you, Agent Hunt," Ernie said hoarsely. "I barely survived losing Kimmie. If I'd lost another child…"

"I know," Nikki said. "We'll see you soon."

She ended the call as the paramedics rushed in.

Nikki quickly stepped aside. "She's been sedated and we strongly believe it could be with lorazepam. Do you guys carry flumazenil to reverse sedation?"

"In the rig," the medic closest to Nikki said. "We'll make sure her vitals are good, check for signs of the drugs and then load her up. We can administer it before we take her in if we need to."

"Good," Nikki said to the paramedic. "If you can wake her, I need to question her. Unless she goes into some kind of distress, don't leave before I get the chance to ask her a couple of questions. We've still got a dangerous criminal out there."

She found Liam and Miller in the other bedroom. Aside from the twin bed and old chest of drawers, it was empty.

"Paramedics are here. They should be able to reverse some of the sedation. You guys find anything?"

"Nope, but we need to process the entire house. Nothing that we've found so far tells us where Frost is now…" Liam said. "I'm guessing this isn't Frost's permanent residence. Doesn't look like anyone actually lives here."

Nikki nodded. "I wonder if he talked the previous owner into selling or he just got lucky and the house was on the market?" Nikki mused. "He had to have known whose house it had been."

"But how?" Miller asked.

Nikki leaned against the doorframe, fatigue sinking in. "I think he was here with me when we were kids."

Both men stared at her.

Liam spoke first. "What?"

She told them about the memory of an older boy trying to smother her in the snow in the front yard. "I was younger than Lacey, I think. Maybe four. I remember an altercation with a boy on this property, I remember being scared."

"Could he have been a neighbor?" Miller asked.

"I have no idea." Nikki hugged her chest, fixated on the memory of her mother on the floor, crying. That had happened here, she was certain. Had it happened during that same visit? It seemed like it had, just later in the day. She could still see her mother on the floor, crying harder than Nikki had ever seen. The sight had terrified her as a child. "Oliver Riley didn't have a record, right?" Nikki asked Liam.

"Not even a parking ticket," Liam replied.

"Look in the other states we know Frost has been. He could have property somewhere else."

"Agent Hunt?" One of the paramedics stood in the hallway. "We've got her in the rig, and the reversal's starting to work. She's asking for you."

Nikki followed him outside to the waiting ambulance, with Liam and Miller in tow. She climbed into the rig and squeezed into the small seat next to the gurney. "Darcy?"

"Agent Hunt," she slurred. "I need to talk to her."

"It's me. I'm right here. We're meeting your parents at the hospital."

"Never…" Darcy said weakly, her eyes fighting to open.

"You don't want to see them?"

"Oliver said… to tell you."

Nikki scooted closer, sweat dampening the roots of her hair. "Tell me what?"

"Never take your…" Darcy's eyes finally cracked open. She grabbed Nikki's hand. "Never take your eyes off your daughter."

CHAPTER TWENTY-SEVEN

Nikki sat in the passenger seat, the sound of her blood pumping through her chest the only thing she could hear. She'd dialed Tyer's number several times, and he still hadn't picked up. "Why isn't he answering?" She kept reminding herself to stay calm, but every unanswered ring sent her anxiety up several notches.

Liam ran a yellow light. "The police are on their way, Nikki. She'll be fine."

A hollow pit had formed in Nikki's stomach. Her clothes were damp with sweat. "They should be there any minute. How close are we?"

Darcy had given her the message forty minutes ago. Nikki had immediately called Tyler, but he hadn't answered, so she'd called the St. Paul police and asked them to check on him and Lacey. Liam had insisted on driving, and Nikki had to admit he'd gotten them back to the Cities in record time.

Her hands trembled as she tried Tyler again. Still no answer.

"Liam, something's wrong. This was his trap. He distracted me so he could get to Lacey." Her voice broke. "If she's gone—"

"Don't say it," Liam said. "He won't hurt her. That's not what all of this is about. She's just a tool to get to you. He needs her alive."

"Right." Nikki was glad that Liam was with her. That had to be it. Better yet, maybe Tyler had taken her to a movie and forgotten to tell Nikki. That would explain why he wasn't answering her calls.

A generic number for the St. Paul police came up on Nikki's screen. "This is Agent Hunt. Did you speak with Tyler and Lacey?"

"We're at the residence," the officer said. "It's dark. No one's answering."

"Is there a vehicle in the garage?" Nikki's heart pounded in her ears. "There's a window on the left side. It's small, but you should be able to see."

"The garage is empty."

Some of Nikki's fear started to subside. "Okay. Can you put an APB out on a Ford Escape, license plate 623 LYS. Oliver Riley—the man we know as Frost—may have done something to them. Run the APB. And check the movie theater on Cleveland Avenue. That's the only place Tyler would be where he wouldn't answer the phone." Tyler's parents were out of town, and he wouldn't have ignored her calls if he were with them, anyway. "Call me the second you hear something." She hung up on the officer and called the field office, hoping one of the technical people was working late. She and Liam had left their laptops at the sheriff's station, and they couldn't access the FBI's system on their cell phones. "I should call the Minneapolis police too."

"They'll get the ABP faster than anyone," Liam said. "Call the state police. They're your best shot at finding him."

"Good idea."

"My cousin's a state trooper She's getting ready to go on maternity leave, but she's still working the desk." Liam fumbled in his coat pocket and then tossed Nikki his phone. "Maura Wilson."

Nikki scrolled until she found the number and then put the call on speaker.

"Hey, Mr. Bigshot FBI Agent."

"Hey, listen. We have a possible missing child," Liam said. "Can you run reports for a Ford Escape, license plate 623 LYS."

"Sure." Maura was quiet, but Nikki could hear her quick typing. "Okay, you're in luck. There's a report here."

"What does it say?" Nikki choked out. "Is it an accident report? A ticket?"

"It's an incident report from about three hours ago," Maura said. "The SUV was found at a rest area north of the metro. Police got a tip about a suspicious vehicle. They found an unidentified white male, deceased. No sign of foul play. Responding officer noted needle marks on the arm."

Nikki leaned forward and rested her head on the dashboard, trying to breathe. What if Tyler and Lacey… no. Nikki refused to finish the thought. They had to be all right.

"No sign of a little girl?" Liam's voice cracked.

"Not on the report."

"Where is the vehicle now?"

"Impounded."

"Where?" Nikki finally managed to speak.

"It's currently sitting at the state patrol's impound facility near Princeton."

"Do me a favor and make sure it stays there until our crime scene people arrive," Liam said.

"I'll call over to that impound and tell them to expect federal investigators. Do you have any idea what the child was wearing?"

Nikki realized she hadn't even seen Lacey since this morning—hadn't video-chatted with her as she normally would. "She was still in her butterfly pajamas when Tyler picked her up."

"Butterfly pajamas this morning, with her shoes," Liam said.

"Where is the body?" Nikki barely managed to get the words out of her constricted throat.

"The Anoka County Medical Examiner's office. I'll call and tell them to expect you."

Nikki spent the rest of the drive to the medical examiner's office struggling to stay calm, her warring mind rendering her mute. The cop in her reasoned that they had every available resource looking through Oliver's life, searching for any clue as to where he might have taken Lacey.

But the mother in her was paralyzed with fear. They were at least two steps behind him already and the words "deceased white male" ran through her head on repeat.

By the time they arrived at the Midwest Medical Examiner's office in Anoka County, a statewide manhunt had been issued for Oliver Riley and Lacey, but no progress had been made, and every minute that ticked by not knowing where Lacey was felt like an eternity. They'd all suspected Oliver had laid a trap. Why hadn't she listened to Liam?

This time of night, the medical examiner's office was closed to the public, but the death investigator on call had agreed to meet Nikki and Liam.

A gray-haired, tired-looking woman waited at the back entrance. "Joanne Pitman, RN. I'm a part-time death investigator for Anoka County."

"Where is he?" Nikki asked. "I need to know if it's Tyler."

Pitman wore the same pitying expression Nikki had seen on countless medical examiner's faces. This was the first time she'd been on the receiving end since 1993.

"I have a picture if you'd rather look at it," Pitman said gently. "The autopsy isn't until tomorrow."

Nikki realized what she was saying. "Get him out of the cooler, please."

Pitman nodded and directed them to the room at the end of the corridor. "The viewing window's in there. I'll bring him in."

She and Liam went into the room and waited. Liam sat quietly beside her, his calm presence the only thing keeping her sane. Her head felt like she'd just experienced a fast ascent and it had filled with pressure. Was she really here? Surely this wasn't actually happening to her. Not again.

On the other side of the window, lights flickered to life, and Pitman wheeled the body into the room. A sheet still covered him, but Nikki had been with Tyler long enough to recognize his stocky form. An iron vice seemed to be closing around her, but she knocked on the window to signal that they were ready.

Pitman rolled the paper sheet back to reveal the man's face.

Crushing grief almost brought Nikki to her knees.

Tyler was dead.

CHAPTER TWENTY-EIGHT

Saturday

Nikki sat in the task room at the sheriff's station, panic ringing steadily in her ears. Lacey had been missing for roughly ten hours. Miller had gone to check in with Darcy Hoff, and Liam was currently coordinating with the state police and the department of transportation. Nikki stared at her notes as though some new information would manifest. Every possible law enforcement resource was being utilized to find Lacey, and nothing was panning out. Just as he'd done all the other times, Frost had vanished. She'd got up to go to her jeep several times but she had absolutely no idea where to head to.

She'd called Tyler's parents on the drive from the morgue to Stillwater. They were distraught and rightfully blaming Nikki. Why hadn't she just stayed with Lacey and let Liam find Frost? Rory had been right about her pride. She'd been so caught up in being the one to say "gotcha" that she'd destroyed everything.

Her second call had been to Ruth Todd—a call she should have made days ago. She didn't answer, and Nikki left a message, praying that she would call back.

She called Rory next, and he'd begged her to let him help search for Lacey, but Nikki had put her foot down and told him to stay away, to remain safely at his house. She couldn't lose him too.

"You all right?" Caitlin sat across from Nikki, looking nearly as bereft as she had when Zach had been taken. Liam had called her from the car, and Caitlin had been waiting at the sheriff's station when they arrived. Nikki had initially balked, because Caitlin was still a member of the media, but she'd promised she was there only as a friend. Nikki had been surprised at how much she wanted her to stay.

"Just trying to figure out what I missed," Nikki replied.

"I keep thinking about Annmarie's tattoo," Caitlin said. "Who gets their boyfriend's middle name tattooed on them? I guess he must have gone by that name."

Nikki shrugged. "Well, Oliver Lyle Riley seems to have disappeared after grad school. We've searched every variation of the name and haven't gotten anywhere. Of course, he's probably got other identities. Maybe even social security numbers. If he's smart enough to hack into The Pointe's security system and shut off specific cameras, who knows what else he can do."

"What about Mankato State?" Caitlin asked. "They might be able to cross-reference—"

"They're going to try, but it's tedious." Nikki dragged her hands down her face. "I can't stop thinking about Lacey, imagining her wherever she might be… I can't think straight."

"Stop," Caitlin said. "He won't hurt her. You're the one he wants."

Nikki could feel the room getting smaller, the walls closing in as time to find her daughter alive ticked away. Her chest felt tight, and the back of her neck was damp with sweat. "I'll be right back."

She exited the room before Caitlin could respond, racing down the hall to the restroom. She splashed cold water on her face and then braced against the counter for support. She had to find a way to stow her panic. Lacey needed her more than ever.

Her phone started ringing, and Nikki's blood pressure spiked when she didn't recognize the number. "Hello?" she answered.

"Nicole, this is Ruth Todd." Ruth's warm voice jarred with Nikki.

She shut the water off and stood, making sure to avoid the mirror. She couldn't stand the sight of herself, of the person responsible for losing Lacey and Tyler. She hadn't used any names in her message, but she'd made it clear that Ruth might be able to help find a missing child. "Ruth, thank you for calling me back. I know I'm the last person you want to speak with, but this is strictly police business."

"Rory told me that your little girl is missing." Ruth's voice was softer than Nikki remembered. "I wish to God he'd said something earlier, because I need to tell you something…"

"What are you talking about?" Nikki gripped the sink for support.

"Your mom and I were close once upon a time. We went to high school together, just like you and Mark." Ruth paused. "I should have said something earlier, but I had no idea that you believed this Frost person could be connected to your family. I haven't been following the news and when Rory talks about you, I change the subject." Her voice broke. "I am so sorry."

"I don't blame you," Nikki said. "Don't feel bad about that now," she insisted. "Just tell me what you know."

Ruth sighed. "Your mother got pregnant during our freshman year of high school. She'd never tell me who the father was, but when she started to show, she went and stayed with family in Michigan. An arrangement with family friends was made, and after your mom had the baby, he lived with them. He visited your mom and grandma sometimes, and he was always introduced as a cousin, I think—"

Nikki's head was spinning. "I have a sibling?"

"Half-sibling," Ruth said. "Don't judge your mom for letting him be raised by someone else. She did what she felt was best for him."

"That's the last thing on my mind… Did my father know about him? Why didn't she ever tell me?"

"Because of the accident. He's several years older than you, but when you were really small, he'd come down to stay for the holidays."

The memory of her mother curled on the floor at Grandma Jenny's came back to Nikki, the hairs on the back of her neck standing up. "What accident?"

"Your mom was on a ladder hanging up Christmas lights and she fell." Ruth sniffled. "She was eight weeks pregnant and lost the baby. She never spoke about it much after, but she said Oliver had pushed her... He was never quite right, always seemed jealous if your mother spent time with anyone else. After that, I believe he visited less and less. Over time, he kind of became a taboo subject. Your dad was certain he'd hurt your mom on purpose. They were afraid he'd hurt you too. He'd already tried more than once."

Nikki couldn't speak for a moment, her body frozen with shock.

"Oh Nikki, I'm sorry. Rory has been telling me to swallow my pride and talk to you, and he was right more than he realized. If we'd spoken sooner, I would have told you about Oliver, because you deserve to know that you have a half-sibling out there. And now... he's done something to hurt someone again. He must be the person who has taken your little girl."

The mention of Lacey snapped Nikki back into reality. She'd deal with the emotional end of the news about a half-sibling when she had Lacey back. "Ruth," Nikki said. "Do you remember his name?"

"Oliver Hennessy. I remembered because Hennessy whiskey was my dad's favorite. Oliver's no relation to them, of course."

Nikki thanked Ruth quickly and put the phone down, leaning against the wall to take a breath. She slipped the phone into her back pocket, running back into the conference room and opening her laptop.

"What is it?" Caitlin almost spilled her tea.

"I know his real name," Nikki said. She found the database she needed and quickly accessed it with her credentials. For the first time in nearly twelve hours, her fog of grief dissipated enough for her to see clearly. The page loaded with Oliver's other name, and an address was listed. "And I know where he has Lacey."

CHAPTER TWENTY-NINE

Nikki gripped the steering wheel, following the jeep's navigation route. Antler Lake was over two hundred miles from Stillwater, deep into the North Woods, where a person could drive for hours and not see another vehicle. Fishing resorts dotted the scenic highway, and homes were scattered with miles between them. In the summer, the area was flush with green and blooming wildflowers, but it was barren and gray during the winter.

Caitlin had tried to stop her from leaving, begging her to wait for Liam and backup, but Nikki couldn't sit around while Lacey was being held by a killer. She'd known that Caitlin would give her location to Liam, but Nikki had only told her that she was going to Itasca County. Caitlin couldn't pull the address herself, and she'd need Liam to access the database. Nikki wanted to buy some time, and she didn't want to put anybody else at risk.

Despite the navigation screen, Nikki almost missed the turn for the narrow dirt road that led to a private dock. She drove into the clearing too fast, her tires skidding on the slushy ice.

Her heart lodged in her throat at the sight of the docked Wilcraft. She scanned the nearest shoreline for any sign of Frost hiding but didn't see anyone in the thatch of woods and overgrown vegetation.

Nikki secured her weapon and extra ammunition and then slipped a utility knife into the side of her boot. She grabbed her phone and turned the GPS back on, and then sent Liam the address and the information he needed to make it to Frost's cabin.

She couldn't stop replaying the memory from Jenny's house. She'd spent more than five years chasing Frost, and he'd been a ghost from her childhood the entire time.

She opened the door slowly, her gaze on the side mirror. There was no sign of anyone in the woods behind her, either, but there were so many places to hide, she had to assume Frost was nearby, watching.

Nikki exited the jeep and crouched behind the open door, cold wind making her eyes water. Nikki found the makeup compact she'd taken out of her bag earlier and then balanced it on the inside of the door. She didn't expect Frost to sneak up on her, but she still wanted some sort of visual.

The Wilcraft shifted, sending her heart back into her throat. The wind might have done it, but it was a heavy vehicle, and the movement had looked more like...

She saw the heavy winter boot first as the man stepped carefully out of the craft and onto the slick dock. He wore the same dark, trendy-looking coat, and aviator sunglasses blocked his eyes. With the door still acting as her shield, Nikki moved into position in case she had to take a shot at him.

Hands tucked in his pockets, Frost strolled up the dock. He reached the end of the dock and walked toward her with a pleasant smile, clearly expecting her. "I knew you'd find me."

"That's far enough," Nikki said when he was just a few feet away. She rested the gun on the door and pointed it at him. Like her and Lacey, he had her mother's fair complexion and dark hair. She wondered if he also had the same blue eyes. As he drew closer, Nikki finally recognized the boy who'd been so cruel to her that day at Grandma Jenny's.

"Please, little sister." His words were partially broken up by the wind, but she'd read his lips. "We both know you're not going to shoot me, so let's act like the intelligent people we are."

Keeping her gun at the ready, Nikki stepped slowly around the door. Her blood rushed in her ears, her scalp sweating beneath her hat. She didn't think he would shoot her, but she had to be ready for anything. If she had to fire her own weapon, she'd take his knees out and make him tell her where he'd hidden Lacey. She could see no sign of her daughter, no sign that there was a little girl here at all…

"That's better." He took off the sunglasses and slipped them into his coat pocket. Nikki felt a tiny pang of relief that his eyes looked nothing like her mother's. Her mother's had been soft and kind, and Oliver's held only menace. "Why don't you put your gun on the ground along with that little knife in your boot? Leave your phone too."

"Why would I do that?" Nikki asked.

"Because I have your daughter, and the only way you're going to see her again is by doing everything I tell you to do," he snapped.

Nikki knew that she could shoot him now, incapacitate him. But there was no guarantee she would be able to find Lacey—he'd brought her to a remote area, an area he likely knew well. Nikki gave him a bitter look as she removed her gun and the knife, followed by her phone. She placed them all on the ground as Frost directed.

"Where's Lacey?" she asked.

"She's safe and sound, I promise. Smart cookie, that one." He smiled. "I bet she wouldn't have forgotten all about me," he said, wagging his finger at Nikki in an accusing manner.

"I was three or four the last time you were around," Nikki said. "What do you expect?"

"Not true," he said pleasantly. "I came to our mom's funeral."

"I don't remember much from those days," she replied, thrown off by his referring to her mother as "our mom." Valerie might have been his biological mother, but she'd been Nikki's mom, not his.

"I'm sure you can understand how difficult that was for me…" She wasn't sure what she should do. If she should try to appeal to his humanity—if he had any—or come in strong. He was clearly a complicated individual, and he knew more about her than she did him. So she asked the question that had been nagging her since her conversation with Ruth. "Why didn't anyone introduce you to me? Why didn't I know who you were?"

"Aunt Mary forbade it," he said, shaking his head. "Even though I promised to say I was distant cousin Ollie from Michigan. She didn't want anything of it. You weren't in a good place, and Mary didn't trust me not to tell you the truth. It was ridiculous…" He sneered.

"And Annmarie?"

It was barely perceptible, but Nikki caught Oliver's recoil at her name. Did he regret what he'd done to her? "I loved her," he said quietly.

"Then why did you kill her?"

He flinched, but quickly regained composure. "I'm surprised you don't remember my nickname, Little Lying Ollie. Your dad gave it to me."

Nikki wanted to check her watch, but she didn't dare. She had to keep Frost talking until Liam arrived. "What did you lie about?"

"Stupid little things," Oliver snapped. "He never liked me, either."

"Because you hurt Mom and made her miscarry."

"Try to see things from my position." His voice ticked up a notch. "I'm ten years old, and I know I'm the black sheep of my family. I can't figure out why, but they just don't like me, no matter how good I do in school or anything else."

Nikki was still trying to process that this man shared DNA with both her and Lacey. Right now, he wanted her empathy, and if that's what helped her find Lacey, she'd give it to him. "You mean the family in Michigan who raised you?"

"Family isn't the word I would use." Oliver sneered, shaking his head. "I found out the truth about my parentage by accident when my so-called grandmother was talking on the phone to her sister, Jenny, who, of course, wasn't actually her sister but a close friend. I'd been spending part of my summers and school breaks with Jenny for as long as I could remember. I guess she wanted to know her grandson even if Valerie couldn't stand the sight of me."

"Because you tried to hurt her?"

"Because I was her bastard child that came from rape," he snapped. "High and mighty Jenny couldn't let that awful truth be known about her daughter, so they came up with the alternative and left me in Michigan. I found out the truth right before I last visited Jenny."

Nikki's legs weakened. Her mother had been raped as a teenager, when? By whom? "But Mom did want you in her life," Nikki tried. "That's what she told her friend."

"She lied," he said. "After the incident with the ladder, I confronted her and Jenny about it. They both went on about how much Valerie did care about me, but when I was born, she was still in high school and couldn't cope with the thought of raising a baby from rape. I asked why we couldn't be a family now, and they went on about turning everyone's life upside down and all that. Jenny said it could be our secret, and Valerie and I would get to know each other. But I was never invited back after that visit. My adoptive parents said they all decided it was best to cut ties, and that was that." His eyes narrowed, and Nikki thought she spied moisture in them. "Imagine my shock when I read that Valerie Walsh's *only* child had found her and her husband murdered."

"That's why you came to the funeral?"

Frost shook his head. "I've thought about telling you this for so long, and I can't believe the moment is finally here." He took a deep breath. "Here's the tragic part of my story. A month or so before the murders, I came to town and asked our mother to meet for coffee. To my surprise, she agreed. I wanted to make her understand that I hadn't really been a bad kid. I didn't feel like I fit in with anyone, and when I found out she was my real mother, I thought things might be different. The last time I saw her, I promised that I just wanted to be part of the family, and that was the God's honest truth."

Nikki caught the crack in his steely voice. She could see the pain in his eyes. "What did she say?"

Frost's jaw tightened. "She'd promised to talk to your dad. She could see that I was different. I was in graduate school and already had a good job lined up. I hadn't been in trouble in a long time. She told me that she was proud of me. I thought we were finally going to become a family, and then she died…"

"I can't imagine what you went through, but why did you murder those women and make them look like Mom in the casket? They had nothing to do with what happened to you."

"Oh please." He looked at her in disgust. "You're a psychologist, for God's sake. What does your training tell you?"

Nikki tried to gather her thoughts and think of an answer that would keep Frost talking without making him any angrier. "Despite what popular culture tells us, most people with terrible childhoods don't end up being killers. Did you ever find your biological father?"

"I have no interest in meeting a rapist." He practically spat the word out, and Nikki finally understood why Frost's crimes weren't sexual in nature. He likely saw rape—and himself—as an abomination. Nikki hoped she could use that to her advantage.

"Do you believe you're a bad seed, destined to kill?"

Frost snickered. "Well, I have killed, haven't I?"

"Everyone has a choice."

"I didn't," he yelled. "No one wanted me."

Nikki seized the opportunity to dig at his weak spot. "Annmarie did."

"I don't want to talk about her." His voice quivered, and Nikki saw her opening.

"Because you cared about her, didn't you?" she asked. "Why did you kill her?"

"She gave me no choice."

"What about Tyler?" Nikki's control started to crack. "He didn't deserve to die."

Frost shrugged. "Maybe not, but he lied to me when I tried to see you all those years ago. Surely you realize that the women I've killed all came after that. If Tyler hadn't been so selfish, they might still be alive. He might too. But he wasn't just going to let me take Lacey, was he?"

"If she's hurt," Nikki started, fighting not to think about Tyler lying in the morgue and her daughter all alone wherever Frost had her.

"She isn't. I'm not a kid killer. I do have some morals."

"Why kill all those women?" Nikki said. "I still don't understand."

"They were the only way to get your attention," he snapped and stepped closer.

"You want to kill us to wipe out the side of the family who betrayed you," Nikki said. "Kill me if you have to, but not Lacey. She's an innocent child."

Frost cocked his head. "You have the wrong idea, sister. I want all of us to be together as a real family. I'm going to take you to Lacey. Then the three of us can escape. I'd initially planned to take you both at the same time so she wouldn't be so scared, but I have to admit, your determination to track me down forced me to change tactics. But we can still be a family, right?" He looked at her with pleading eyes.

Nikki felt like her throat might close up. She'd been prepared to bargain for Lacey's freedom with her own life if she had to, but this? "Where are you taking us?"

"Wherever we want." He smiled, revealing crooked teeth. "That's the beauty of it."

Terror pierced her resolve. "Lacey won't understand. She's just a little girl, and her father's gone."

"She needs her mother," Oliver said. "You of all people should know how much a girl needs her mom."

His words burned like salt in an opened wound, but Nikki refused to give him the satisfaction. Where the hell was Liam? Why had she allowed her pride to overrule reason? Coming up here alone had been foolish. She prayed Liam was getting close.

Behind Oliver, something moved through the barren woods, darting between the drooping branches that were still covered with ice and snow.

Nikki was certain she recognized the lean figure.

"Come on, Nicole. Think of all the things I know about our family that you don't. If I'm gone, those secrets all go too."

"I want proof that Lacey's still alive." She couldn't see the figure anymore. Doubt began to creep through her. She was tired and emotionally exhausted—had she just imagined the person?

"Figured you'd ask that." He reached into his pocket and held up his phone. "This is a live feed straight to her. She's sleeping. And no, she isn't drugged."

Nikki inched forward to get a closer look. It was Lacey, curled up in her normal position, covered with a blanket. Struggling not to sob with relief, Nikki squinted at the numbers on the bottom left of the screen. "Is that a timestamp?"

Oliver nodded. "We can be with her in less than ten minutes. What's it going to be, sis?"

Nikki looked at the shoreline again, praying for another sign of movement and trying to think of another stall tactic. "I'm still deciding," she said evenly.

Oliver's dark eyes narrowed as he pulled a dart gun out of his pocket. "Then I'll make it easy for you. Start walking to the Wilcraft, or I put a strong sedative in you and toss you into the lake."

She didn't have any other choice. Lacey was alive, and Nikki needed to be with her. If she had to endure Frost to do that, then she'd play along for now. She walked carefully onto the slippery dock and glanced down at the water. This lake had thawed more than the ones further north, but it was still patchy with ice and very dangerous. If she fell in, Nikki doubted she would survive long enough to swim to the island.

"Am I supposed to get inside?"

"Not until I do." Oliver approached her slowly, clearly expecting her to try and ambush him.

Nikki put her hand on the craft's top for balance and opened the door. It was too dark outside to see the details of the Wilcraft's interior, and Nikki didn't have her phone or flashlight.

"Wait right there." Oliver kept the dark gun level with her face. "If you try anything, I'll shoot."

Nikki stood at the end of the narrow dock, with her back against the water, still clinging to the craft's top. Frost was less than a foot from Nikki when she saw the figure emerge silently from the woods, gun in hand. Struggling to keep her tone level, Nikki addressed Oliver. "Is Lacey on that island?"

Oliver smirked. "Yes, she's just over there, across the water. She's maybe five hundred yards away from you."

"Then take me to her, please." Nikki edged over to her left so that she was in the far corner of the narrow dock, leaving him enough room to maneuver and get into the craft.

"Good girl."

He was only a few inches away now, and their window was closing. Nikki held her breath as Caitlin stepped onto the dock.

"Can I go too?"

Oliver's head whipped to his left, and Nikki launched herself onto his back. She managed to get him into a decent chokehold, his reflexes quickly kicking in. He still held the dart gun, but his fingers dug into Nikki's coat, struggling to find a grip.

Caitlin approached from the opposite side and stepped onto the dock, her little silver pistol clutched in her hands. Frost shifted and dropped his shoulder, slamming Nikki's back into the docked craft. Pain shot down her back, and her arm muscles begged for relief. He finally managed to get a good grip on her left elbow and yanked hard. Nikki's fingers relaxed, but she held fast to his neck.

"I'm going to shoot him," Caitlin yelled.

"No," Nikki grunted as Frost dug his elbow into her chest, trapping her between him and the Wilcraft. "Lacey's somewhere on the island. I have to find out where she is."

"It's not that big," Caitlin said. "We can find her without him."

Oliver roared and slammed his left fist into Nikki's head. She sagged on his tall frame like a rag doll, red stars swimming all around her. Not stars, she realized. Nikki summoned the last of her strength and wrenched the dart free, plunging it into the artery in Oliver's exposed neck.

"Bitch." He hit her twice more. She could feel his muscles giving in to the sedative, but he stayed on his feet.

"What was that about you not going to prison, Lying Ollie?" she hissed into his ear.

"You won't be alive to see it." He shifted, and Nikki realized his intentions too late.

Her head smacked the dock pole. Her arms went limp, her vision nearly gone. Frost howled in pain, and then Nikki felt herself flying through the air. She hit the thin ice several feet in front of the dock hard. It splintered, and the freezing water took her breath away, soaking quickly through her layers.

"Hang on," Caitlin was yelling. "It's not deep. Just don't pass out. Do you hear me?"

The cold water felt like millions of needles being jabbed into her skin, and her head seemed like nothing more than a giant cotton ball. She stared at the sky, amazed at how dark it had gotten, before realizing that her eyes were closed. She tried to open them, but the cold water was all-consuming.

"Find Lacey," she gasped.

Caitlin shouted something at her, but Nikki sank into unconsciousness.

CHAPTER THIRTY

Nikki had never been so cold. Every fiber of her body seemed to be frozen. She didn't know if she were alive or dead or someplace in between. She knew only the relentless cold. Even her eyelids seemed to be frozen shut, just like Frost's girls. He must have won. He'd killed Nikki and left with Lacey. Who would save Lacey now? If Caitlin were still alive, she would keep trying to find Lacey. But what if Frost had killed her too?

Nikki couldn't let Frost have Lacey. She struggled against her frozen prison, pain lashing at her from every direction. Her arms finally began to move, and she forced her way through the cold water, fighting to get to the surface. She must be getting closer, because she heard voices. Someone was saying her name over and over.

Lacey.

Small hands patted her face. A familiar scent, the most beautiful smell in the world, urged Nikki to wake up.

"Mommy." Lacey's sweet little voice took care of the rest.

Nikki peeled her eyes open to see a worried little girl staring down at her.

"I knew you'd find me," she said.

Nikki held out her arms and Lacey fell into them, sobbing. For a few minutes, Nikki breathed in her scent and held her close while they both cried. She didn't care where they were right now, as long they were together.

*

The next time Nikki became aware of her surroundings, she was staring up at the emergency room ceiling with no idea how much time had passed or even what hospital she was in. How much had been real and how much had been a dream?

"Where's Lacey?" she asked frantically, noticing a figure at the end of the room.

"She's in the other trauma room getting checked out," Caitlin said. She was standing a few feet away. Nikki could see that she was shivering, and she had a hospital blanket wrapped around her, but it didn't seem to be doing much good. "Rory's with her. She refused to leave you until he went with her."

"Did you fall in too?" Nikki asked. She realized that she had no true recollection of what had happened—she remembered the cold and seeing Caitlin as she fell. How much time had passed? What had happened to Frost?

"I pulled your ass out of the water," she said. "Thank God for that emergency box in your truck. I managed to scrounge up enough stuff to cover you and keep you from freezing to death."

"Is Oliver dead?" Nikki asked. She was so grateful to Caitlin for following her out there, likely saving Nikki and Lacey's lives.

"No," Caitlin said. "But he cried like a baby when Liam read him his rights." She smiled. "My phone was dead, or I would have recorded it for you." She came next to Nikki's bed, and Nikki felt Caitlin's hand on her arm.

"Now that would have been one hell of an exclusive," Nikki mumbled.

"Exactly." Caitlin shook her head. "I've been kicking myself ever since."

Nikki's head still felt like it was bogged down with water. "Has anyone told her about Tyler?"

"I don't think so," Caitlin said. "Tyler's parents showed up not long after we got to the hospital and wanted to, but Rory wouldn't let them. He said it had to come from you."

Nikki nodded, a fresh wave of sadness nearly choking her.

Caitlin yanked a tissue out of the box next to Nikki's bed. "I can help you with that."

Grief that Nikki had been burying fought its way to the surface. She pressed her hands against her face to keep from crying. How was she going to tell Lacey that her daddy was gone forever?

Nikki must have fallen asleep again, because the next thing she heard were Rory's and Lacey's soft voices.

"But Mommy's okay, right?" Lacey asked.

"Yes, Mommy's just resting now," Rory said gruffly. "You both need to rest."

"I want to stay with her."

"We'll stay until she wakes up," Rory told her. "But Mommy might have to spend the night, so you might have to go with your grandparents. They want to spend some time with you too."

"Because of Daddy." The pain in Lacey's voice broke Nikki's heart.

She peeled her eyes open and saw Rory sitting in the nearest chair, still in his work clothes, his long legs stretched out in front of him. Lacey was curled in his lap, a blanket wrapped around her.

Rory locked eyes with her, the emotion on his face matching everything Nikki felt. She reached out a weak hand, and he leaned forward to grasp it tightly. "Lace, look, Mommy's awake again."

Lacey's head popped up from his chest, and she shimmied onto the bed.

Nikki scooted over to make room for her. "Hi, Bug. You feeling any better?" Nikki tried to sit up, but the pain all over her body was excruciating.

Lacey could see her struggle and moved over, burying her little face in Nikki's neck. "That man made Daddy go to sleep, didn't he?"

Nikki hugged Lacey as tight as she could without hurting herself. "Yes, he did," she replied softly. She had no idea what Lacey had seen, and the thought of what had happened in that car with Tyler terrified her. She tried to ignore it for now and just hold her daughter for a moment.

In the following days, Courtney's DNA results proved what Nikki already knew: Oliver was her half-brother. Courtney had run Oliver's results against various DNA databases, but so far, no other matches had come up. If Oliver knew who his father was, he wasn't telling anyone. Nikki knew she should probably drop the idea, but part of her wanted to know who had raped her mother and set off a chain of events that led to six women's deaths, Tyler's murder, and countless ruined lives. She wanted more people to blame.

Darcy Hoff and her parents had stopped by to say thank you, and seeing Darcy safe in her parents' arms had eased a little of Nikki's grief. But she still had pounds of baggage to work through.

Annmarie's funeral was small, as per her will. She'd also named Nikki as executor to her estate and requested that Nikki look after her father. Nikki had been relieved when she heard Annmarie's last wishes. Even after everything she'd gone through and the fear she'd probably been living in, she still tried to warn Nikki with the card and by leaving the fabric. If Annmarie hadn't done those things, Nikki and Lacey probably wouldn't have made it out alive. She'd gone to see Howard a few times since Oliver was arrested. She never knew if he was going to recognize her, but he seemed to enjoy the company.

Tyler's parents were still angry with her, and she knew they were going to be even more upset when they found out that he and Nikki had never changed their wills. He'd left everything to Nikki and Lacey.

Her daughter shifted in Nikki's arms, her thumb firmly in her mouth. Nikki had been concerned when Lacey started sucking her thumb again, but the child psychologist had said it was a temporary coping mechanism, and with the right therapy and some time, Lacey would give it up.

Rory appeared in Nikki's bedroom doorway with a cup of coffee. He'd stayed with them as much as possible since they left the hospital, but as Lacey wanted to sleep with her mother, he'd insisted on crashing in the guest room so that Lacey could have some sense of normality. Nikki loved him for that, and she'd told him so the day they left the hospital. Even if he couldn't erase the pain, his being there helped to ease it. He'd kissed her on the forehead and said he loved her too.

"Good morning." Rory set the coffee on the nightstand. "I let you sleep as long as I could, but you wanted to be up by 10 a.m."

They were burying Tyler today. Nikki still couldn't believe he was gone, and she knew once the shock wore off, a new round of guilt would take its place.

Rory sat on the edge of the bed beside her, careful not to wake Lacey. "It's not your fault," he reminded Nikki.

"I know," she said. "But it still feels like it."

"I'm glad you're going to therapy with her," Rory said.

Nikki smoothed her daughter's messy, dark hair. "She's lost her daddy at such a young age. What if she's never the same?"

"She won't be the same," Rory said sadly. "But eventually she'll be happy again, I promise. We all will."

Nikki felt the tears building in her eyes. "You didn't ask for any of this. If it's too much, I won't blame you for stepping away." Her stomach knotted at the idea of Rory taking her up on it. He'd become her anchor.

Rory leaned down and kissed her softly. "I'm not going anywhere. I love you. Both of you." He brushed one of Lacey's tangled curls off her face. "I want to be in her life, as long as it's okay with you."

"Of course it is." Nikki took his hand and held it tightly. "We love you too."

Tyler wouldn't want her or Lacey to be sad, and as much as Nikki's moving on had upset him, she knew he'd be relieved to know that Rory was around to help. Life after Frost was never going to be the same, Nikki knew. Her mother had loved the poet Robert Frost, and Nikki still clung to one of his famous quotes.

"What are you thinking about?" Rory asked.

"Robert Frost."

"The poet?" Rory pursed his lips, confused.

Nikki nodded. "He was once asked about the things he'd learned about life, and he said, 'In three words, I can summarize everything I've learned about life: it goes on.'"

A LETTER FROM STACY

I want to say a huge thank you for choosing to read *Lost Angels*. If you did enjoy it and want to keep up to date with all my latest releases, just sign up at the following link. Your email address will never be shared, and you can unsubscribe at any time.

www.bookouture.com/stacy-green

If you loved *Lost Angels*, I would be very grateful if you could write a review. I'd love to hear what you think, and it makes such a difference helping new readers to discover one of my books for the first time.

I love hearing from my readers—you can get in touch on Facebook or my website.

Thanks,
Stacy

 StacyGreenAuthor

 @authorstacygreen

 @StacyGreen26

 stacygreenauthor.com

ACKNOWLEDGMENTS

As always, thank you to my readers for their support of the Nikki Hunt series. *Lost Angels* has been a long time in the making, and I hope it lived up to your expectations! Your continued support means more Nikki Hunt books, and I can't thank you all enough!

Thank you so much to my editor at Bookouture, Jennifer Hunt, for her support and guidance. I am so lucky to work with such an amazing publisher and team.

Thank you to my husband and daughter for their unwavering support. Thank you to Kristine Kelly for her support and friendship. A special thanks to aviation specialist Brad Kutz for his guidance on landing the ski-planes. Many thanks to the rangers at the Boundary Waters Canoe and Wilderness for helping to pick the perfect location for the all-important opening scene. Thank you to Kim and Greg Crawford for their help with all things northern Minnesota.

Maureen Downey, you're a rock star as always. Thanks to the staff at Poised Pen for all their marketing help. Special thanks to the amazing Lisa Regan for her continued support and friendship.

I hope you loved this chapter of Nikki's story, and I can't wait to share the next one with readers!

Printed in Great Britain
by Amazon